Helena Kelleher Kahn comes from a middle class Irish background. She trained as a nurse at Charing Cross Hospital in London. Helena married Jacob Kahn, a biologist. When their three sons were old enough to make it possible, Helena trained at the London School of Economics as a social worker specialising in work with disabled children. Helena and Jacob retired to Ireland in 1994. Helena joined local writer's groups. Her work has appeared in the magazines History Ireland and The Holly Bough of Cork, a celebrated Christmas annual.

This story is dedicated to the people who try to help deprived and disabled children.

Helena Kelleher Kahn

THE SILVERCAGE

AUSTIN MACAULEY PUBLISHERS™

LONDON • CAMBRIDGE • NEW YORK • SHARJAH

A CIP catalogue record for this title is available from the British Library.

ISBN 9781398466067 (Paperback)
ISBN 9781398466074 (ePub e-book)

www.austinmacauley.com

First Published 2022
Austin Macauley Publishers Ltd®
1 Canada Square
Canary Wharf
London
E14 5AA

I would like to thank my son John and daughter in law Teresa, for their assistance in this book reaching publication.

25 March 1974

When the child ran out in front of the car, I only saw her head and her arms, and oh God oh God I braked, I didn't even think. So there was no real danger, just the shock to me of her being there at all. I was sitting shaking, but the little girl, she didn't seem afraid, for she turned around to look at me and gave me a smile like a real welcome.

My official welcome had already taken place twenty minutes earlier when Lillian Saye rose from her flower-laden desk to greet me.

"Mary Delancy. Good afternoon. Do sit down. Sit here. Now, was it hard to find us? Good. You see, I thought Dr Gomez really should meet you as well. Unfortunately, he's late, doctors always are, as you know. You've been a nurse, and so you know. Charing Cross Hospital, wasn't it?"

"No," I said, "Baron's Cross Hospital. And I don't—"

"Tea or coffee? We have time, I think."

"Tea, please. But I don't remember—"

Lillian silenced me—never difficult to do—by raising a hand while she spoke into the intercom and ordered tea. But I did remember something to do with that out-of-season big bunch of lily of the valley between her and myself. The scent was distracting, and for me, it brought too much of the past into the present.

"You're admiring my flowers. One of my team brings them in. I always think we need something to keep us, well, calm. Balanced. We give so much, do we not? We give so much to others. Thank you, Sylvia, just here. Wait—perhaps you'd better give Dr Gomez a ring. He's probably forgotten."

Silvery fair curls lay on Lillian's blue silk-clad shoulder, her eyes, blue also, narrowed under even pencilled brows. Talking all the time, she offered me the tea with Nice biscuits, but not one single crumb of her attention. I wanted to ask her why we were here at all, why she had sent for me.

My references were in order, and in my bag was the letter confirming that I was to start my first social work job next week, with Doctor Morgan's paediatric team at Riverdale General Hospital. So who was this Dr Gomez? And what had gone wrong, for I knew something certainly must-have.

Perhaps it was only the scent of those flowers, debonair little white bells with their stiff leaves and invasive scent, they're unlucky for me. This is nonsense, I told myself, that's all over with now.

There was a rush of footsteps outside, and a man came in very quickly without knocking.

"Ah, Dr Gomez, this is Mary Delancy—you don't mind if we call you Mary, do you? Mary, Dr Paul Gomez from Sladebourne."

We shook hands, and I murmured something, but my mind was busy with the unfamiliar place name, for I couldn't recall any Sladebourne Ward in the children's unit. With some dexterity, Lillian extracted a stacking chair from a pile of these beside her desk, and now she handed it to the doctor, who sat down facing me, his warm brown eyes fixed on mine.

"Miss Delancy—Mary—I'm so delighted to meet my future helper in the field. You are interested in working with these parents, Mrs Saye tells me—I too am keen to work with them. We must start a group. Parent power! I believe that is the key to the whole thing.

"We will certainly do better than that other chap, the nursing officer, who only had one reply to all the letters he sent out to parents. He really, let me say, got nowhere." I looked at Lillian, but she was concentrating on pouring tea for Gomez.

"I'm afraid," I said, "I don't understand at all. I don't know what Sladebourne is, or what it's got to do with the Paediatric Unit."

Dr Gomez's mouth opened, then closed again. Lillian put down the teapot. With a serious air, she addressed us both, her gaze avoiding mine and seeking, as it were, the middle distance.

"Well, actually, Mary, there's been a slight change of plan. You did say at the interview that you wanted to work with children, and I thought at the time— only thought, mind you, for there wasn't anything in writing, was there—that Celine would be leaving Paediatrics. Well. But now Celine's withdrawn her notice.

"We're in the hands of bureaucrats since Social Services took us over! The trouble I've had with Richard Sawney. He's our director now. Doctor, you wouldn't know him. Mary, you won't actually be here with the Paediatric Unit as we had thought. You will be a part of our Paediatric family, most definitely. But your base will be at Sladebourne House."

"And that is?" My mouth was so dry, I could hardly get the words out.

"For children, Mary, children with mental handicaps. They're all children— and of course, they'll stay like that, like children all of their lives. They're from, let me see, about four or five up to nineteen, or twenty, or thereabouts. The work you'd have would be with the parents of course. Dr Gomez came to me to ask for help with setting up a Parents Association for them, and I thought of you."

Here Gomez cut in so that I could not say much of what I wanted to, but at least I could now understand why Lillian had made sure to have him present for her revelation. She had correctly guessed that my feelings would not be very readily expressed before a stranger.

Gomez, recovering quickly from his surprise, began an appeal to my better nature: "I promise you, Mary, you will have much interesting work, helping the families of those poor little ones to come to terms. Many of the parents feel broken and rejected, so I myself have already taken them on."

A shy smile of satisfaction appeared beneath the drooping moustache. "I did not always work in this discipline. Formerly, I had a good job with the Ministry of Supply at Porton, but I asked myself sometimes, what does that do for the soul, for the character, even?

"So then I went back to school, to study for DPM, and now I'm at Sladebourne with Dr Nicholas Hanafin, our senior consultant. He himself may be said to have vast experience of many years working in this field. I cannot of course speak for him, but I know that I will welcome your help. The thing is, are you still prepared to come?"

I could not be said to be prepared for anything. While they were speaking to me, my mind went very rapidly through several changes, which must have been reflected in my face. Surprise followed by disappointment and anger were the main emotions. The anger was directed about equally at Lillian and at myself because I felt shame at my own lack of caution.

It was not as if I had not been forewarned about Lillian and her ways, but still, I had allowed myself to be manipulated. Sladebourne was obviously unpopular. No existing staff member wanted to go there, so the choice was to send the new girl, recruited on a semi-informal basis (my practice tutor knew Lillian socially), and with no written contract yet in a time of changing masters. The looming reality was that I needed a job, and the positive side was that Paul Gomez, unlike most doctors I had met, actually seemed to want a social worker.

"I'll try it," I said slowly, "but on condition."

The look of relief beginning on Lillian's face creased back into a near frown.

"On condition that I can change to some other social work post after one year, if I don't like this job or if it doesn't like me."

"This is not usual, of course, ah—Mary. However, we can discuss it again. After all, you will be on probation for the first six months anyway."

This means I thought: 'Give me any trouble, and I'll fire you'.

Doctor Paul Gomez looked pleased as if he had got what he came for. What was that really, I wonder. Did he want a friend, a secretary, or a serf who would do all the running around and leave the credit to him? Probably he'd like a mixture of all three, but time alone could tell that.

Now, he was encouraging me to come to next Wednesday's Case Conference. "We have them every week—everyone is there!" It sounds something of a social occasion. And then, as Gomez was about to leave us, he asked when I would come to see Sladebourne.

"I will take her there today," announced Lillian, "and we must go now, at once. You'll have to follow me, Mary, I can't give you a lift because I'm going straight on to another meeting after."

Five minutes later, we were speeding through the outer London suburbs. Lillian drove so fast that I could barely keep her yellow Mini in view, indeed I twice lost it and only caught up with it by good luck. We came to the outer reaches of the city, going south. There were more trees and fewer buildings, then there were distant woods spaced out with what I took to be common land; finally, there was a stretch of sandy open heath.

In the middle distance, a water tower in the surprising shape of an Italian Renaissance belfry arose from a cluster of trees. Around them, I saw a wall, waist-high, brick-based, and topped with six-foot ornate railings shining silver in the uncertain spring sun. We were at Sladebourne House.

As we drove through impressive gates, in tight convoy behind a builder's lorry and the hospital group's mail-van, I noticed some movement in the window of the gate lodge, movement like the withdrawal of a face, followed by the lifting of feet from a table-top. A sallow man in dungarees came slowly out to collect mail from the van, which had stopped abruptly and was holding the rest of the queue up.

Lillian waved to him, and he made a gesture which could have been acknowledgement, but his eyes were not on Lillian. They were on me, with an inquisitive and somewhat puzzled stare. Presently, the van moved enough to let us by.

A narrow drive curved before us now, with thick shrubbery on either side, then came to a crossroads where we turned left. A fair-sized house, mid-Victorian I thought, could be seen about two hundred yards ahead. A sign just before it pointed to Administration.

Bushes to my left parted abruptly, and a child sprang from them out in front of the car. I braked hard. As I was going fairly slowly, there was probably no danger to either of us, but there is always an if—. I sat stunned and shaking, feeling what could have happened.

The child, a blonde girl of nine or ten perhaps, stood still in the middle of the road and stared at me. Her eyes were puckered against the sun, her blonde hair was uncombed, the shapeless faded pink dress she wore almost reached her dirty plimsolls. As I started to get out of the car, she suddenly thrust one hand into her mouth and began to bite on it, making at the same time a high-pitched, whimpering sound.

A stout young woman emerged from the shrubbery, glanced doubtfully at me, then grabbed the child by the shoulders and marched her back into the bushes. The child looked at me over her shoulder then and smiled, a charming smile I involuntarily returned. As the shrubbery closed again behind the pair, I heard the sound of a slap on flesh, followed by a single sharp cry.

This encounter gave me something to think about, as I parked beside Lillian. "I wondered where you had got to," she said. I told her, but she had not seen the girl in the pink dress.

We went through a pillared porch with an open door, into a long, ill-lit hall. There came no sound from the high doors on either side of us, and now for the first time, I saw Lillian hesitate. After a moment to consider, she went to the first door on the left and knocked. It opened for us so promptly, that I could not help feeling someone had been waiting just at the other side.

Leonard Locke, the Hospital Secretary, is one of those who make a handsome first impression. He is not very young, but at first, this is not noticeable, so straight and slight is he, and with such an easy, smiling air about him. The hospital administrators I have met up to now are harassed people who look as if they dealt perpetually with complaints.

Locke is not like that. Locke is elegant, leisured, relaxed, expensively suited and silver-haired. He shook my hand and introduced himself as if he liked meeting people, which is probably the case, and his eyes looked twinkling into mine when he expressed a particular delight at meeting me.

"You'll join our committee of course," he said. "The Friends of Sladebourne. We raised three thousand last year for the Adventure Playground, and now we're working for the therapeutic pool. Great fun."

"I'm not really into fundraising," I replied.

"Oh, but you Lady Almoners, you're too modest. You're *all* marvellous at raising money, experts at it, I'd think—aren't you, Mrs Saye?"

Lillian did not reply. One thing we evidently share is a desire to escape from the stereotype of Lady Almoner, a figure from the pre-NHS past, formerly an assessor of patients' ability to pay towards their treatment costs. Means-testing, in the current moral code which Lillian and I both nominally hold, is now a grave sin. Good, I thought, at least that's one thing I won't be obliged to do here: fund-raise.

"Have you seen…?" Locke lifted a humorous eyebrow at each of us.

"Not yet," said Lillian, "if you mean Mr Paigle. We're going there now. Unfortunately, we're short of time today, Leonard. Mary will start here on Wednesday, so she'll be coming to your next weekly meeting, your, your—"

"Our Case Conference," confirmed Locke. "Look forward to seeing you there, Miss Delancy. You'll find this a friendly place, everyone does. We all pull together. This sort of work calls out the best in people, in everybody working here. Yes, we're a loyal team."

It did crazily occur to me to ask: loyal to what, or to whom? But I resisted the impulse, and to control it better stared for distraction at an engraving on the wall before me. Contemporary with the house, it showed a forlorn maiden comforted by the attentions of a spaniel.

That dog had something about it which reminded me of Locke. I looked at Lillian. She was explaining to Locke how to get to the venue for the next interdisciplinary meeting, which he is supposed to attend, having apparently missed the last two. When she had finished, we crossed the hall, and Lillian knocked on the opposite door.

"Come in!" Max Paigle, Chief Nursing Officer, rose slowly from his desk to meet us. A short, frowning, bald man, he accepted my introduction to him in the manner of a potentate receiving a new servant. He was distant, dignified, and disinclined for conversation. Wishing to lighten the atmosphere, and not being able to think of anything better to say, I made some foolish remark about the beauty of the room we were in, which was indeed very impressive.

From the spotless plasterwork of the ceiling to the red and blue Turkey rug on the polished floor, it looked like a genuine Victorian office adapted unobtrusively to the modern world. There were repro telephones for internal and external lines, modern radiators disguised by antique-seeming grilles, and that desk lamp was surely converted from a genuine *art nouveau* piece.

This much I took in, and it was not until later that the probable cost of it all occurred to me. But I had somehow found the right thing to say this time. Paigle actually smiled, seeming to grow inches taller as he did so. I'm sure he would have taken us both on a detailed tour of his den if Lillian had not been so obviously anxious to get away. As it was, when she had left us, he offered me a guided tour of the whole place.

20 March 1974

The territory covered by Sladebourne House is large—I do not know how large. It appears even bigger than it probably is because it's planted so closely with trees and overgrown shrubs. There are no vistas here, no views, nothing to indicate where you are or to make any connection with life outside. Once past the entrance gate, which is apparently the only way in, the visitor enters an enclosed world, secret and apart.

Walking through his territory with Paigle yesterday afternoon was not entirely comfortable. He kept too close to me, I found, and once or twice I felt almost as if in the company of a dangerous large dog. The few people we met eyed us warily and showed no desire to stop and chat. When Paigle greeted anybody, it was with a sound resembling a growl.

From time to time, I would ask him something, and he worried it and turned it about, doglike, before giving his response. But for all that, I did at least get some idea of the history of the place, for Mr Paigle likes history, and he also likes to display what he knows.

Sladebourne began as an estate formed by the marriage of two Huguenot families. The bourne, or intermittent stream, flowed in winter only through the deep valley, or slade, crossing and dividing the estate. Both these features of the land still exist—somewhere. Somewhere also in the neglected woods are ruins of the original mansion.

The road from the entrance gates is the former carriage drive. The present administration building used to be a Manse, added in the 1850s when the estate's owners were still rich, but Calvinist no longer. The family ran to daughters at the time, and when the one male heir died of fever in the Crimea, the title died out. This part of the estate was left to the War Office, and while the government of the time was making up its mind what to do with the unsought legacy, the mansion mysteriously burned down.

Eventually, the surviving Manse became a convalescent home for officers. Other buildings were added to house staff. Between wars, nothing very much happened here, and it was not until 1940 that the first children came.

A city institution had to evacuate seventy disabled children from London, and Sladebourne took them all. To these, over the next years, were added children from all over southern England. Antibiotics developed during the last war helped them to survive diseases that had ravaged institutions of the past.

So, according to Paigle, with life expectancy grown longer, there aren't many vacancies now, and as fast as eighteen-year-olds are transferred to Mount Vervain, their places are filled again. Mount Vervain is the local institution for mentally handicapped adults.

"Children come to us," concluded Paigle, "when other places have given up on them. Runners. Kickers. Biters. Children with all sorts of violent behaviours. We don't give them up. Young people unmanageable elsewhere are managed here. You could say it's our special talent."

I said that must be very gratifying, and asked if it was difficult to find suitable staff. Paigle pursed his lips and puffed out his cheeks as if to blow away any hint of difficulty.

"Our staff, I may say, are all exceptional people. Of course, you have to be a special sort of person to work here. D'you see, you have to be a little bit mentally handicapped yourself to do it. I mean, clever people wouldn't do. People with those bits o' paper, degrees and that, wouldn't do. No, no, we want people here who are qualified in the University of Life. Who's got real-life experience."

"But you've some people working here who are, well, officially trained—nurses, for instance?"

"Oh yes, we have some, we have some. But what I'd call the real backbone of the place is the ordinary person. The ordinary person with what it takes."

It occurs to me that it would take a good deal of confidence for an ordinary person to challenge Paigle about anything, and in his eyes, this would be an excellent reason to employ as many untrained workers as possible. I begin to suspect also, that Paigle is himself without qualifications—in fact, he later told me so. He comes from rural Dorset, where he began his career as an attendant in the local mental hospital. I reckon he owes his advancement to other factors than formal qualifications.

As he was telling me all this, we reached a row of big red-brick villas with high gables, their white-painted trim giving them the spruced-up look of old-fashioned seaside boarding houses. The first house, I was told, was a staff hostel, the second a staff canteen. We did not go into either. I began quite consciously to prepare myself for what I might see in the children's houses. As unobtrusively as possible, I took several deep breaths.

"This is Waverley," announced my guide. He added, with some pride, that he had personally renamed the wards, changing A, B, C and D into names which he was sure I would recognise as having literary associations. Besides, Waverley, there's Ivanhoe, Kenilworth and Midlothian—I had a fleeting fear of being expected to discuss Scott's novels with Paigle. But I would like to know sometime, why those particular names.

We entered Waverley through a lean-to conservatory. Appropriately enough, this was full of plants and flowers, but as we passed toward the dim regions at the back I realised with a kind of shock that all the plants were artificial and all the flowers silk. Wafting scents came, not from living blossoms, but from incense dwindling in a clay holder, and from the fragrant melting wax of scores of votive lights.

All over the crowded walls and shelves were images from many faiths: pictures of Moslem, Sikh and Parsee sages beside the Sacred Heart and the mother of Dolours; a Hindu goddess between a gold-painted Buddha and a porcelain Kuan Yin. In what little space remained, perched dolls and small toy animals dressed as people. Untouched and somehow expectant they looked, these worshippers at a complex shrine!

Distracted by them, I was startled by a faint noise. A small dark-skinned woman appeared suddenly before us; she wore a long blue dress, and her head was covered by a white veil, beneath which her dark eyes shone with the reflections of candle flames.

"Sister Daroga—Miss Delancy, social worker," said Paigle, introducing me.

Light coming through a swinging inner door dispelled any half-formed illusion—Sister was simply wearing the traditional uniform of a ward sister, and its archaic appearance was exaggerated by her tiny size. On her, the dress was ankle-length, the veil reached below her waist.

For one moment, I had had thoughts of an apparition of the Blessed Virgin and was relieved to know myself mistaken. Sister Daroga acknowledged me with a nod and a brief glance, a look not dismissive exactly, but one putting me 'on hold' for the time being because she wanted to turn her full attention to my escort.

"Mr Paigle, what do you think I am? Answer me! Yesterday you take away my staff and today you send me more children, two respite children. Just look, look anywhere, where to put them? Answer me! I'm the hard one, the one who tells off, but the one who gets work done. No one dirty, hungry on my ward. But I do it—I have to do it—with no help from anyone."

She paused, not because she had finished, but because she needed to draw breath. "Now, you're bringing people in here when we're changing the children, without asking. You don't let me know ahead, even."

Paigle seemed unsurprised by this onslaught. He stood quietly under it, saying nothing, very slightly embarrassed and that only, I feel because I was a witness. Sister returned to the attack.

"And you don't answer me when I ring you up about those three girls, Caro, Lolly and Vera. That secretary, or whoever she is, always answers instead. She's no good to me. I need to speak to you about them. Today. Now."

Paigle's colour abruptly changed, the pink of his face deepening into an angry red. His pale eyes blazed, his sullen self-control abruptly deserted him, and his role as guide and host went overboard.

"Daroga, you're always complaining about everything but if you'd play ball with me I'd play ball with you. These girls shouldn't be here still, you know that. Nor that boy, come to think of him.

"Taking up staff time here, and all Mount Vervain material, all four of them. And if you didn't have them here you could fit in more respites, easy. Now, if you can't see that…."

In a moment, they were shouting at each other. It may be that this scene occurs regularly, still, I felt as if my presence had somehow caused it to happen. I willed them both to stop and looked pleadingly at Sister, who suddenly ceased her tirade, shrugged, turned away and led us into the main ward.

The first impression I got there was unexpected; it was one of complete silence. Where were all the patients? I looked around, puzzled. There was certainly colour, light, and warmth, there were pictures and posters on every wall. Mobiles dangled from the ceiling, trembling and tinkling before barely opened windows.

A giant television set in a corner talked faintly to itself, but there was no other human sound at all, and no movement either seemed to take place in that large, low-ceilinged room, filled with hospital beds and cots, in each of which, now that I was close enough to look, could just be seen the outline of a small recumbent body. Sister vanished, followed by Paigle, into a room at the back which I guessed to be the office. I did not feel that I was meant to follow them there, so I remained where I was, and looked about me.

A silent door opened and two women, one black and one white, both in blue overall dresses, entered dragging between them a trolley laden with incontinence pads and washing materials. They paused at the bed nearest me and turned back the covers. I could not see what they were doing and involuntarily moved closer. Then, one woman left the bedside to fetch something, and I could see a face on the pillow, a young girl's face with dark eyes, a wide mouth and dark hair.

The face and head, which seemed large, belonged to a dreadfully thin body arranged in foetal position upon pillows and wearing only a nappy and a washed-out pyjama jacket. A thin hand lifted from the bed and wavered towards me. Without thinking, I held out to it my own hand, which it grasped. Pulled by the hand, I moved closer to the head of the bed.

"She does that to everyone," said the white care assistant, "she can't talk."

"What's her name?" I asked, and then thought I should at least have pretended to ask the girl herself, as we do with babies.

"That's Vera," said the black care assistant shyly, "maybe she can't talk, but she knows how to get what she wants."

They both laughed and Vera with them, but seconds later her laughter turned to moans as the women lifted her. I introduced myself, both women smiled politely but I do not think they took in what I said—they were busy, and I was just another visitor. Vera's hand, a bundle of little bones, clasped mine.

Her eyes moved restlessly, not focussing on anyone, and the thought came to me that she might be blind. I was now aware that Paigle was back and was waiting impatiently to go on with the tour. Vera carried my hand to her face, stroking her face with it in a seeming attempt to draw a caress from me. I patted her cheek before slipping my fingers out of hers and returning to Paigle's side.

There were faint noises now in the room, but still, no one moved about, much less sat up. Twenty-five severely disabled children live in these two adjoining rooms. They lie in bed for most of the day because there are seldom enough people on duty to get them up, and very little space, either, to put them in when they *are* up.

They don't all attend school. Some respond to attention—some don't. Is this from lack of stimulus or intellectual deficit? Paigle, I feel, is unlikely to be able to tell me this.

As we were leaving, Sister Daroga rejoined us, and now I noticed that whenever she spoke to a child they seemed to respond to her voice. Paigle, on the other hand, as if to make up for lack of interest in the individual patients, told me how much he had spent recently on paint and new curtains for Waverley.

However, when he called attention to the big new television, he was swiftly deprived of credit by Sister, who explained that she had bought it herself, with money raised over months of selling home-made samosas in the local street market. It was no thanks to anyone else, according to her, if the children had something to look at beside bare walls!

Leaving Waverley by the back door, we struggled through a small enclosure filled with laden rotating clothes dryers. Facing us across a stretch of trodden grass was Kenilworth. It looked far shabbier than Waverley; indeed, from the side, its only conspicuous features were a battered swing in a wire enclosure, and a neatly piled heap of broken chairs reaching up to first-floor level. Kenilworth was clearly a place where residents took out their frustrations on furniture.

As we walked to the front door, I had the sensation of being watched. Almost before Paigle could touch the door handle it was opened by a girl with long fair hair and a fringed mini-dress. She held a mug in one hand, and her round blue eyes looked surprised to see me.

"Michelle, this is Miss Delancy, our new social worker," said Paigle importantly, "You here all on your own, Mitch? I thought Duncan's supposed to be on as well."

"I dunno. Anyway, he's not come yet." Mitch nodded at me and put her drink down.

"Kids still at school? I suppose you were just going to put out the medicines."

"OK, Mr Paigle. The medicines. And the pills. I'll put them all out now."

"Show Miss Delancy round first, there's a good girl. I've a call to make."

With an awkward glance at me, Michelle finished her tea. Passing by Paigle, she gave him plenty of room, something I could not help seeing. How is it that I always notice things like that, which are not really my business, instead of other things like the records system, which should be? On this occasion, I did not take in the location of patients' files, but I saw that telling gleam in the eye of the nurse manager, and I think he saw that I saw it, too.

Michelle and I left Paigle in the office shouting down the phone to someone called Den to 'get off the outside line'. Kenilworth was fairly clean but very bare.

I've never seen inside a prison, perhaps they are like this, with the bareness so deliberate.

No sign of pictures, books or toys. Anyone shut up in such a place as this would have a great need to look out, indeed, would have no other diversion, but Kenilworth windows are placed so high up that nobody under six foot tall can see out of them.

My visit did not take long, for with all the children still at school there was little to see. I tried to draw Michelle out, and she told me that there are twenty-five children living in Kenilworth, and she doesn't know much about them, really, since this is only her second week at Sladebourne.

The job she had before this one was at the Sea Palace Takeaway down the road. Yeah, it's alright here. No, she hasn't had any induction course, 'but you don't need to know much, to look after these kids'. How did she get the idea of coming to work at Sladebourne? Her uncle knows one of the porters, he fixed it up.

Michelle asked if I wanted to see 'the upstairs. I followed her up an uncarpeted staircase to five bedrooms, each with five beds in it and nothing else, all bedspreads and window-curtains made of the same ugly patterned fabric, and the whole effect impersonal, like rooms in one of those tourist hotels where no guest stays longer than one week.

"How do the children know their own beds?" I found myself asking.

"They don't," replied a surprised Michelle, "but it's us who put them to bed, so it doesn't matter. Some of them," she added, as if in explanation, "some of them are mongrels."

"Oh, you mean they've Down's Syndrome," I said before I thought. Michelle had clearly never heard of Down's, and then I began to feel how unfair of me it was to quiz the girl, new as she is (and she can't be much over sixteen, surely).

But does Paigle risk leaving her in sole charge of so many children? I was relieved to see, as we left Kenilworth, three other people coming on duty. Two were middle-aged women in blue care assistant's overalls; the other, male and rather sheepish, I guess to be the missing Duncan. Paigle ignored him—I suppose his telling-off has already been delivered, by phone.

Ivanhoe came next on our tour, and it was very like Kenilworth except that every window and door was wide open, and there was nobody at all in the building. Paigle said that Sidney and the staff must have gone to collect the children from school for lunch, which they take in their own houses.

I asked how far away that school is—apparently not far, it is on the site. One thing about Ivanhoe, the colour scheme is really odd! The hall is painted maroon, the playroom (or living room) lime green, and the office cobalt blue with pink woodwork. Paigle agreed that the décor was unusual:

"It's done by a member of our staff, a talented chap, friend of Sidney's. I like to pick up people who can make themselves useful, and he used to be in the decorating business, so we paid for the paint, and he did it for us all by himself. Brightens the place up wonderfully, a bit of colour."

I did not think Ivanhoe was either bright or clean. Its miasma of the less attractive human odours was barely overlaid with the sickly scent of a popular disinfectant. Not even large open windows could take that away; the smell hung in the building like a cloud.

Now, I begin to understand the Victorian preoccupation with bad smells as the cause of diseases. Something else bothers me too—the bareness. Where on earth are the children's clothes, their personal belongings? I did not see any lockers in the bedrooms. Is it worthwhile to ask Paigle about such matters, or would it be more sensible to ask care staff?

I will have to think about that…

"We'll just take a look into Midlothian, Miss. Terence—my deputy—he'll be there."

On our way, we passed a small, strongly constructed building right on the drive, but on the opposite side to all the other houses. There are no shrubs or flowers outside this one, and some of the windows have bars. I asked what it was.

"It's our special unit for disturbed children. Our Time Out room, you could say."

And Paigle looked very keenly at me as if he hoped I would ask for an explanation of the unfamiliar term. As I already know what it means, I did not take the bait and instead asked him if there was anyone living in there now. Paigle said quickly that there wasn't, but as we passed by I heard the sound of voices. It is clear that this place is not to be included in any official guided tour, and so I've decided to put it high on my unofficial list of places to see at Sladebourne when I start work there in earnest.

Perhaps it is under the supervision of Terence, who met us on the threshold of Midlothian. Terence would be in his early forties, smooth face, smooth fair hair, and something watchful about him. That sort of person, I think, who will

23

always be prompt to escape responsibility, to avoid being caught out. On this occasion, he beamed at us above the high burden he carried in his arms—a pile of folded cotton velvet curtains, in a harsh purple shade.

"More new things, Terence? He's always got something new."

"Yes, sure, Mr Paigle. Curtains for the bedrooms; brand new and cut price cause of the colour. Sorry I can't shake hands with you, Miss Delancy."

I told him that that was all right, but my mind was busy. He knew my name, but how—who told him?

"The curtains look washed already," I said.

"Had to take them all to the washeteria this morning. Some kids wiped their bottoms on them last night. We're not used to things posh, here."

Terence grinned at me, and I returned his grin, feeling ashamed of doing so. He has the ability somehow to make one feel collusive and uneasy at the same time.

"Mr Paigle, can I see you for a sec.? There's been this phone call."

"Don't mind me," I said, "I'll just have a look around if that's all right."

Before I'd finished speaking, they were in the office with the door closed. I moved uncertainly towards the stairs, which I now know to be at the rear of each villa. From one of the doors I passed, came a rhythmic noise, no doubt of some cleaning operation in progress. The next door was open, and what I could see of the room beyond drew me in at once.

The walls were covered with frescos—acrylic paintings of animals and birds in a woodland setting. These creatures were shown much bigger than life-size, in fact on a human scale. At ground level sat rabbits with predatory faces and long, sharp claws. (I tried, but failed, to remember if rabbits do in fact have big claws.)

A robin, perched on an overhead branch, had claws as well. A huge toad, with claws, of course, waited in ambush behind a realistically rendered clump of Deadly Nightshade. Farther on, a serpent displaying eighteen-inch fangs entwined itself in an oak tree. I feel it might have had claws also, had the artist been able to find a good place to attach them.

I was reminded at once of a visit I'd made some years before to an exhibition of patient's art, held at a famous psychiatric hospital. Surely, I exaggerate to make such a comparison? No, I don't exaggerate. Who would decorate a playroom for children in this disturbing way, if they didn't have a number of unresolved mental difficulties of their own?

A raised voice could be heard through the open transom above the office door. Paigle was giving off about something, and Terence seemed to be trying to placate him. Feeling slightly guilty at remaining within earshot, I moved along the hall towards the kitchen. As I had expected, it was bare in here, except for the heated trolley containing the dinner, a Formica-topped table at which places were set, and an assemblage of somewhat battered chairs.

Opposite the kitchen was a lavatory, and so far, Paigle had left these out of the guided tour. Idly I pushed the door open, expecting to see something like the toilet annex to a hospital ward. What I saw was more like a run-down public loo, except that as Midlothian inhabitants can't write, the tiled walls were adorned with faeces in place of graffiti. The floor was wet and slimy, and slimy also the lengths of rope dangling from the overhead cisterns.

A heap of torn-up newspaper rested in an orange box on the floor. There was an ancient washbasin, with no hot water (I tried it), no soap, no towel. The shower cubicle was lined with chipped and broken tiles, the doors of the stalls had been wrenched off; a broken hinge caught my sleeve and tore it as I turned to go. And somehow, I was not as surprised as I should have been.

My suspicions well awake now, I left the annex quickly and made for the door from which that regular thumping sound still came. It was locked, but the key was in the lock. I opened it and saw a very big room with several windows, plastic-covered easy chairs, and a wooden crate holding a mass of broken toys. In the centre of the room stood a solitary chair like those against the walls, and tied into it with belts and straps was a thin young man whose shock of mousey hair swung across his face as he rocked the heavy chair, edging it by centimetres across the room.

I wondered if he had any purpose in doing this, other than enjoying the motion and the noise. I went over to him with no plan either, only the feeling that he should not be tied up like that. As I reached him, he ceased to rock and looked anxiously up at me. A sound behind me drew my attention. Paigle and Terence were standing in the doorway, watching us. Terence's bland expression had not altered but Paigle looked very angry.

"Who is this?" I asked, trying to keep my voice steady.

"Matthew, Matthew French, isn't it, Terence? He has to be restrained. Staff shortage. I didn't think you'd go poking around on your own, Miss Delancy. After all, it is the children's home. Private. *You* wouldn't like—"

"Mr Paigle, this is a ward of a hospital. I can visit children on the wards. Hospital social workers are allowed to do this now, and this is what I am doing."

I was angry now, as angry as he, and just as illogical because obviously I hadn't known of Matthew and my visit if it could be so called, was accidental.

"That may be or may not," retorted Paigle, "but there is such a thing as politeness, as asking permission. And anyway," he added triumphantly, "he doesn't belong to Dr Gomez, who *you're* working for. He's Dr Hanafin's patient, he belongs to him."

The senior consultant, I thought, was the one with vast experience.

We left the room. Terence was about to relock it when he saw me looking at him and didn't. He showed me around upstairs in a perfunctory way, while Paigle retired to the office again. When we came down a few minutes later, he had gone. My guided tour was evidently at an end.

22 March 1974

The dignified shabbiness of north London basked temporarily in the spring sun, as Nilla Ryan and I left Camden Town tube station and made our way uphill. Presently we drew level with a curious, shallow shop, all window with almost nothing behind, and the little space there was, crammed with fabric remnants. My kind of shop… Nilla gave a cry of recognition.

"That's it. That's the place. Stop, Mary, you can go in the shop afterwards, but we've got to eat now or it'll be too late."

She made for a doorway leading, apparently, to a cellar beneath the shop. I followed reluctantly. Down some steps, we found ourselves in a small and not overly clean basement room, containing travel posters of Greece, tables clothed in green plastic, and no sign of a waiter. The only other customers were four unshaven young men seated together; they were eating some indefinable meat dish with the wholehearted and silent concentration I had up to now only seen in hospital canteens.

"Why did we have to be here so early? It isn't one. And Nilla—would this place have any connection with Haverstock College?"

"Well, yes. If you're a student and you get in here and give your order by 1:00 p.m., they take ten per cent off. And what's wrong with students, then? You were one yourself not long ago."

I was about to tell her what was wrong with them when a bearded giant appeared who seemed to be a personal friend of Nilla, so I postponed it. Over the next few minutes, some matters became clearer. George the Greek is the sole waiter, proprietor and chef of The Pavement, and he has been Nilla's pupil when she was teaching English to foreigners.

He insisted that he owed her a great deal, some of which he proceeded to repay by adding to our meal a bottle of very dark wine strong on tannin and piling our plates with the day's speciality, overdone pork chops. Later, when we were alone in the café, drinking the coffee which was definitely the best part of

George's cuisine, I started to tell Nilla about the previous day's introduction to Sladebourne. She listened in silence to begin with, then—

"You are a total fool, do you know that?" she said.

"Yes," I answered meekly, "I'm aware of that."

We have known each other since we were both ten years old, and Nilla is the one who tells me the home truths as a sister would.

"You let yourself be conned by that one at the hospital. I'm talking about Lillian, she saw you coming. I'd consider getting her for breach of contract, you know if I were you. Then that doctor, the Goan. They're worse than the Irish, you know, real, bigoted Catholics.

"That institution you're going to work in must be full of weirdos, not the children I mean, but the adults as you have described them. The bottom-pincher who showed you around—he's probably got form! His sidekick obviously has something to hide as well. And to put a finish on it, the head bottlewasher is your old pal Dr Hanafin. Now, don't you think he will be a treat in store?"

"I won't have anything to do with his patients if he doesn't want me to, and he won't want me to because he does not want a social worker. You forget, that it's not as if I were helpless. … I already know enough about him to place him, although he probably doesn't realise that. And you're talking now as if I'm totally clueless."

But I was laughing. I could keep up no pretence of being hurt because it felt comfortable to me really. Being slagged off this way suggests to me that what you are doing actually matters, and you might be getting something right.

"I don't think you're clueless, but you're an awful masochist. You haven't any method, you know, you can't set yourself boundaries, and as for others. You never can say no. I am worried about you, Mary, I really am. I foresee trouble coming, of which you have had enough already."

"And so have you. We've both had too much."

"Now, now, I'm the one making the personal remarks at present. You'll get your turn soon."

Nilla's fuzzy, fair hair shook energetically as she spoke, as her head and her hands jerked, to emphasise every point she made. She's trying to persuade me, I thought, as I knew she would. She wants me to insist on my rights, and hold Lillian to the original agreement. But actually, I probably don't have any rights, for Lillian is cute enough to get out of any sort of agreement! Nilla suspects this also and does not really think I'll take her advice.

Still, she's trying to put me in the right. I know Nilla, almost as well as she knows me. The two of us came together from Ireland six years ago, ostensibly to get the training we needed for the callings we wanted to follow—teaching in the case of Nilla, nursing for me.

A motive acknowledged by neither of us at that time was the desire to get away from our old lives. Today, the future still means something positive to us, it is still exciting and full of unlimited possibilities, although there have been, and still are, a few difficulties along the way.

Nilla is involving herself in my affairs partly to forget her own. A disastrous recent love affair made it necessary (or she thinks it has) to disappear for a time. Nilla gave up her job, her flat, her acquaintances—and joined a commune, something she had always said she could never do. She sees herself now as one who, having experienced much and lost a good deal, has had to start life over again but thanks to what she has learnt from bitter experience is qualified to undertake the direction of others.

About that conclusion I am not so sure, remembering what Mother Bonaventure, teaching us English long ago, called 'Dr Manette Syndrome', after the character in Dickens who thought (mistakenly) that his time spent in the Bastille had given him enormous powers of moral persuasion and a charmed life. Still, if it relieves Nilla's mind to advise me, I cannot find it in my heart to object. Using the actual advice offered is, of course, another thing.

To change the subject, I asked her how her current job search was going.

"Not too bad," Nilla said. "I'm seriously considering the ILEA Tutorial Centre in Ashgrove Park. They've made an offer."

"At any rate, it would be entirely different to anything you've ever done before. One to one tuition, where else could you give that? Apart from the Prison Service and the older universities, that is."

"It won't be easier. Those kids may be few in number, but still able to take it out of me. Anyway, we'll see; I can give it a go. Just by the way, Mary, what's the hospital school at Sladebourne like? Because they've put in an ad. for a temporary post."

I had to say that I did not know.

"Any news of your whatever-you-call-it coming through?"

"No news, but they did say it'd be at least six months longer."

"Oh well. And anyway you're still seeing Phil sometimes, I take it. Perhaps it's just as well somebody is a Holy Molly, though I never thought it would be you. Not so easy to be that, here and now. Not fashionable."

"Not easy at all, but then, it never was. And I never was what you thought me, either."

'Holy Molly' is Nilla's name for any believing Catholic, and although I felt surprised and touched by what she had just said to me, I still found myself responding in the defensive way that has become a habit.

"Come on, then, finish up that coffee. George doesn't like to see anything left over. Stick the cork back in the wine bottle if you don't want more now, we'll take it along with us." Afterwards, we went to a local street market and bought blue chenille curtains, cushion covers with little tassels on them, and a set of coat hooks, all to beautify my new flat.

It was not until much later, when Nilla had gone back to the glorified squat she shares with all those other people, that I began to think about what she had said, and to allow myself, by degrees, to feel a bit anxious about the nature of what I have taken on. When I feel anxious I have this habit of going to look at myself in a mirror. The mirror I choose for my inspection, a small oval glass in a giltwood frame, hangs in the hall, and apart from clothes and books is the only thing I have brought from Ireland, from what was my home.

I put the overhead light on, to see better the face of one starting a new life in a new place. The face I saw looked relaxed, rosy, almost peaceful; the eyes were clear and the frown lines above them did not show. The hair needed cutting— but that would do next week. On the whole, then, I felt the sight—and the future—were not looking too bad.

After that personal inspection, I went slowly from little room to little room of the shabby flat, trying to see it through Nilla's eyes. It had seemed important to me, first to live alone, then to live near where I worked. But, since encountering Lillian and realising the need to take into account her vagaries, I've arranged to lease the flat for only six months to begin with. The owner agreed to this; he's in America for a year, but might need his place again at short notice, or so the agent said.

I enjoy the sense of freedom the flat gives me. After years of sharing living space with others, now, there will be no one having to be considered apart from myself. And, of course, Molly, a one-year-old white female cat, was given to me by a fellow student who has already named her.

30

I've never had any pet animal before, so Molly is educating me, moulding me nearer to her heart's desire. Living in the flat for much less than one week, Molly has already learnt to depress the lever handle on the bedroom door so that she can get in to share my couch whenever she wants to. Molly is beautiful to look at, which goes a long way with me, I love her clear green eyes, the sleek white of her coat, and the way the sun shines through her little pink ears when she basks out on the fire escape in the afternoons.

Molly, at least, has adapted wonderfully quickly to her new world. And Molly is now demanding to go out on to the fire escape again. As I open the kitchen window for her, I enjoy seeing the roofscape of differing slatey or tiled slopes and heights, valleys and ridges, varied by glimpses of garden trees. Over in the direction of Sladebourne House can be seen more trees, whole trees this time, in early leaf, and even the very top of the institution's water tower is visible.

The sight does not in any way threaten peace. Set in its cul-de-sac, this whole apartment block is secluded and surprisingly quiet. It should not be hard to get to sleep at night. Absently, I wander into the bedroom and start to unpack a few belongings.

I open what I take to be a wardrobe, and find part of it occupied by a coat; a grey duffel coat that looks really old could even be a genuine antique left from World War II. I take it off its hook and transfer it to a hook on the door between the hall and kitchen. As I'm doing this, the telephone shrills suddenly from the bedroom. I am so unused to its tone that I'm slow to answer it, and perhaps that's why, when I involuntarily give my full name, there is silence for a long moment before the unknown caller hangs up.

As I've inherited my landlord's number, the call was doubtless meant for him, still, why did they not *ask* where he was, or who I was, or say *something*, other than leaving a silence? Unpacking once again, I arrange my diaries, which take up one entire shelf of the little empty bookcase. They're not the printed kind, but simply very thick notebooks; I owe the whole idea of them, to a counsellor who favoured the recording of each day's events.

Between these dull covers are stored the outlines of a life in exile. Sometimes I want to get rid of them, but realise how difficult that is in practice. How can you tear them up, they're so thick; and as for burning them, who has a real fire now? Besides, they hold useful detail, needed for example when I applied, eighteen months ago, to have my marriage annulled.

It is an odd comfort to read the old diaries, for as the mirror does, they reflect me to myself, when I summarise my past and type it in italics. To dignify it, I suppose. On this particular evening, inspired by something Nilla said, I've picked out this year's diary and taken it to the sitting-room, which is cold, for there is no warmth yet in the spring evenings, and I have to search for matches to light the gas fire.

How pale that flame is at first, flickering on the fishbone-white element! Molly, who has come in again, loves this fire and rubs my hands with her head to express gratitude. The poor creature has probably never known a real fire! Subsiding onto the smooth, slightly chill surface of the couch, I open this year's diary and make the entry for 22 March. Later, if I feel like it, I will open a past volume, to read about when I first met Philip.

Autumn 1968

At Baron's Cross Hospital, you had to stay on and work for a year after qualifying for the General Nursing Register. This custom was described, inaccurately, as 'giving the hospital a year'. In reality, you didn't give them anything, but they gave you a staff nurse's post for one year. How sweet it really was, that transition after three years of poverty to something resembling an income! People reacted recklessly by taking an exotic holiday or putting a down payment on a car.

I decided to leave hospital accommodation forever and, with a friend Tina Taborelli, to rent a flat. For several evenings we travelled all over South London inspecting flats, and we settled at last for the basement flat in a Victorian house in Earl's Court—39A Tullamore Crescent. It seemed funny at the time, I remember, to live in a central London street apparently called after an Irish midland town.

Previous tenants of 39A were art students, and all the cheaply carpeted floors were splashed with clots of oil paint in every colour. After much discussion with the landlords, we persuaded them to abate some rent in exchange for our help with redecoration. When we'd finished doing all of that, we gave a party to celebrate and invited all the other tenants of the rest of the house. That is how I met Philip, who was living in an upstairs flat all by himself.

I cannot say that I felt an instant attraction to Philip, but I did feel, straight away, the light and heat of his attraction to me. I felt it on that first evening. Over the noise, the excitement, the smells of cooking and cigarette smoke, scent and sweat, the sense of the silver-grey London day gracefully dying outside; there existed unexpectedly something more: the presence of desire, like a spotlight, focused (or so it seemed to me) on me and on me alone.

I was aware of this before I even took in its source, Philip himself. When I did look, I saw a big young man, slightly stiff in attitude, sallow-complexioned, with soft black hair and large brown eyes fixed on mine. When he saw I'd noticed him, he came over and began to talk to me, in his coaxing Welsh voice—and it seemed to me, even then, that I had no choice in the matter, as if our meeting was already planned, decided about somewhere else. But I can't, in fact, remember what we talked about.

"That chap couldn't take his eyes off you," Tina said afterwards, "when are you seeing him again?"

Tina spoke with forcefulness. A recent romance of hers had ended badly, and she thought if my love-life went well it would somehow bring good luck and improve hers also, there would be hope for her. I answered that I did not know, which was true then, but the next day, when Philip rang and asked me to a dance at the Civil Service Club I felt no surprise, and again had the feeling that this was inevitable, it was meant to happen.

I love dancing but am a poor dancer, nervous, ungraceful, and lacking a true sense of time. Philip danced well, steering me expertly, patiently, through a crowd of couples mostly older than ourselves. It was a formal dance, and I wore a borrowed green strapless dress, the skirt fashionably puffed out with home-made petticoats of green gauze pilfered from the stocks of a hospital's ENT Theatre, where I worked at the time.

Beneath the bodice a strapless bra, also the fashion and also borrowed, compressed my breasts uncomfortably. My jewellery consisted of an imitation emerald necklace, with matching drop earrings—they belonged to Tina, like the little silver bag dangling from one of my wrists. Relaxed for once, revolving easily in Philip's arms, I smiled at the thought that only the shoes were mine—everything else visible on me belonged to others.

"Something amusing you?"

"Only something silly."

For I did not know what he might think of girls scrounging from each other the component parts of an outfit. He might not know that this was something all *hard-up girls did all the time. Later, as we were sitting over a drink, Philip told me a bit about himself.*

His father was dead, his mother was nursing in London, but North Wales was where the Parrys came from, and Philip was their only child. Trained as an accountant, he worked in the civil service, in a department to do with Inland Revenue. So I thought, he probably does know that nurses are poor!

Our courtship, to look back on now, seems distant and unreal, like something I've heard of rather than experienced. It followed nevertheless a traditional, conventional pattern. There still were, in the sixties, couples who didn't sleep together right from the start of their relationship. And Phil made clear from the beginning that it was a wife he was looking for, anything else was less, and not to be considered.

Wasn't a commitment to permanence and security what I also wanted? It must have been, for when, after a few months of going out together, Phil asked me to marry him, I felt it was what I'd expected and hoped from the first would happen, and I knew that of course, I would be saying Yes.

I'd met Philip's extended family, with his aunts and myriad cousins, soon after I first met him, on the convenient occasion of a cousin's wedding. The Parrys were by religion Baptist, they were accepting if not exactly welcoming to a Catholic. I did not expect more. It was less the religious differences and more the cultural ones that bothered me, for the latter are less easily discoverable.

Would there be attitudes that, once part of the Parry family, I'd be called on to assume, like somebody else's clothes, whether they truly fit me or not? I was concerned to know what the Welsh really thought about Irish people. Did they look down on us? See us as violent, unpredictable, contrary—as a few of the journalists writing then apparently saw us? See us as an inextricable part of the violence going on in the North?

Well, no, they did not seem to see us like that. Philip's mother Susan even seemed pleased, as if I brought relief to her; appearing somewhat better than she had expected.

My own dead parents had been, for their country and time, what used to be called 'broadminded'. Religiously mixed marriages were not unknown among their friends and seemed to work out no worse than average—though I always felt that was due to the extra work put into them. That work, I was arrogantly sure that I could give.

And did I love Philip? As much, I suppose, as I could have loved anyone then. Hardly enough, as things turned out.

We began our married life in the simplest way, after a small wedding at which both families contrived to behave well, and the Irish contingent said nice things to the others, once or twice going over the top in this, as we tend to do. There was no honeymoon because we couldn't afford one. I moved into Philip's flat, and after a few days off went on working just as usual, for an agency that found me night-duty at the local general hospital.

We were, or rather, I was, accustomed to managing on very little money; poverty was a nuisance, nothing more. When you are so young, there is always the hope that change, which must come, always comes for the better. Mostly we stayed in—I was learning to cook, and wanting to practise my new skills—Philip seemed happy just to be with me, and I, well, I saw myself at last secure and starting to become the strong and confident woman I had always wanted to be.

Six months went by, and then, one day Phil came home early. It was afternoon, but I wasn't asleep because I'd had the previous night off, and I greeted him with enthusiasm: "Oh good, you're home nice and early—" something like that. Phil did not answer me. He stood and stared at me, almost, I felt, as though he had forgotten who I was, even as if I were some kind of the interloper.

"What's wrong? Phil, are you all right?"

He still stared, then he said: "I'm OK," and went into the bedroom, and I thought I could hear resentment in his voice.

Recently, Phil had gradually seemed rather preoccupied and unresponsive, and I had put it down to pressure at his work, which I really knew very little about. After a couple of minutes, I followed him into our bedroom. Philip was lying fully dressed on the bed, or rather, in it with the duvet wound tightly around him. He had pulled the window curtains across, yet in the light there still was I could see that his eyes were wide open, but not looking at me, or at anything.

Near to the pillow, his little radio made a whispering sound, a sound so low that surely he could not hear it properly, he must have accidentally turned it on. When I involuntarily reached for the knob and turned it right off, Philip's expression did not change, but at once he reached out for it and turned it on again, to whisper as before. I spoke to him, asked if he was ill, then if anything had happened to upset him, and was there anything that I could do? Without looking at me, Philip said: "Nothing," and the word seemed to be forced out of him.

I did not think that he wanted me to be there at all. Anxious, and by now rather frightened, I went slowly back to the sitting-room and tried to think. Something had obviously happened to my husband, and it must be an unusually bad experience, to make him behave in this strange way. Should I ring his work?

Find out what the matter was? Something felt wrong to me about doing that. Call a doctor? We had no telephone in the flat, and the nearest working public one was ten minutes' walk away. Contact my friends? Nilla was on holiday in Ireland, Tina was at work. But help for Philip I must have, so at last, I went out and rang my mother-in-law.

Susan was at home, and when she heard my voice her voice changed and became as anxious as I felt mine was. I started to tell her about Phil and had the impression that she knew already what I was going to say, that it did not come as a surprise. She tried to reassure and more, she was going to help.

"Dear! Now, don't let him go out, Mary, Keep him there until I come. I'll come right away, now, promise. I'll see to him."

I heard myself say: "I've to be at work at 7:30—"

It had not occurred to me to call the agency, and it wasn't the fear of losing money really. I wanted to get away from whatever was going to happen, I did not feel able to face it. The resources I had thought I had were quickly coming to an end.

"Yes. Well, you'll want to go to work, so I'll be over straight. He'll be all right with me, and if you're gone by the time I get there, remember I've the key I've always had, to get in."

"Has—I mean, do you know if Phil's been like this before? Not talking, I mean, and a bit, a bit strange?"

"Yes," she said, "he has been like this before. If I don't see you tonight, Mary, I'll see you tomorrow morning when you come home, and then you can put all the questions you like. Bye."

I put down the receiver, feeling sick. Philip had been 'like this before'. And what was 'this'? I could not let myself imagine, and my nursing training, general as it was, had not included anything significant about mental illness.

Over the following days, by degrees, I learnt from Susan Parry what she could tell. Philip had had a 'breakdown' at eighteen, following a party where he and his friends, unknown to parents, tried out cannabis and a few other things.

Treated by the family GP, supervised by a local psychiatrist, he apparently recovered, took his A levels and passed them.

At college a year later, Phil had a longer episode and was admitted voluntarily to a psychiatric unit just after the start of the summer vacation. As it was brief, this admission did not appear on the patient's CV. He took his prescribed medication, and seemed well for the rest of his training. After graduation, Philip went to work for an accountancy firm based in France.

A year later, he took himself off medication and relapsed. Susan was sent for, and when she escorted her son back to Britain, she demanded to speak with the psychiatrist who had seen him first. She wanted to know Philip's original diagnosis—which she had, apparently, never been given, since her son did not want her to know it and political correctness demanded that his will should prevail.

The information she was given was not reassuring. Philip had schizophrenia, a chronic disease with psychotic episodes, subject to relapse. There was as yet no cure, but Susan was told that the symptoms could be controlled by medication.

I had not the heart to ask her, but it must have been around then, I think, that Susan took the decision to keep Philip's diagnosis a secret, even from her family, always hoping as she did, that each psychotic episode would be the very last.

1 April 1974

The first of April is not a fortunate date on which to start a new job. So, when I drove to Sladebourne this morning, finding the big silver gates shut and locked with nobody visible at the gate-lodge did not come as a complete surprise. After a half-minute wait, I pressed the horn, and all the other people in the short queue of vehicles behind me pressed theirs.

The result was impressive enough to rouse an elderly porter with a serious red face, who hurried from the back regions of the lodge to open the gates, calling out something by way of apology as he did so. He added an aside which sounded to me like: 'Child got out'. I waved to him and drove on towards Administration to let them know that I had come.

At the place where the drive forks a procession came suddenly into view. I stopped to let it pass. First, crept a superannuated ambulance painted yellow and decorated with the logo of a children's charity. After it, straggled a line of children, some pushed in wheelchairs, others swinging awkwardly on crutches, or walking hand in hand with care workers.

One big boy rode an adult-sized tricycle with his feet strapped to the pedals. These children were mostly boys, they were silent, shabby, and all looked pinched with cold. The morning was grey and chill, as April often is, yet they wore no coats or jackets and the few girls there had no tights or even socks. There I sat in the car, warmly wrapped, caressed by the heat from the engine, and gradually feeling really ashamed.

One black youngster—he looked about eighteen—broke ranks suddenly and made for my car. He did not look at me, but with a rapt face examined, in turn, the bonnet, the radiator, the headlights and the wheels. I put down the window.

"Hi," I said, "you like cars, then?"

He did not respond and seemed totally unaware of me, but his hands sought and felt the edge of the open window as though it were something new, which, in a sense, it probably was to him. One slim hand entered the window and felt about as if seeking the inside door handle. What was I to do now? The dilemma was solved for me by the appearance of a harassed-looking man in a white coat, who grabbed the boy's other hand and led him firmly back to the line.

When the children had gone past me, and down a turning to the school, I felt a sense of disappointment. I had expected to see again the girl who ran out in front of my car last week, and she was certainly not among these children. Perhaps, though, she was a temporary resident and now back home; as Sladebourne does take children for respite care.

Parking spaces outside administration are all reserved—a fact which escaped me before—and they were already occupied. I drove cautiously around the building. At its rear, a curved wrought-iron staircase rose to a first-floor balcony with a stylish front door complete with knocker and letter-slit.

Flanked by potted shrubs, the door had a foreign and formal look; in the middle of an institution here is someone's own very private territory, and rent-free no doubt. I edged the car into a space beside a Lancia convertible. This, I think, must surely belong to Dr Gomez, and is a souvenir of the good life at Porton.

And as I was locking my car, there suddenly came to me again, as once or twice on my first visit, that unmistakable feeling of being watched. Involuntarily, I looked up. There *was* a watcher on the balcony. But from where I now stood, all I saw was a flutter of green as she disappeared, and a quivering of the brasses on her hall-door as it rapidly shut.

Lillian, when we have talked about the matter, was vague as to where my Sladebourne office accommodation would be; saying that she was still arranging this with Locke. So to his office, I went, and as I knocked, half-caught an impression of movement and of the colour green, this time on the dark upper landing right at the back of the hall. Somebody wanted to get out of the building, but not to be seen doing so. Well, why not, and none of my business. I can't help wondering about it, all the same.

In Locke's office, I found his secretary, a large young woman with big grey eyes, who introduced herself as Lynn Rodgers. Lynn was expecting me and appeared to know exactly what she was doing, which was, in this case, deputising for Locke.

"He asked me to look after you," she explained, "and show you your office because he can't be here this morning. I've got your keys for you," producing them as she spoke. I took them and thanked her, and said that I was sure that there would be a lot of things I would need to ask about. As soon as I had said that, I knew it to be somehow wrong, but not why. Lynn gave me a deliberate and condescending smile.

"I'll take you to your office now, Miss Delancy. It's just where you come in, you know, back of the gate lodge."

As we went out, I asked her: "Who lives in the upstairs flat here?"

Lynn started to say: "Why—" then quickly produced another little smile instead.

"Mr Paigle lives there—the Chief Nursing Officer. And Mrs Paigle too, of course."

"I think I saw her just now," I said, "at the top of the stairs."

"You can't have. Mrs Paigle," said Lynn, "is away at present in Corsica. She's Corsican."

The voice did not sound quite so confident or friendly as before.

On a bench outside the lodge sat the porter who had admitted me, doing something with a screwdriver to the innards of an electric plug. At our approach, he stood up.

"This is Mr Aitken, Miss Delancey," said Lynn, "our Head Porter."

Aitken acknowledged us politely, but his face had lost nothing of its morning anxiety.

"That kid—they still haven't caught him, have they? That worries me. We've got a runner here, Miss, can't keep him in. Goes all over the place, and with the main road so near—"

"But are you sure he went through the gates?" said Lynn, "maybe he simply headed for the woods at the back." Aitken shook his head, unconvinced.

"That road down there. He'd only have to see that, know how he is about cars. He'd only have to try to cross that, and—"

Aitken brought a heavy hand down on the wooden arm of his seat, evidently with greater force than he intended, as he grimaced and wrung the hand afterwards. Sighing, he beckoned us into the lodge. I was aware of a dim, low-ceilinged space, made large by removing the partitions of several small rooms.

"I can see the post is sorted here," I remarked, looking at an array of lettered pigeonholes.

"Not altogether, Miss. Mr Paigle comes down and takes all the rest when we've picked out for Mr Locke and the school. Will your post be going to Mr Paigle or Mr Locke first?"

"To neither of them. I don't come under Mr Paigle, or Mr Locke either, but under the Social Work Department at Riverdale General, and any post coming here for me, I want to come to me directly. I mean, I don't want it to go to someone else first." I am certainly not going to have anyone else opening my mail. Aitken said nothing.

My eyes had grown accustomed to the gloom, in which I could now see a little man seated at a rudimentary switchboard. This was Fred, another porter (how many more of them are there?) taking his turn at dealing with incoming calls, though plainly disconcerted by our presence. Aitken was meanwhile making tea in a damp-looking recess at the back of the lodge.

Lynn refused it, but I accepted the strong brew in the stained mug as 'token hospitality'. We were taught, on my social work course, how important it could be not to refuse offers like this. So I sat down on one of an assemblage of old chairs and drank tea with the porters, disregarding Lynn's obvious impatience.

Anyone who has worked in a hospital knows the importance porters have in the institutional system, and I guess they can be rated very high in the scheme of things at Sladebourne.

"Aitken," I said suddenly, "the boy you said got out—is he a big lad with no speech, about eighteen, and black?"

"That sounds like Eugene alright."

"Because if it is, then he's back here, safe." As I described to him the boy who had examined my car, Aitken's expression changed. He reached for the internal 'phone, rang one of the wards, and somewhat to my surprise roundly told off the person who answered him because she had not let him know about Eugene's return.

Lynn's face showed amusement, and when I looked enquiringly at her, she told me that Aitken's stepdaughter works on Midlothian Ward, where Eugene lives.

Presently, Aitken escorted us through an archway at one side of the building, to a little courtyard furnished with swings, a shelter, and doors labelled BOYS and GIRLS.

"This was the Deaf School," said Aitken, noticing my surprise. He explained that in the fifties a short-lived boarding school for deaf children occupied the gate lodge and what is now a staff hostel.

"Here's the rest of it," he added, leading the way through another arch, to another small court of whitewashed walls and buildings as old as the lodge itself.

The place was melancholy and neglected, shaded by trees growing outside of the mossy walls crowned with ferns. In one of these walls were two doors, newly painted a shining green. Lynn indicated that I should unlock the second of these.

"What's in there?" I asked, pausing at the first door.

"Night staff's office," said Lynn shortly. Her mood had changed, I felt, and now she was impatient. I unlocked the second door, opened it, then hesitated. Aitken, in the background, looked expectantly at me over Lynn's shoulder.

"Go on," Lynn said to me, "take a look."

I must have been unconsciously expecting something rather like the lodge interior, so I was speechless when I saw what was actually there: a vision from the past, a crowded, colourful Victorian room like those I saw when I went with my father on business visits to elderly customers of the Bank he worked for. I have had to wait, time after time, in rooms very like this one.

I looked up at the ceiling with its decorative mouldings, around at the high walls, papered above their ornate tiling in a Morris design of green and grey leaves. A composite-marble mantelpiece, its polished grate framed in turquoise tiles, enshrined an early gas fire; the gilt-framed mirror above it easily assembled our three faces in its wavy depths. To one side of the fireplace stood a leather armchair, facing it, an easy chair covered in red plush.

At the two big windows, red curtains hung down to the Turkey rug on the polished floor. A second glance, it is true, revealed shabbiness; the wall's half-tiling chipped here and there, the once thick white paint of the woodwork faded to cream, the original bright colours of the rug subdued by age. But it was still superb, and the centrepiece of this room was an antique desk, only to be surpassed in size by those of Locke and Paigle. Overcome, I sat down in the wooden revolving chair behind it.

"I don't know what to say. I've never had anything like this before. It's so, so—I don't know. Gorgeous. Unexpected."

"I got it cleaned up for you," said Aitken.

"That was very kind of you and I'm really grateful. It's just such a surprise."

"Glad you like it, Miss. There's central heating, but it's on the blink, so the gas fire was left. It works," added Aitken as an afterthought.

"Thank you," I said again, and pulled at the drawer handle of a polished wooden filing cabinet, "do you know if there are keys to this?"

"Don't worry, Miss. I'll get 'em open while you're at the meeting later on."

"I will need a cabinet that can be locked, for client's files. If this doesn't lock, Lynn, I'll have to ask you about ordering one that does. You don't look hopeful!"

"It's only that we have been trying to get new ones for ourselves for ages. But maybe Riverdale General will send you one. They have everything over there."

This is a remark which I am sure that I will hear often over the next few months. Riverdale, the parent hospital of the group, is evidently seen as a Cauldron of the Dagda, from which you can extract unlimited goodies if you know the right magic words.

"Lynn, do you think that you could let me have some stationery? Just to start with. I'm not sure who does the ordering for stationery here."

"I order all the stationery for Sladebourne, but I haven't yet been told anything about ordering for a social worker."

"Then, would you please put in an order for me and see what happens? I'll just need some report sheets and a spiral-backed notebook to begin with, nothing very special."

"I don't know. Perhaps if you were to ask Mr Locke yourself. Anyway, we don't stock the notebook you just asked me for. You'd best talk to Mrs Saye about that."

"All right, I will. Today."

When they had gone, I explored all the drawers on my desk. The top left-hand one was shallow, and partitioned into spaces for pen nibs and paperclips. It was empty now, except for a white card the size of a postcard. I picked this up, turned it over and read in shaky black capitals: WE DON'T WANT YOU HERE.

When I rang Lillian a few minutes later, and she was asking me if I had found everything all right, I thought it better not to mention that card.

This afternoon, the Case Conference was held in the big room in Midlothian, where I had found the rocking boy.

When I came in with Paul Gomez, the room had been transformed into something between a lecture theatre and a courthouse. Rows of seats were arranged in a semi-circle around an arena space, into which the room door also opened. Gomez seated himself in the front row, insisting that I sit beside him. Paigle soon joined us, nodded severely to me, and sat on my left. He was followed by Locke, who placed himself as far as possible from Paigle—but still in the front row.

I was surprised to see so many people and to find that most of the seats far back were taken. Among the takers I saw Fred the porter, the mailvan's driver whose name I don't know, and Nola, the black care assistant I've met before in Waverley. There was continual talking and laughing, a relaxed air, and somehow a real feel of a social occasion taking place.

The ward meetings I've been at during my life as a nurse were hurried affairs in the ward office following a consultant's inspection of his patients, the Case Conferences I attended as a social work student were longer and more formal than the ward meetings, but also more tense and wordy. This meeting was clearly going to be a completely different scene, and who, I wondered, was going to be the one to set it.

I was not left to wonder long. As a distant clock struck the hour of two, the door opened and a procession entered. First came a child, a black boy of thirteen or fourteen, blinking behind glasses with abnormally thick lenses, and accompanied by Michelle from Kenilworth. Just behind her came Lynn, eyes modestly cast down, but equipped for action with a new spiral-backed notebook, of exactly the sort she had told me she could not get me.

And lastly, a familiar figure, sandy, self-conscious and vulpine, Dr Noel Hanafin, senior consultant psychiatrist at Sladebourne, an occasional lecturer on my social work course, and, very much further back in time, a neighbour's son from Co. Tipperary.

At college, Hanafin had never shown any sign of recognising me, indeed he never showed the slightest personal interest in any individual student. But whatever hopes of anonymity I might have nourished died straight away when the doctor stopped and, scattering a sheaf of papers onto the floor with a theatrical gesture, glared at me as if he could not believe his eyes and in that high-pitched incantatory tone disliked by so many people, addressed me directly:

"Miss Delancy! An unexpected pleasure to see you here! As an honoured guest, no doubt? Was it my colleague Dr Gomez who invited you, perhaps? Or was it you, Paigle?"

I felt my colour rise, and shrank back into the chair, wishing I had ignored Gomez and gone to sit somewhere else. I had quite forgotten as well, Hanafin's trick of drawling one's name out, to give it a sarcastic emphasis.

"Oh no, doctor," Gomez beamed, "Miss Delancy is not a guest. She is here to work. You will be glad to know that she is our social worker."

"Our what?"

"Social worker. The one I told you about. The one Mrs Saye found us."

"Found you, you mean. I've never had one or needed one either. Any time I want a few letters done, I can get this young lady to oblige."

This he said with a distinct leer at Lynn, who was picking up the papers he had let fall. Beside me, Paigle swallowed uneasily, then turned around to glare at some of the audience who were making appreciative noises.

"Where's the first patient?" demanded Hanafin, seating himself by the table on which Lynn had placed his notes. He was looking pleased with having demonstrated, as openly as possible, his status and my own. The patient was still standing, no seat having been provided for him. But now Michelle gently pushed him forward to a position where everyone could see him. That she pushed instead of instructing him, suggested to me that he might be deaf.

Paigle stood up, and ceremoniously read the patient's name aloud from a list he held: Ivor Smith, birth date and a home address. Gomez, also standing, produced a battered folder with Ivor's name upon it, and began to read aloud a condensed version of the boy's history.

Ivor's parents come from Grenada, but Ivor was born in London. He has been at Sladebourne for the past five years. He was a typical 'Rubella Baby', an infant whose mother contracted German Measles at an early stage of pregnancy. The unfortunate effects—of hearing and visual damage, plus intellectual handicap— were transmitted to her child.

West Indians, said Gomez, were especially vulnerable to rubella because it was so rare in their part of the world that they acquired no natural immunity to it. When he said this, I felt rather than heard a little stir of interest in the crowd behind us, where there were several people from the Caribbean. Gomez heard it too, I think.

He went on to say that as a result, Ivor was born with a profound hearing loss which meant that he had not been able to acquire speech. Gomez had examined him just that morning at Bourne School, and Ivor was otherwise healthy.

As the effects of Hanafin's rudeness wore off, I began to question what was happening. What *were* all these people here for? How did a physically handicapped child (for such Ivor appears to be) come to be living in an institution mainly for children with intellectual disabilities? I must ask Gomez a few questions. As he finished speaking, a woman's loud voice, coming from the back of the room, began to deliver a report on Ivor's school progress.

It was not detailed, nor was it long—and the conclusion went something like this: "Ivor is in Rosebud group with Miss Macleod. He receives every encouragement to practise his self-care skills. He takes part in all group activities. He has now reached a peak in his development."

I could not see the speaker, but something in the confidence of the voice struck me. It sounded as if it could belong to Mrs Bailey, Head of Bourne School, whom I have yet to meet. And, as Ivor stood near me, I was able to notice how he was reacting, and I thought he was aware of loud voices to some extent anyway—enough to be frightened by them.

There came a sudden shout from Hanafin, at which Ivor jumped and so did I.

"No mother presents? Where's this chap's mother, Paigle?"

Paigle swiftly withdrew the hand which had rested, in an absentminded way, on Lynn's thigh and replied: "Nobody has seen her, doctor. She never visits."

"We'd better do something about that, hadn't we, Paigle? That's your job, you know. Not now, man, not straight away (for Paigle had risen). Later will do. But Dr Gomez here will want to see the lady about her son, as he's taking over the case from me."

From the way Ivor turned his head slightly towards anyone who moved suddenly or gestured, as Hanafin had done, I felt sure that he could see something of them. Deafness protected him from the verbal part of the proceedings, but then I had to ask myself if anyone would have spoken differently, had Ivor been able to hear them.

A discussion followed between Hanafin, Paigle and Michelle about Ivor's challenging behaviour. (This convenient new term, I am learning, covers everything from nose-picking to the infliction of GBH.) Ivor has developed the habit of ripping his cotton shirts into strips about two inches wide. As punishment, he is made to sew the strips together again with needle and thread.

No one commentated on the surprising fact that a blind child can, apparently, see well enough to sew. Nor did anyone remark that boredom might play some part in Ivor's desire to tear things up. Paigle expressed concern about the expense and difficulty of replacing the torn shirts, something which, said Paigle bitterly, was almost impossible at present. Locke, silent until now, made as though he wanted to speak, but was quickly silenced by Hanafin who briskly dismissed both Ivor and Michelle and then asked Paigle to call the next patient.

Paigle obediently called out: "Next," and nothing happened. Paigle called again, a temper flush showing on his round face. This time, the door opened, there was a scuffling sound, and Terence entered backwards, dragging a child who was trying to refuse to come. Gomez put a chair for him, and Terence sat down, the child standing before him, held by one arm. I knew her, she was the girl who had jumped out in front of my car.

"Stella Wilson," read Paigle, and then a birth date, but no address.

"In the workshop, I presume?"

"In the workshop, Dr Hanafin."

Stella Wilson turned her blonde head and looked around the room as I have seen an animal looking for a way out of a cage. Her appearance brought matters to a head with me; I was already revolted, and only a strong effort at control kept me there at all, feeling as though I gave approval to the scene by being present.

To me, this was no longer a meeting, but a circus in which the performing animals were children. And there was, I saw, no quick way out for me now—literally none, for the room, big as it was, was full to the door and Terence sat in front of that door. Whatever took place here, we all had to stay and see.

Gomez read that Stella was admitted to Sladebourne eighteen months ago when she was nine. Her behaviour on admission was—he paused to find the most suitable term—challenging. Challenging in the extreme. Stella was hyperactive and almost uncontrollable in any setting.

It had been impossible for her mother to look after her. At Sladebourne, on the other hand, where it was possible to isolate her, she has become easier to manage. Gomez examined her recently: she has no apparent physical disabilities and is healthy.

Here Paigle smiled a justified smile. However, Gomez went on to say that Stella now self-mutilates. To illustrate this statement, Terence silently lifted up Stella's bitten and scarred left hand. Stella snatched the hand back and put it in her mouth. Released by Terence, she sat down on the floor and began to rock herself to and fro. As she did so, it became evident that she wore no knickers.

"Why has this child no underwear?" asked a faintly embarrassed Gomez.

"Got them wet," responded Terence, "we had to take them off."

"Or a tracksuit, as it's cold," from Gomez.

"Only if she stops wetting. They cost to wash *and* to dry, and we don't have all we need, unfortunately."

I looked up at this point and intercepted a surprisingly vicious glance from Terence to Locke.

"No workshop staff here?"

"Coming now, Dr Hanafin, just coming now."

A lean, brown woman somehow slipped between the chairs and into the circus ring. Hanafin looked a question at Paigle.

"Louise," explained Paigle, "new care worker. The last one was—"

"Yes, yes, no time for that now. Louise, can you tell us how you manage this girl, give a report on her, can you do that?"

The woman compressed her lips and nodded. She could have been almost any age between thirty and fifty, she had long dyed black hair and very bright blue eyes, and her thin, flowing clothes and open sandals suggested hippy identity. Squatting down beside Stella, she coaxed the hand out of Stella's mouth. Only then did she address herself to Hanafin.

"Stella has her good and her bad days. This is a bad day, so she won't talk. But she can talk all right when she wants, she certainly can, and sing too. She's always worse when there are men around, plays them up, screaming, hiding, wetting and soiling herself.

"Running away, even. On times when it's only girls on duty, she's really good, and she'll do what you tell her. But even then, if something happens, she doesn't like; she plays us all up. In fits." And in a gentle, almost motherly fashion, Louise stroked the hair out of Stella's eyes.

"Fits, you said," from Gomez, "what fits? What do you mean? Does she fall down? Pass out? I would like to know details."

Gomez, he has been telling me, is professionally very interested in epilepsy. But it seemed that Louise did not understand what he was asking her. After some minutes of confusion, it became clear that 'fit' was just a turn of phrase, and Stella shows no epileptic signs.

"Stella, will you sing for me?" asked Gomez suddenly. To the surprise of everyone she obeyed, and in a hollow but tuneful little voice she began the Squirrel Song:

When cold winds did blow, and the leaves began to lack,
A beggar-boy found me and put me in his sack,
He brought me up to London, a lady did me buy,
She put me in a silver cage, and hung me up so high,

There were apples by the fire, and nuts for me to crack,
And a little feather-bed, to rest my little back.

"All right, thank you, thank you that's enough," cried Dr Gomez, "you've sung enough for me."

I clapped, as did several others, and then Gomez looked as pleased as any snake-charmer might be. He riffled through the papers on the table and asked Paigle if anyone ever came to visit Stella.

"To see her? No. No, no one. Ever."

Paigle then looked in a questioning way first at Louise and then at Terence; they answered 'No' simultaneously. I wonder how they can be so positive, for neither of them spends the whole day with the child. When Hanafin asked suddenly how Stella behaves during the night, Paigle rushed to answer him, saying that at no time was Stella left alone, and Hanafin would be glad to learn that there had been no more dangerous behaviour either…

"You mean, like with the bag?"

"Yes, I can safely say that."

A few of the surrounding faces looked blank, others knowing. I remembered the warnings printed on plastic bags.

Under the influence of Louise, her stroking guardian, Stella gradually lifted her head from her chest and then her whole body from the floor. She is a real blonde, I thought, the tresses framing her little face much fairer than, at first sight, they had seemed to me. Her features were too pinched to be pretty until she smiled, as at last, she did.

Then, with her face animated, the green eyes shone too, and she was enchanting; faded clothes and dirty shoes no longer taking anything away from the impression she made. As Stella raised herself on tiptoe like a bird preparing to fly, everyone in the room looked at her, unable to keep from doing so. Having gathered their attention, with amazing speed Stella launched herself at Gomez head first.

He had risen and was now standing directly between her and myself. He sidestepped, and Stella's head hit me in the midriff, knocking all the breath out of my body, and sending me, chair and all, into the lap of the woman seated behind me. While we both picked ourselves up, Stella was led away, laughing loudly and persistently.

This evening, back at the flat nursing bruised ribs, I keep wondering if the child hurt herself. She laughed, but that means anything—a child like her might as easily cry, and with as little reality of feeling. She has no understanding that she can hurt someone else. She's so thin—and in those awful clothes thinner still, like something out of an illustration to *Oliver Twist*. Whoever is responsible for looking after her, they don't seem to be doing it properly.

2 April 1974

Last night, I thought I would certainly sleep, but found that I could not. Whatever vague premonitions I had about that weekly conference did not come anywhere near to reality, and my tired mind could only focus obsessively on the outdated nature of the whole event. Nowhere else in seventies London, I am sure, could such a meeting be staged—it belongs to the time of Queen Victoria, the heyday of institutional living.

And if the so-called conference is bad now, what's it going to be like when parents are encouraged by Gomez and myself to attend it, only to be ticked off by Hanafin and Paigle? Yes, we'll certainly see the parents involved—once. No part of me wants to be involved with a spectacle so lacking in human sympathy. It is far, far away from my recent training, light-years from the statements of intent we received: *We take the side of the most vulnerable, or We don't make life harder for unfortunate people,* which are supposed to be our own guiding slogans.

Moreover, from even my very limited contact with the children at Sladebourne, it's clear that they are really *not* well cared for—even physically. Some people here must realise this, but think it does not matter. To change *that* part of the situation means involving powerful individuals who are often difficult to reach and then to convince. Ultimately, it means confrontation, and how my heart sinks at the prospect.

There is still more. Something about my new place of work is ominously, tormentingly familiar. In my sleepless state, I acknowledged this idea without knowing where it came from; then mercifully I slipped into sleep, and it was not until morning that memory provided the answer to my question. Memory reminded me of Mount Alverno.

Mount Alverno was a neglected demesne, about three miles from the small Tipperary town where we lived when I was about twelve. My friends and I spent hours there after school, the short hours of winter days even when we were supposed to be walking family dogs. The sense of remoteness, of mystery, which was a quality of that place, rises up in me like a sigh whenever I deliberately call it into memory as I am doing now.

Now, I can see in turn the entrance gates; elegant, broken and perpetually shut (we had our own ways in); the dark woodland paths intruded upon by outsize camellias, giant laurels, towering araucarias, alongside river channels and backwaters running, like the waters of Lethe, into perpetual gloom. From these shores, banked with rich-smelling mud, the boys launched crude rafts; in the sunless clearings, the girls attempted to build shelters.

When the rain came, as it frequently did, we retreated to the haggard where we sat on lumpy heaps of swede turnips covered in straw. There we sang against the noise of rain beating on the iron roof, or played Consequences using an old Bridge scoring pad and pencils purloined from Nilla's mother.

We were innocent, ignorant, and, it seems to me now, totally free from care. Mount Alverno was our chief refuge and the most secret place we knew. Apart from farm sheds, there weren't any buildings left. The estate house, mentioned with respect in nineteenth-century gazetteers, burned down during our Civil War; a huddle of brick heaps and hollows now represented the cellars and foundations.

A sloping meadow, once a lawn, was strewn with limestone cylinders, the former sections of broken pillars. The desolate garden still held a few neglected plants, the names of which we did not know. I was always curious about this place, the more so because local people, when asked about it, did not want to even mention the name of the house, calling it instead by the name of the townland, Rossmore.

The person I can best remember my asking about it was Cait, who was my own age—but went to a different school. Cait lived about a mile from Mount Alverno, she was a daughter of schoolteachers, and I questioned her because I thought her on that account to be above the common prejudices and fears of others, so I hoped that she would understand my curiosity and see it as natural. My interrogation was not very sophisticated.

I asked if she knew who had lived in the house, and how it had come to be so completely destroyed—that was all. Cait's expression, usually pleasant and open, changed to stillness and a wariness I had not seen in her before. She said that she could not tell me anything at all about the house.

"But maybe you know about the family. What were they like?"

Suddenly Cait spoke, with the air of one delivering judgement:

"They took the land from the people, and God cursed them. Whatever happened, it was the price of them, so."

Foolishly, I began to contradict her at once, saying that God did not personally intervene to burn Mount Alverno down. Then I remembered what we were being taught about the Divine use of human hands to execute justice and said no more.

It was always possible that Cait's father and her uncles had given God a hand, but I knew I was not going to hear if that was the case. So there was a mystery about the place, and perhaps more than one.

Isolated as Mount Alverno was, people other than ourselves sometimes came there. Members of gun clubs came to shoot rabbits and pigeons and, although tolerant, did not really like our being around, in case they shot one of us by accident, I suppose. There must have been fishermen there as well, for in a remote clearing in the woods we came one day upon the grey body of a pike, jaws half-open, suspended by rope from a branch as if it had undergone execution.

The fishermen did not interfere with us, and somehow their unforeseen presence was reassuring; nevertheless, Mount Alverno was not a place to which any of us ever chose to go alone. Its mystery was not a benign one. Even if nothing terrible actually happened to any of us there, we felt certain that something could be waiting to happen in the future.

Only at Sladebourne yesterday, have I felt the same sense of menace. Both places have a scarcely known past, are isolated, are self-contained and self-containing, apparently needing nothing from outside. Both have an air of keeping guard against people who want to change anything about them; and they send out the same message, that change means danger.

Yet the same half-understood attraction—risk, which once drew me and others to Mount Alverno, is drawing me powerfully to Sladebourne. Only this time, it seems I am facing into the wilderness alone.

9 April 1974

Yesterday, I went to see Stella for the first time since she headbutted me over. My authority to do this rests on somewhat shaky ground for although, as I argued in the case of Matthew French, permission to interview a child in an NHS hospital unit can be assumed by the social worker attached to the same unit, yet at Sladebourne Dr Hanafin makes the rules, and if he denies me access to his patients, what can I do about that? Not much, probably.

The idea of asking his permission first did cross my mind, but I did not entertain it long. Hanafin is virtually impossible to get hold of except on Wednesday afternoons when he attends the weekly conference. But, as an attempt to supply a strong motive for my visit, I have sent a formal letter to the Director of Social Services in Hoxton, the new name of the re-shaped borough from which, Terence told me, he believes Stella came. (Terence has actually unearthed an address for her, a house number in a street demolished over a year ago.)

Besides introducing me, my letter enclosed a list of the names and original addresses of the several Hoxton children at Sladebourne. I trust that someone somewhere in that bureaucracy will get the message and respond.

The workshop where Stella lives is indeed the building that Paigle left out on the conducted tour of his kingdom. Backing onto woods behind Midlothian, it is a small brick house which, according to local folklore, was once a cobbler's workshop where the shoes of a whole community were mended.

Now a modest prison, it consists of two rooms and a bathroom. It has few windows and only one external door, usually kept locked both night and day— Midlothian care staff have the keys. Secure, bleak, unobtrusive, it is a disturbing place to find as part of an institution for children.

When I knocked at the door of the workshop today, it was opened by Louise. If she was surprised, she gave away no trace of it; even remembering my name. I asked if I might come in, and she made no demur. Stella was not so civil. Fixing me with her wary gaze, she simply retreated into the room's farthest corner and sat down there on the floor.

"I wanted to see how you are and where you live, Stella," I said when I had told her my name and who I was. Stella made no reply.

Louise sighed. "It's another bad day with her, she isn't talking to anyone. And I haven't been able to get her to say sorry about knocking you off the chair."

"Well, it's a pity if Stella can't talk because I'm just going to take a picture of her, and when it's finished I'll want to know what she thinks of it."

Without more ado, I took out my sketchbook—the last remnant of a childhood ambition to be an artist—and without another look at Stella began to draw her face from memory. As I was doing so, the bleakness of the surroundings impressed itself on me. The room was small, and in addition to three people, all that it contained was a battered table, three kitchen chairs and a few broken toys in a cardboard box.

Grime-grey institutional lino covered the floor. There were no curtains at the window. Through the open doorway to the inner room, I saw an iron bedstead, an old cupboard, another kitchen chair. No pictures or posters, no colour, no interest anywhere—why keep a ten-year-old like this? A prisoner in jail would have more.

My drawing took shape, the thin, almost angular face with its little nose, sad mouth, and alert eyes. As I worked on the hair, I could sense Stella's footsteps, quiet though she tried to make them (she isn't very good at being quiet).

A moment later, I was only just quick enough to stop her snatching the book away from me, and only just observant enough to catch the pure amazement on her face as she saw what I had made of her. I held my work high out of her reach, and was rewarded by the cry:

"Let me see it, Oh, let me, let me have it!"

Louise sucked her breath in audibly. She had watched the scene until now with her usual calm.

"I don't want it torn up, Stella!"

She had stayed within my reach until now but was always ready to retreat quickly.

"Give it to me; please give it to me. I won't tear it. I'll call you Mary if you give it to me."

I made her promise not to tear it, then gave her the drawing, and she carried it away with her into the bedroom and closed the door.

"Perhaps she will come back." But all Louise's skill could not coax her back.

"Louise, there isn't much here to occupy Stella—so what do you do with her all day?"

"Talk to her, mostly. Take her for walks. And we do exercises to music, I've a cassette player I bring—"

"Stories, books?"

"She doesn't want them. She can't read them." Or you can't, I thought. I felt I'd stayed long enough for a first visit. Calling a goodbye to Stella, I paused at the outer door, uncertain how to ask what I wanted to know.

"Louise, do you have any information about how Stella came to be here, where she's actually from, what her family's like—that sort of thing?"

"Not one thing. And she's had no one from her family visit her since I've been here, that's certain."

Today I met Louise again, in the canteen. This is a big room constructed from the whole ground floor of one of the Sladebourne villas. Unfortunately, the meals served there do not live up to the surroundings, being overcooked, long on grease and short on anything fresh. Louise was sitting with a group of care assistants, she smiled at me when I came in, and when they all got up to leave, she came over to the table where I sat alone.

"I was wondering when you'd be coming to see Stella again," Louise said.

"Is she going to stay in that little place?"

Louise nodded. "Terence Brady doesn't want her back in Midlothian. You can see why. It's all boys now, and they'd make her worse. She's not so bad on her own."

So I said I'll call in early next week. I don't want to fix a regular time. And I've got to think about where this is going, anyway.

30 April 1974

Over the last weeks, I've learnt more about Sladebourne. I have talked to Paigle, Locke and Lynn politely when we met. I have visited all the children in their houses after school. I have eaten in the canteen and chatted with the porters in their lodge.

I've met the therapists—some of them, anyway. Conclusions? The physical layout of this place is not hard to follow, once you know the boundaries and the principal paths, but the way in which the whole community of patients, staff and hangers-on actually works day to day will take me much longer than a week to puzzle out.

Nevertheless, I've made some early discoveries. The first is that Locke and Paigle do not communicate with each other at all. I don't mean only that they do not speak. They do not acknowledge each other to exist.

They send no memos back and forth as managers do elsewhere. They deliberately keep clear of each other, to the extent that the one does not emerge from his office if the other is present in the hall.

That sounds funny but is actually very serious because Locke controls all the finances, and it explains to some extent the bare and poverty-stricken settings in which the children live. I asked how this state of affairs was allowed to go on, as it apparently has, for years, and then I found out a little bit more. Lynn Rodgers is delegated by Locke to administer the budgets of individual wards.

So if, for example, she disagrees with a charge nurse on Kenilworth who maintains that the children there need new clothes, no money will be forthcoming to buy these. And Lynn does not have to answer to anyone else about her decisions, either!

A second discovery, arising from the first one, is that Locke's view of social workers as fundraisers is widely held. Every member of the care staff, from Paigle down, thinks that raising money for them is what I am here to do.

Fundraising is so important because, in the general climate of poverty, it's the one hope care staff have of getting their hands on petty cash; moreover, they enjoy the whole income generation scene: raffles, sales of work, dances, and charity concerts since these are held near enough to where they live for them to be able to take part. Sladebourne House thus provides its employees not only with work but with play.

And I have tried to make it plain to everyone I've met that I am not here to raise money for them!

From one viewpoint, it's an advantage to have an unknown role. As no one at Sladebourne really knows what I'm supposed to do, I feel free to attempt anything. Who is going to stop me? Not Lillian, though she won't support me either. When I went to see her recently for my first supervision, the way things went told me that. She listened to me for only about five minutes, before her feelings overcame her:

"But Mary, Mary—these are very critical comments about a place you've only known for a few days. You must not be too hard on Mr Paigle. Remember the enormous, positively enormous changes he's had to take in recently. Including the appointment of yourself. Now, I grant, he is something of a rough diamond, but Leonard Locke always strikes me as a charming person, from the 'old school' of hospital secretaries when they were ex-officers and so forth.

"If he is having trouble with managing finances—well, aren't all of us? There is no bottomless purse in the NHS, you must know. But you probably don't know. That's what I feel about the new social workers. You don't—I don't mean you personally of course—you don't think of realities. Of making do with what is there…"

By the time she had finished what she had to say, all I felt I had gained was the half-promise of an allowance for stationery, and an awareness of the need to change tactics for the next session.

We never even got to the question of access to patients' records. To write to all parents, obviously, Gomez and I must have their addresses. I'd have thought there should, in a long-stay hospital like this, be some filing cabinet somewhere containing this kind of information—but there isn't. You don't expect a proper Records Office, but you expect *something*.

All there actually is, on each ward, is a meagre, stapled bunch of daily report sheets for each patient. These bundles, usually kept in a desk drawer, don't always include histories. In other hospitals, therapists and social workers have easy access to reports and records.

Not here. A new physio assistant yesterday was refused access to notes on Kenilworth, and the ensuing row was exciting enough to reach even my ears, courtesy of Aitken.

After some thought, I have decided to start my record research with Waverley.

Sister Daroga received me in her office, where, in brooding silence, she was completing the detailed menus for next week's meals. I carefully explained why I was there. Sister heard me at first without comment, but as I went on to explain the reason for what I was doing, she listened, nodded agreement, and caused me to feel grateful to her in an almost emotional way, so anxious have I been without being fully aware of it.

Waverley records are kept in Sister's office, in a metal contraption on wheels; it would make sense to look at them where they are, but I asked if this would not disturb her?

"No, no Miss Delancy. Fine. But perhaps you have time for me to speak with you first?" Of course, I said yes, and hoped that she was not going to ask for my help in a fund-raising project.

"I am very angry and distressed" (To my view, she did not look either, just tense.)

"They are saying, Dr Hanafin and our Chief Nursing Officer, that some of my children cannot go any longer to the Bourne School. I know, I know, Vera's eighteen, and maybe one or two of the others are that age, but so what.

"Are they adults? Have you seen the size they are? You have? Can they go out to work? I do what I can, and so do we all, but everything, everything you see here, *we* got for them, the girls and I, with some help from therapy and from nowhere else. Their home is here. Miss Delancy, *where will they go if they can't go to school?*"

Daroga's voice shook and shrilled on the last few words: I think she knows as well as I do the answer to her question. Paigle and Hanafin intend to transfer all the over-eighteens to Mount Vervain, where Hanafin also holds a consultant post. They want space, on Waverley or elsewhere, to accept new admissions and so to justify Sladebourne's continued existence.

Mount Vervain, to the local Press known as Vampire's Castle, is a large institution described as a subnormality hospital, part of a circle of similar places around Outer London. It certainly would seem to offer even less to Waverley residents than their present placement does. But what no one working here seems to be aware of, is that reform of the whole institutional care system, which the politicians are promising, is going to involve shutting down Mount Vervain as well as Sladebourne House.

Daroga stood facing me, her whole tiny body trembling with her distress and frustration. Up to now, she has been able to provide some compensation for the restricted lives of her charges. Now, an obstacle has arisen which she can see no way around. For myself, all I could think about at that moment was the urgency of getting parents involved in care plans being formed, and decisions are taken, about the future of their children.

Legally, full-time schooling for children with special needs may continue until nineteen, depending on the child's ability to benefit from it. I found myself, against all the rules of reason, dreadfully tempted to make promises to Sister which might be impossible to keep.

"I need to see now what you've got on file about all the Waverley children," I said at last, "and I'll talk to Mr Paigle and the consultants about the older ones. But I can't promise anything." And as soon as possible, I must visit Bourne School.

7 May 1974

Bourne Hospital School stands on a small hill at the end of the road which opens to the right just before the Admin building. A big gate in a high wire fence is the only entrance to a wide gravel path that runs all the way to the top of that hill. When you get there, what a marvellous view over South London, almost to the Thames! And air seems all at once to be cleaner and fresher than elsewhere at Sladebourne.

The school itself is a typical nineteen-sixties construction; angular, one-storey, panelled outside in blue plastic which has weathered badly and lost most of its visual impact. Nevertheless, what I saw there today was unmistakably a school building and was relatively new. My heart lifted at the sight, as I went up the slope towards it, passing on the way a direction sign to therapy, where I had been invited to lunch today.

I know that special schools for disabled children rely greatly on the help of therapists, and it seemed a positive sign for one unit of Sladebourne to acknowledge the presence of another. (By now, of course, I was looking, perhaps rather too eagerly, for some positive signs.)

I walked around that whole school building twice, seeking an identifiable way in. Doors and windows of buildings from the sixties look very much alike. Direction signs there were none. Through the ceiling-to-floor-length windows, I could see spaces with people in them, but no one seemed to notice me, the stranger peering uneasily in.

At last, I came on an unlocked double door, opening into a corridor painted in several equally ugly shades of blue. As I entered and walked down it, all that I could see around me were successive unmarked blue doors, and all I could hear were occasional faint noises. I had never before been in such a silent school.

That silence broke suddenly when a door was flung open, and a sandy-haired, bearded man ran across the corridor in front of me to the entrance of a walk-in cupboard and disappeared into its depths. Either he really had not seen me, or it was his habit to ignore people: either way, I felt, he should not be allowed to get away with it. So, after a moment's hesitation, I knocked on the door of his refuge, introduced myself, and asked where the office of the school secretary was.

He muttered something I didn't catch, and gestured towards a recess a few yards on, then shot back to his class in response to a rise in the noise level there. I caught a faint scent of alcohol as I passed the door of the classroom, where I could see him attempting to pick up a boy considerably larger than himself, who had fallen prone over another child lying on the floor.

There were two unlabelled doors in the recess. I knocked at the left-hand one and obeyed an invitation to come in. Two women looked up at me from desks, one of them, shy and grey-haired, smiling uncertainly. The other was the woman I had already glimpsed twice, once on the balcony and once on the stairs to Paigle's flat. I told them who I was.

"Miss Delancy? I'm Lucinda Grant and I'm Deputy Head. Mrs Bailey is busy just now—but I'll show you around the school."

Lucinda was a surprise; very tall, thin and elegant, stylishly dressed and somehow, not at all like a teacher. Her glowing, skilfully made-up features, faultlessly arranged wings of straight black hair, with her beautiful clothes came from an altogether different world to the one I know.

I thought suddenly: she's been a model, no, she *is* a model! I met some models when I first worked in London, and I know that they don't look real. Lucinda was smiling, evidently aware of my amazement and enjoying it; she rose gracefully, introduced me to the shy woman, Ann Tillot, who is the school secretary, then led me out of her office, and back the way that I had come.

Although they are all supposed to share a common philosophy, each special school reflects the mind of its headteacher. And it is possible to pick up much information about a school by studying the décor, plus the level of the artwork displayed outside as well as inside classrooms. At Bourne, there are few clues of this kind to be found in corridors, where the only decorations are a few tired-looking plants.

We went into five classrooms, all there are I think, and each was much the same, with hardly any colour, little equipment, and a pervasive musty scent which I recognise as the smell of human saliva. I saw physically disabled children lying in groups on mats on the floor with plastic toys lying beside them; mobile children sitting at tables, fitting puzzles together, sorting wooden beads according to colour, or just sitting.

Occasionally, a floor-dweller raided the territory of the others, grabbing at legs or clothes. When this happened, a teacher intervened to keep the peace; otherwise, they kept it at a distance from their charges. There don't seem to be many classroom assistants, and I wonder how teachers manage when they must leave the group in order to attend to one child.

Apart from Vincent Snape, the man I'd already met, there appear to be women in charge throughout the school. I put it that way, 'in charge' because they seem to be child-minding rather than carrying out any kind of educational plan.

The one possible exception was in the second last classroom we visited, where a plump, fiftyish woman, one Mrs McLeod, had organised her pupils to assemble bouquets of paper flowers for sale at a forthcoming charity fair. While they were doing this, she was telling them a story, which our entrance interrupted.

Ivor Smith was part of this group, I caught his eye and smiled at him. He gave me an oblique look, then turned his face away, his delicate fingers meanwhile sorting the flowers into regular bunches as quickly as anyone of his age, anyone not disabled that is, could have done it. Again, I am reminded that I must ask Gomez about Ivor.

A boy sitting beside Ivor was trying to attract my attention. Fixing me seriously with his great brown eyes, he addressed me with a flood of sound which, indistinct as it was, resembled speech.

"Trev can't talk," interposed his teacher, who was now occupied gilding plastic detergent bottles to serve as containers for the paper bouquets.

"He seems to be trying hard to talk," I said. "Does he have speech therapy?"

"No. Not here. Not so far as I know."

Her accent wasn't English or Scottish, but different—perhaps Spanish, or South American?

"We don't have any speech therapists here," stated Lucinda. "We've never had them."

Trev was pulling at my hand. It was hard not to think of him as a toddler, but in reality, he is probably ten or eleven. Close to him, I could not avoid being aware of the child's shabbiness, his washed-out faded shorts and jersey, odd socks, thin plimsolls, unappealing haircut. The other children, now that I looked at them, were not any better.

Regarding them, I felt an odd sensation of pain, an almost physical pang, just as though for a moment only, I too, wearing other people's castoffs and shoes that did not fit, sat in that bare room at a rather pointless occupation. This child must have a family, where are they?

"What happens about the parents?" I asked. "Do they come to see you, or can you do home visits? When are Parent's Evenings held?"

Mrs MacLeod glanced at Lucinda, who responded smoothly:

"Our children come from all over London, Miss Delancy. Most parents cannot get here easily. As you know, it's right off a bus route and the train station's miles away. They don't all have cars… of course, they're free to visit at any time, by appointment. And no, we don't do home visits, and we don't have Parent's Evenings."

"Progress reviews?" I knew these to be a feature of special schools.

"Oh, we don't have those here. It wouldn't be appropriate, in a hospital school."

Lucinda spoke with such a decision that I was silent. I had meant to ask if they produced school reports but realised in time that Bourne was unlikely to do this either.

We reached the last classroom. Here were the biggest children, most of whom have physical as well as intellectual disabilities—I recognised two from Waverley, as well as Jonathan, the tricyclist I'd seen on the first morning. Jonathan apparently does not walk.

He sits on the floor, shuffling around on his bottom and grabbing, like a human crab, at anything or anyone within his reach. The other children were all trying to keep clear of him, which suggests that he is able to inflict pain.

A boyish-looking blonde girl appeared in the doorway, carrying a large cloth bag in each hand. Evidently recognising her, the mobile children dropped whatever they held at the moment and made for her. Laughing, greeting each one by name, she at first defended her bags from them, and then by degrees disclosed the contents.

These looked simple enough—samples of the fabric of different textures, unusual-sounding home-made rattles, and stuffed animals whose Velcro'ed limbs part from their bodies with a most satisfying ripping noise. These riches went to the more passive children. The active ones were organised into play with a huge soft-ball; rolled, pushed, sometimes even thrown between them.

Children called and laughed, and for the first time, an air of normality came over the scene. The magician responsible for all this? The new physio assistant is Vicky Grainger. She stayed half an hour with that class, while its teacher was immersed in what looked like a ledger. Interesting. Pausing in mid-corridor, on the way back to the office, I suddenly decided to take control of our tour.

"Lucinda, at this stage, I really need to ask you a few more questions—"

"Oh, I can't answer anything, Miss Delancy. You'll have to ask Mrs Bailey."

"Do you think she's still busy?"

As we spoke, a thickset woman with a grim expression emerged from the door opposite Lucinda's.

"This is Mary Delancy the social worker, Mrs Bailey, and she wants to ask you some questions." With that, Lucinda turned smartly on her heel and disappeared. Mrs Bailey looked me up and down.

"Well?"

"Could we go somewhere else to talk?"

Silently, Mrs Bailey led the way into her office, silently she seated herself behind her desk and indicated to me a chair in front of it. I felt like a naughty small child, sent to the Head for correction because she had 'given cheek' to a teacher.

"Lucinda," I began, "has been showing me around the school."

"So I see. It would have been more polite if you'd given me prior notice of this visit. I like people to contact me first."

A Scots accent frosted Mrs Bailey's voice, and her eyes were bright with indignation.

"I did ring your secretary a few days ago, and she said that I could come this morning."

"No message about you came to me. However, now you're here, you want to ask me something, is that right?"

"I'd like to ask about one or two specific things. Lucinda has filled me in already about the, well, the contact between the school and parents. But there are other matters. Stella Wilson, that child who lives in the workshop. I did not see her here. Doesn't she attend the school?"

"No, because I won't have her."

"Do you mind my asking why?"

"Yes, I do mind. And I've got work to do. And I don't see what it's got to do with social workers, who goes to our school and who doesn't."

"It has to do with both of us because each child here in Sladebourne has a legal right to be educated. If Stella isn't attending school, I'll have to let Hoxton Social Services know why. She's in care to them, and they placed her here. They have a right to know the situation, and I have an obligation to tell them about it."

I really didn't know if Hoxton gives a hen's kick or not, but I was not going to let this woman define my responsibilities to me. There was a pause. Mrs Bailey looked down at her clasped hands and sighed a gusty sigh. Then she looked back up at me again, and some of the annoyance had gone from her face.

"This is a curious place you've come to, Miss Delancy, it's not like the outside. Rules that work very well *there* don't work *here*, and the opposite applies too. People here don't want anything to change, and to get on with them you'll have to remember that.

"But you want to know about the Wilson girl. That child's not mentally handicapped, that's about the size of it. She's maladjusted—disturbed—call it what ye will. But not mentally handicapped, so Bourne school is not the right place for her. If I had her attending here, you'd have good reason to protest about it!"

"If that's the situation—can you tell me why Stella's at Sladebourne at all?

"You're asking me? You should ask the London Borough of Hoxton; they'll have tried a good few places for her. If you want my opinion, it's that nowhere else was prepared to take her!"

"I see. Now, about the Waverley children, Vera and some others, I'm told they've been excluded—"

"Now, that is altogether a different matter, the over-nineteens with complex needs. They are too old for her, but they could maybe go to day centres outside. Over nineteens should not be here in the school.

"Now, that would be your business to arrange: Day Care. Your responsibility and the doctor's and Max Paigle's. So you'll have plenty to do without worrying too much about what's going on here."

"I don't think all the Waverley children who've been excluded are over nineteen."

"Well, we don't have proper facilities for multiply handicapped children here anyway, or the staff for them either. Children like these take up a lot of staff time with very little result. Now, if you'll excuse me—I've to make a phone call."

Unlike the Sladebourne wards, therapy has no Scottish name. It is housed in a low, single-storey building with a cluster of pointed roofs which make me think of tents and pavilions. Inside, a gallery of small rooms surrounds a central working space.

In one of those small rooms half an hour later, I sat, lunching on sandwiches and coffee with Margaret Tobias, the senior physiotherapist. So far, this grave-eyed, diffident woman had not asked for any of my impressions of Sladebourne. For that reason alone, I felt driven to open the subject.

"I've just been at the school, and I saw your assistant Vicky in action—but actually, I'm feeling puzzled by the whole set-up. There does not seem to be much going on here anyway—I mean, in the way of training or instruction—and I would have expected more to be happening at Bourne School, but it seems unfair to be critical, especially when they're so isolated from other schools."

My voice trailed away uncertainly. Margaret glanced at me, evidently picking up the lack of confidence and courage. Then she seemed to make her mind up and said:

"They're not all trained teachers, you know."

I said that I hadn't known.

"I think Carol Bailey and Lucinda have qualifications they don't use, but I know the others haven't any. That may account for some of the difference—or oddity—you noticed. They were taken on at the time—and it's not so long ago—when there were no Special Schools, just Junior Day Centres, staffed by people who went in for occupying rather than educating children.

"When ILEA wanted the centres to change function, staff were offered training as teachers on full pay and on courses especially for them. At Bourne, nobody wanted to do it."

"But why ever not? They'd be more secure, better off financially—"

"Not according to them, they wouldn't. Too much extra responsibility, that's the problem. You'd have to be prepared to work overtime, to do things like seeing parents. And as it is, they already get enhancement, so it wouldn't make much difference, moneywise."

I had never heard of enhancement. Apparently, it is an extra payment to some of the people who work with severely disabled children.

"I don't get anything like that."

"I don't either," said Margaret, "it seems to be for people who don't have relevant qualifications. It means that they can earn almost as much as they would get if they had them."

That would explain a lot, I thought. But it would make it harder to get trained people if you took away the pay differential.

"What happens about school inspections, do you know?"

"I don't know, for I've never been around when the school had one. But, going back to when I worked in Richly Manor School a few years ago—and that's a similar patient mix to the one here—inspectors pussyfooted around, not actually saying anything that might be taken as criticism. They wanted to find everything was OK I guess. Or maybe felt out of their depth, with kids as disabled as some of these are."

I shook my head, not to disagree, only to order my thoughts and to make sure that I was still awake and actually hearing what was being said. Then I realised that time was going on, and I hadn't yet asked what I had come there wanting particularly to know.

"You've shown me such a lot here, and given me an idea of what you do, but still, do you—I mean, can you tell me—are there difficulties getting people who work here to carry out what you suggest? When it comes to it, I mean?"

Margaret's normally gentle expression gradually altered from the consciously patient to the withdrawn and preoccupied. I thought I might have gone too far in what I asked because, after all, she does not know me or what use I might make of what she had just said. Then she smiled, and I felt it was all right, she had decided to trust me.

"The other day, Mary, we all went to Ivanhoe to help with feeding dinner; Vicky and Terry and Maureen and I, four of us. You know, some of the older children there can't feed themselves, and we try to be available to help out at lunchtime because food gets cold, standing around. And some children have trouble with swallowing and chewing, so it's a good opportunity to demonstrate ways to help them, or so you'd think.

"Anyway, we tried, Vicky and the rest of us, for half an hour, and after we'd left, I had to go back for my notebook. Before they realised, I was back, I heard one care assistant say to another: 'Now, the physio's gone, we can hurry up. You don't have to do it the way she said, do it the way we always do and do it quicker.'"

"I would be furious," I said, "I would tell them—"

"But Mary, what would the effect be? People don't always know how to change, or why they should. Perhaps we're all like that, in some ways."

68

I felt uncomfortable. Was Margaret actually suggesting that there should be no change to the system? Ever?

As I left, she evidently felt she'd been a bit hard on me, and invited me to join Vicky and herself for lunch there whenever I like!

21 May 1974

I have now been at Sladebourne for almost six weeks. And as most of the children here are described as having 'challenging behaviour', a term I'm not over-familiar with, I rang Nilla today to ask her what *she* thought it meant.

"Life getting difficult? I said it would, you know."

"No, I just really want to know what's meant by that term. You know more about things like that than I do."

"You should be more confident. But anyway, it's makeup. Wholly subjective, in fact. The challenge is not to the children, it's to the staff. It's the name they give to anything they can't deal with or can't understand. No, I don't approve of terms like this one because they label people—"

"Labels are useful, Nilla. To keep things from getting mixed up."

"Labels are divisive; they only foster discrimination and should not be necessary. If people behave, say, dangerously it's either because they don't understand the effects of what they're doing or they do understand very well, and they don't care. Either way, something has gone wrong, very wrong, for them and needs putting right. A label won't change all that."

"But the way they are situated, their deprived material surroundings, Nilla—"

"Only up to a point. After all, I suppose environments to blame for most antisocial behaviour, although there certainly seem to be a few people around still with inborn attitudes you can't change."

I reflected that Nilla's own Catholic attitudes are still there, swelling secretly like mushrooms under the repressive pavement of current behaviourist theory.

And then I had to think of a way to refuse her invitation to the Gathering of Peace and Love, taking place next weekend in rural Berkshire, a county that, whatever the season, I always associate with ankle-deep mud.

4 June 1974

Nilla asks me every time we talk if I'm still finding out Sladebourne's secrets. Every time, I have to say that I'm trying to but am not there yet, and she says that it must be a welcome distraction from personal troubles of one's own making.

One of these troubles, I've discovered, is that my mental picture of the NHS still comes from a nurse's viewpoint. There is structure, sure, there are rules, but they are all there for some reasonable purpose. They are necessary. And the degree to which they are applied, as well as the manner of the application, depends on the personality of the individual who has enforcing power—line manager, senior administrator, consultant doctor.

Most nurses can work with this. What helps is, that nursing as an occupation is terribly open. Everything you do is public, seen by everyone, noted by most and particularly by your colleagues, whom you cannot deceive. They know, and quickly, who is thorough, who slipshod; who is compassionate, who is uncaring; who leaves unpleasant tasks to others, and who takes on, often unwisely, more than their share of work.

My new calling—social work—is, by contrast, a solitary one, largely unsupervised, and remotely managed by people some of whom feel that to comment adversely on the work of others is judgemental or, to use the out-of-date expression, wrong.

An open secret of Sladebourne is that the staff truly do not want any change. Most of them, having had little or nothing in the way of training, shaped their roles to suit themselves. For years they have been secure and out-of-the-way on a kind of desert island surrounded by probably the last patch of common land south of the Thames.

The local inhabitants, whatever their private doubts, choose to regard the Sladebourne staff as a model, moral beings, with more than a touch of sainthood about them, caring tenderly and devotedly for the rejects of society. The staff accepted this view of themselves at first with complaisance, but now some are beginning to feel a cold wind of change blow upon them.

Paul Gomez and I are the advance guard of that change. We might truly prefer to be seen simply as the bearers of good news, but our chances of that can't be rated high even, it appears, in the case of the very people we are trying hardest to help. Something that took place yesterday showed that to us both, plainly enough.

Waverley has the highest visiting numbers of any Sladebourne ward. Sister Daroga and her team certainly do not discourage visiting since, apart from meeting some of the emotional needs of their patients, visitors give money to Daroga's projects, and a few have taken on the status of regular volunteers, to help feed the children, and perhaps even play with them and take them out.

Fiorina Cassati, dark and gentle, is one of these helpers. In fact, she is the one I know best because she is here so often. Her sons, twin boys with a rare and destructive syndrome, sit like statues in their identical wheelchairs and don't respond very much to anyone but their mother.

"A charming woman," says Gomez admiringly, watching a smiling Fiorina spoon food into waiting, birdlike mouths.

"A good parent," agrees Daroga, adding "and a good helper to me."

Bourne School, it appears, also finds Fiorina useful. She never makes an unwary comment or expresses an opinion, and is always unbelievably patient, tactful and discreet. She knows her place, as Head Teacher Carol Bailey would say. As for me, well, I begin to wonder if Fiorina is allowing herself to feel anything at all.

Yesterday, as previously arranged, the Cassatis were the first parents to be interviewed by Gomez and myself. Leo came straight from the merchant bank in the City where he has a senior post. His formal banker's clothes looked right for Paigle's beautiful office, our temporary venue if somehow they were not quite right for the occasion.

Fiorina, seen for the first time without her helper's overall, wore a city suit tailored, unlike English ones, for the female figure. On one elegant lapel was a cameo of gold and jet—an emblem not so much of wealth (though it was that) but rather, I felt, of mourning. Both Cassatis were pale, and Fiorina kept licking her dry, reddened lips.

Gomez introduced himself and myself, and then he took charge, explaining that we wanted to enlist the help of parents to improve long-term prospects for their children. In a time of great change, there would be difficulties to be faced, but also opportunities to be used, so the outlook could be seen as positive. He spoke on warmly, occasionally casting an eye at me to check that I was not so lost in admiration that I was forgetting to take notes.

The expressions of the couple he addressed did not change. Gomez brought in the concept of partnership, explaining that he wanted comments, suggestions, *ideas* from parents. Parents must be active participants, not merely receptive. The tense expressions on the faces of Fiorina and Leo did not alter unless just to become more tense, and not a word came from either of them.

"Perhaps," I put in, "we need to stress the positive aspect—"

"Of course, of course. We understand that you may have doubts—this new approach—after so many years of—of nothing much happening for your children, could it be making way for some terrible upheaval in their lives? That is not so, let me assure you. It is not what we intend."

Gomez paused, but still, no response came. With an air of slight desperation, he went on to what I think of as the technical stuff. He referred to the rarity of the syndrome affecting both Cassati boys, talked of a new chromosome research project, quoted statistics. In passing, he mentioned the age of the boys: Roberto and Riccardo are almost fourteen.

At these latter words of Gomez, Leo Cassati's mouth opened, and he grasped the arms of his chair as if about to rise from it. Carried away as he was with his subject, Gomez, at last, caught my eye and stopped talking.

"Well, now, Mr Cassati, have you anything you want to ask me, so far?"

"Yes, doctor, I have, of course. About our children."

Leo's English was as perfect and polished as his appearance. Gomez nodded at him encouragingly, and I found myself following his example.

"Can you tell us please, doctor, when are they going to die?"

"When they're—when they're going to—I'm not God, Mr Cassati, I can't tell you that!"

"But you must know," cried Fiorina, suddenly agitated, "you or someone else here must know. It was in all their notes. When we brought them here, we were told? By a big man—"

"Yes, you see, I remember it well, and my wife remembers it also. We could not forget it. Six years ago, we saw a man who was in charge here, he wore a white coat, and we were told he was a doctor, but I can't remember his name. He said to us: 'You know, these boys will not live to grow up. They'll die before reaching fifteen', he said, 'such children always do'. So the age they are; surely, it can't be much longer now."

Companions in distress, Gomez and I looked at each other. Then Gomez found his voice, his authority and his doctor's *persona*.

"Mr Cassati, Mrs Cassati—up to a few years ago the estimated lifespan of a severely disabled child was indeed very short. But now we realise, such is not always the case. With antibiotics, with all the treatments, we have today, people in institutions do not die as prematurely as they once did.

"With your sons, I can't of course predict absolutely their life expectancy; I can only say that there is nothing in their histories that would make me expect either of them to die at fourteen or at fifteen."

Looking at the stunned expressions of those parents, I did not know if what I saw there was a relief, disappointment, or perhaps a blend of both. They did not want to talk about anything else, but thanked us and went away.

I've got to work something out with Gomez. He finds the way we are doing things at present professionally satisfactory, but I don't. Taking notes of our interviews is fine, but what I want as well are outlines of family circumstances and history, especially the circumstances leading up to admission to Sladebourne.

Why do I need them? Not just for Gomez to read. The past history of every child here is needed if we're to sell local authorities the idea that they should take responsibility for educating 'their' kids and finding them somewhere better to live.

I've begun to educate myself, to look beyond Sladebourne, not to other Mount Vervains, but too small children's homes, places where our patients would have the chance of some individual attention. I've read and heard of the successful emptying of institutions, and I don't see why it cannot be done here.

17 June 1974

Berkshire is the part of England that gave Paigle birth, but he does not fit the traditional insulting rhyme from there, about being 'strong in the arms, and weak in the head'. He is not stupid, but he is a nuisance because he keeps intercepting my mail.

As the days go by, it comes ever more erratically, sometimes very late, later than anyone else's, and occasionally it comes not at all for several days and then in a large bundle. Aitken, when questioned about this, says he doesn't understand how it can happen, but he looks uneasy at the same time and is probably lying. Yesterday, matters came to a head.

Celine, a social worker from the Paediatric Unit at Riverdale General, called to ask why I didn't turn up at a symposium she'd arranged to be held in one of the District Offices last Tuesday. She had sent me a formal invitation complete with RSVP. An acceptance was returned with an illegible signature.

It seems she wanted me there because I'm the only social worker in the entire borough with a 'specialisation' in children with disabilities—which was what the whole session was supposed to be about. There is a new Government directive on the proposal to integrate services for disabled children with the existing ones for normal kids, which are much better resourced—so it *is* right up my street—and I let them down by not turning up, etc. When Celine had calmed down enough to listen, I explained that I'd never even seen her invitation. Did anyone turn up in my place?

"A strange, stocky guy came. When somebody asked him what he did, he said he did the social work at Sladebourne House."

"Really—and did he say anything else?"

"Not much. He ate and drank a lot—Area Four gave us lunch—and he seemed a bit out of place. Yes, and our team clerk Elsa says he goosed her on the way out."

"Then that would be our Chief Nursing Officer, Max Paigle. I'll have to have a word with him. Elsa's bottom isn't the only thing he's pinched!"

When I went to talk to Paigle, he brazened it out.

"That letter came just addressed to The Social Worker, not personally to you. And I did the social work here, Miss Delancy, for years and years before you came."

I said that as I am actually present now at Sladebourne, I want all of my posts, including anything addressed to The Social Worker. To this, Paigle said nothing. Yet since then, my post has come regularly and, if Paigle still interferes with it he has found a way of doing so that I can't detect.

It is also possible that I owe the improved postal system to the hospital porters. Contrary to expectation, they show no resentment of my presence at all, even of my presence five days per week in what they must have looked on for years as their private territory. Head-Porter Aitken is quite un-nerving fatherly, not only to me but to any distressed parent who comes his way.

When he has administered First Aid to them in the form of a mug of his special tea, he always sends them straight to my office. As well as lodge-keeping, sorting post, the moving of heavy objects and general security, porters here do a lot of locking up.

On a quiet day, Aitken and his henchmen can be tracked by the faint, persistent sound of the bunches of keys with which they are festooned. There are six porters usually on duty in the daytime, but apart from Aitken I only know two of them at all well.

Raymond is a large young man whose frizzy gold hair and beard surround his amiable face as light rays appear to do in old astronomical pictures of the Sun. The light hairy pelt covering Ray's arms and shoulders is set off by his style of dress—he wears a singlet in all weathers and seems impervious to cold. Ray's actions and speech are very slow, which may account for the slightly protective stance of his workmates towards him—he's given routine tasks, usually teamed with others, and never, I notice, expected to work entirely on his own.

A complete contrast to Ray, Steve is a stout, acne-scarred man of indeterminate age, with bushy hair and tufted brows twisted upward at the outer corners in a diabolic manner. He possesses a flat voice and a ready scowl. Never in Margaret's time, and she's been here a few years, has Steve been known to smile.

Steve is Ray's opposite in more ways than one—he is the carer of his elderly mother. He took her up here recently to show her where he works, and I spent a bit of time telling them both about what's available locally for people her age.

Steve still doesn't smile, but now I do always get a nod of recognition.

I'm going for supervision to Riverdale tomorrow. Lillian cancelled the last two sessions ('pressure of work') so I wonder what this one will be like. I will try to meet Celine and her pal from Paediatrics afterwards—misery loves company.

25 June 1974

Lillian and I met this morning. I had brought along some notes for reference—this time, I wouldn't be caught out. I had even decided how I would begin.

"Dr Gomez and I have been making a start on the Parent's Association."

"The—oh, yes. Go on, Mary." Lillian looked at her watch unobtrusively, but I saw.

"Well, it's not been straightforward because we've no addresses for at least fifteen families. I mean, they must have had home addresses once, but now they don't have because whole streets where they lived have been pulled down. So I'm trying to find out if the boroughs, at least the ones the Londoners came from, have any records of them anywhere.

"In some cases, boundaries have been altered, and no one seems sure who's responsible—contacting different Social Services Departments, the response is pretty mixed. Some Principal Officers react, well, as if they're being personally threatened by the existence of a handicapped child. In Thamesbrook, for instance—"

"Surely, you don't need to have anything to do with Thamesbrook? It's outside of London altogether. I was under the impression, in fact, I'm certain Mr Locke *told me himself* that all the children at Sladebourne come from Inner London."

"A lot of them do, not all. I don't think Mr Locke has been kept up to date about the children's backgrounds. And in the meantime," I said cautiously, "there is a problem about getting the circular letters to parents typed and copied. We drafted the model one all right—here's a copy—but nobody at Sladebourne will type it for us. They consider it's not their job. If I could type, I'd do it myself—"

"You can't type? You surprise me. I thought everyone could, nowadays."

Lillian pondered languidly. She looked tired, even sleepy, and for the first time, I speculated about her private life.

"You can ask Phyllis in the typing pool," she said at last, "only this once, mind, and be sure you send her Sladebourne letterheads. And you'll have to write everything down for her because she's deaf."

"Thanks. Oh and there actually is another thing. About Dr, Hanafin. He does not seem to have known that I was coming at all, and he says he has no use for social workers. But he *is* the senior consultant, and it seems so unfair that his patients aren't to be included in what we set up. There'll be trouble when they find out he won't see them, and won't let Dr Gomez and myself include them. And I do get the feeling that it's put down to me!"

As soon as the last words left my lips, I knew they were the wrong ones.

Lillian roused herself and turned on me a blue gaze in which pity and exasperation were about evenly blended.

"Mary," she said, "when are you going to do things for yourself? That's why you are at Sladebourne House. You can't expect that anyone will help you over every little stile along the way. It is not part of my role here to negotiate with Dr Hanafin, a consultant with whom I would, normally, have nothing to do."

He is a difficult man. Consultants are often difficult men. I did not offer him the assistance of a social worker because I knew and everyone knew that he wouldn't accept one. And Dr Gomez was prepared to have you. Has *he* suggested to you to involve others, for instance, myself, as intermediaries?

No, I can't believe he has. He would have sufficient consideration not to do so. It's *your* business to pour oil on the waters, to get on with those men. If you can't manage that, you won't be able to do anything else there."

I was suddenly aware of a threat behind her words and felt that I did not want her to carry it out. My face must have told Lillian what I was thinking.

"Changing the subject," she said, "I've arranged a Visit of Inspection for you on next Thursday morning, to the Children's Unit at Lorne Pond Hospital. Mrs Maze, the senior social worker there, is a personal friend of mine. You must ring her, to confirm that you can come. I trust," she added looking at me intently, "there will be no difficulty about that. No? Good. You will find it a valuable learning experience."

"Do you want me to send you a write-up?" I mumbled.

"As you please." Supervision was over.

In the Riverdale dining room, social workers have their own secluded table, arranged by Lillian, I am sure with the object of turning any meal into a working lunch without attracting too much outside attention. Earlier, she had made it clear that she would not be coming to lunch today. Now, I smiled uncertainly at the man and woman already seated at the table—they looked familiar, indeed, I realised we must have met in the painful recent past when I'd visited the Children's Unit and still thought I was going to work there.

"I'm sorry," I said, "I've forgotten your names." The pretty dark-haired woman laughed, but not unkindly, "That wouldn't be surprising, would it? Everything was so confusing, and we felt sorry for you, and that mix-up since was down to me—"

"Was—oh then you must be Celine. You were leaving and you didn't."

"Celine Jones is my name. And you're Mary Delancy, aren't you? And we've spoken on the phone, about that invitation that went astray. Mary, this is Brian, Brian Haskins. I found I had to stay on here after all, so Brian has to put up with me a bit longer. He says he really does not mind—"

"I said it once." Brian grinned amiably. He's quite a lot older than Celine, I would guess. Probably fifty—but looks more, has a mild, fleshy face, and his hair is grey, and he seems laid-back.

Not for Brien, then, the current image of the male social worker, the flared jeans, the jewellery, the beard and the long, long hair. No, he is more of a suit, shirt and tie man, and his prevailing colour—I nearly said, protective colour, is certainly a pale grey.

I think that most anxious people would find Brian reassuring.

Celine impresses me as being very lively and always speedily at home in a new situation, however it happens to be. That's comforting to me as well. Perhaps her uncommon first name, perhaps a certain style about her, made me decide that she could be partly French and yes, it seems she is. I feel no urgent need to ask why she changed her mind about the Riverdale job. That can wait because another idea has come to me suddenly.

Lillian's evidently not going to be a very likely source of support and information—but why couldn't these two colleagues be? They must know so much that I don't, about all sorts of things. Local resources, for instance, include those belonging to where they work.

"I've been meaning to arrange to meet you both properly," I said, "Mrs Saye did tell me that I'm still part of the Paediatric firm—"

"Lillian Saye," responded Brian firmly, "is not always aware of what she's saying, and where you fit into the pattern is not completely down to her, anyway."

Seeing my expression of dismay, he began to laugh. He got up to get a drink for me, and to fetch the cutlery I had forgotten when collecting my cold-meat-and-salad lunch. By the end of our meal, simply from sitting there between Celine and Brian and hearing them rib each other, I felt myself relax as I have not been able to since I started this job.

They seem to share my view of Lillian, they seem interested in what I hope to do, and perhaps, even, they can give me a bit of the moral support I need so badly. Maybe life does not really have to be as hard as I sometimes think.

"Tell us about Sladebourne, first," said Celine, "what is it really like there?"

"That will take some time," I replied, "but I can make a start today."

8 July 1974

The weeks of April, May and June have passed quickly because I've been imposing a pattern on the work: so many joint interviews with parents, so much time for phone calls and correspondence, so many visits to the wards to get to know the children better, especially the child Stella. Once a week, whether Lillian offers me supervision or not, I've lunched at Riverdale in the company of Celine and Brian and we've sympathised with each other's troubles.

Every week also, the Case Review has been held on Wednesday afternoon and I've attended it. Outside of my two-office windows, lilac and laburnum are in heavy bloom, birds sing and mate and quarrel and rear families. The weather grows warmer by the day, a promise for early summer.

Today Dr Ben Morgan, consultant paediatrician at Riverdale, came to Sladebourne, and I met him for the first time.

By noon, it was so hot that Gomez had prevailed on Paigle to hold the Case Conference outdoors, in a clearing behind Waverley, where the grass had been cut, and there were a few trees to give shade. We were about to start when down the access road bumped a red convertible, taking the ramps at what must have been a highly uncomfortable speed. The car stopped so near to us, that Paigle jumped like a rabbit when the horn suddenly went off.

"So sorry, Maximilian, hope I didn't startle you!" cried a silvery voice, as a blue-clad figure emerged from the car. Paigle grunted, clearly annoyed. Our Chief Nursing Officer was dressed, appropriately to the weather, in white shorts, sandals and tee-shirt, yet the comfortable outfit hardly suited him, the impression he made in it being somehow juvenile and old-fashioned at the same time.

By way of contrast, the newcomer wore a suit of denim wonderfully well cut for his stocky figure. From one of the many gold chains around his short bare neck dangled a large medallion bearing the word Peace in different languages. The face above the medallion was not peaceable.

It was wide-mouthed, with thin lips, a long nose, and large green eyes; the entire impression was almost feline. If, as I sometimes think, Hanafin can easily be reimagined as a bird of prey, Ben Morgan is surely one of the larger cats.

Ben Morgan deliberately holds centre stage wherever he is. On this occasion, he strode rapidly and confidently to the heart of the meeting, where people recognised him, made way for him, and found him a seat. As they were doing so, I recollected what I'd heard about him, from Celine particularly, and tried to connect it with what I was seeing now.

I know that Ben comes from South Africa and that he combines his Riverdale post with an extensive private practice north of the Thames. Some of his juniors speak of him, with a kind of reverence, as one of the richest consultants in London. I also know that he's away from his Paediatric Unit for up to a third of every year, spreading the light of learning elsewhere according to some people, just showing off according to others. As to how effective he is at getting good things to happen—opinion on that is divided as well.

Although I hate the room in Midlothian where Case Reviews are normally held, it has to be said that this alternative wasn't much better. The sun beat down aggressively, we were only partly screened from it by the leaves of young trees.

Powerful soporific scents of lime blossom and freshly cut grass were making me feel dangerously relaxed. Gomez having been called away suddenly, Hanafin was holding forth alone on the history of autistic William Green, eight years old, admitted almost a year ago and now being reviewed for the first time.

William's parents had five children when their marriage broke up each parent took two, leaving William, certainly seen as a contributory cause of the break-up, apparently right out of the reckoning. After a brief stay on the children's ward of a local general hospital, where he demolished every cot they tried to tie him into, William was transferred to Midlothian where, Terence said, he had calmed down to a remarkable degree.

An attractive child of handsome appearance despite his obvious inability to 'meet gaze', William sat quietly before Hanafin while the latter, shirt-sleeved and sweating, castigated the absent Greens for their failure as parents to communicate with Terence, whom Hanafin described as 'the present carer of their rejected son'.

Towards the end of Hanafin's presentation, at the point when I felt sure that Mrs Bailey was going to rise to contribute her share, William started to grow restive. He stretched his arms, then started to pull at his long-sleeved shirt as though trying to take it off. Far from helping him, Terence tried to restrain him by holding both his arms. William whimpered and tried to twist himself away from Terence.

"Hey, Hey," called out Ben Morgan suddenly, "hold your horses !" and jumping forward he seized the child's shirt, unbuttoned it, and eased it gently over William's head. From the opposite side of the meeting came a sound like a universal gasp or intake of breath. What they could see, I could not, until I changed sides and moved to stand behind the people opposite.

William's back displayed two raw, red stripes each about two inches wide, curving around the child's ribs. At the end of the stripes, and just below the right armpit, was a squarish abrasion. I remembered textbook pictures of physically abused children and felt sick. Margaret Tobias was sitting near me, and I found myself trying to see her face as if the sight of her reaction would somehow make me feel better by convincing me that I wasn't dreaming.

Dr Morgan induced William gently to stand up, turning him around so that everyone present could see his back. No one said anything. Hanafin for once looked dumbfounded and Paigle also.

"Well, Charge Nurse, I think that this calls for some explanation. Now."

Ben Morgan's metallic voice had lost its sweetness. Terence, white and determined, confronted him.

"Dr Morgan, I don't know how this can have happened."

"But if *you* don't, Charge Nurse, what conclusion are we to come to? Someone climbed in at the window at night and beat William here with a leather belt? Within the last couple of days too, by the look of things."

"They fight sometimes," began Terence, "one of the other boys—"

"Not possibly a fight, not self-inflicted either. This looks like chastisement to me, eh, Hanafin? Mrs Bailey, can we take it that this couldn't have happened in your school?"

"We don't use corporal punishment, Dr Morgan. Never."

"So what are you going to do about this, Paigle? It's neither my responsibility nor Dr Hanafin's. It's yours. You'll need to look into this; have an enquiry. Write a report, enter it into the book.

"And do be sure to let us all know what happens. And oh, before we forget, Charge Nurse, take William to Riverdale Casualty right now and have the people there put a dressing on. And don't bother him with that shirt 'til his back's dressed."

After the meeting, I was just trying to catch up with Margaret, when a silvery voice behind me spoke my name. When I turned around, Ben Morgan was there, hand outstretched to grasp mine. Before I could think twice about it, I found myself in the canteen, seated with Morgan, Hanafin and Paigle, and pouring tea for all four of us. Paigle, from being somewhat crushed, had recovered enough to be conciliatory.

"I assure you; I had no idea that anything like that—can't imagine how it could happen or who would do such a thing, of the staff we've got on Midlothian."

"Can't you imagine how it could happen? I can. Somebody lost his temper. Not still recruiting night staff from the local bin, are you, Maximilian?"

"No! Never." Paigle reached for the sugar bowl and added three lumps to his cup.

"And just to change the subject, Maximilian, what's to happen about Dr Fermatt—are we to be honoured with a visit from him or not? Sometime will be needed to prepare for him, won't it? You go to all the meetings, Maximilian. According to God's Cousin, he won't get to us before December. Miss Delancy, do you know anything?"

"Nothing about Dr Fermatt, except that he's Minister for Health. But please tell me who God's Cousin is?"

"Certainly. God's Cousin is someone you can never have met, or you would identify her straight away from the title I've given her. But you may have heard of her. She is the Hospital Secretary at Riverdale."

And Ben Morgan went on to relate his struggles with his anonymous opponent over the money needed to print copies of a leaflet for parents of children attending the hospital. He told it so funny that I was sorry when he left in response to a phone call. As he strode out of earshot, Paigle remarked, in the tone of one making an accusation:

"He's doing exercises, you know, to expand his chest."

"I'm not surprised," responded Hanafin bitterly, as the red car bounded noisily past the canteen window.

I went back to the office. On the doormat, which still carries from the pre-NHS era its London County Council logo, rested two objects—an institution-size tin of Nescafe and a jar of powdered milk. Last week, it was a box of custard creams and the week before that a massive pot of Bovril.

I know better than to think these tributes are for me, they are provisions for the night staff, people I never see but who have moved in to share my office at night while their own is being redecorated. After Morgan's mysterious reference to them, I would certainly like to meet them! As I took their food into the office and fitted it into the drawer labelled Night Staff, I thought another session with the therapists might enlighten me.

Tonight, as usual, I put Molly out for a run in the communal garden behind the flats. So far, she has not come back.

17 July 1974

Stella was having a bad day. She sat hunched up in a chair, staring out of the window at the buildings opposite. She ignored my greeting, and occasionally her hand sought her mouth, and she bit at the tags of skin around her neglected nails. I wasn't feeling all that happy myself because Molly is still missing, but I manage to keep it out of my mind while working.

Louise is on holiday this week, so it is Donna who looks after Stella at present. Donna is the care assistant who slapped Stella on the day we met first, so it may be that she is the reason why Stella is so cross. In spite of the slap, though, Donna does not really seem unkind.

She is a blonde, placid girl with high colour and a slow reaction speed—and that's all I knew about her before today when I chose to ignore Stella by giving my attention to her career. Chatting deliberately to Donna, I hefted my heavy bucket bag onto the table with an ostentatious thump. Nonchalantly I took out some of the contents: the plain and patterned sugar-paper, the scissors, the crayons, and the packets of gummed-paper scraps which Stella loves—she makes what she says are pictures with them.

And a few books. I've actually found a charity which pays for books for children in hospital: The Arbuthnot Trust. Today, Stella, though certainly fully aware of what I was doing, at first never moved or spoke to me. I sat down, picked up the newest of the books, and put it on the table where she could see it.

Still, without looking at me, Stella got to her feet and moved a little nearer to the table. Then she stopped. Out of the corner of her eye, she had seen the cover picture of a tiger. She loves stories about animals, preferring them to stories with human characters.

"Read it, Mary," Stella ordered, "please! And with a sweet voice," she added. So I read. As I read, soft rain fell outside, blurring the windows. Donna, seated peacefully in the background, knitted a jacket for her sister's expected baby. And Stella moved gradually nearer to me, to see more of the pictures.

The story is told of a lost animal, a tiger cub with large green eyes. Everyone who saw it, feared it and ran away from it. The cub had several adventures, most of them unpleasant and some frightening. The cub was lonely, hungry and cold. At long last, it was found and comforted by its large, furry, stripey mother.

With a sideswipe, Stella knocked the book from my hands, sprang across the room, and threw herself sobbing onto the hard floor. When forgetting her dislike of being touched, I bent involuntarily to pick her up, she rose with great speed and flung herself into the bedroom, banging the door as she went.

Something made me turn back to the window. On a level with my face, two other faces were looking in at us, two pairs of eyes stared accusingly into mine. Quickly hiding her knitting, Donna opened the door to Dr Hanafin accompanied by Mr Paigle.

"Miss Delancy, why are you here, and who gave you permission to come and interfere with my patient?" Hanafin's voice rose and shrilled on the last words.

"You didn't say I couldn't visit her, Dr Hanafin," I began, but then felt how feeble the remark was, and stopped. Paigle also began to say something, but Hanafin interrupted him.

"I will not have you interfere with my patients. This psychotic child needs the utmost care, and protection also, protection, Miss Delancy, from intrusion like yours. She does not need to be upset. And now you have upset her, haven't you?"

But I had thought of something to say, though it was something not yet completely true.

"Dr Hanafin, Stella Wilson was placed here from the London Borough of Hoxton. Mrs Bailey tells me Stella does not attend school and does not get any tutorial help, and I have to let Hoxton know this so that they can make suitable arrangements for her education. Not to do this, would be to break the law. In fact, I'm just about to notify Hoxton about all of their children, they have five here but only Stella is under your care."

Mr Paigle here interposed his red-faced eagerness to join the winning side (if a little late). He assured Hanafin that I would never be allowed set foot in the workshop again. He would give his instructions and (with a warning glance at Donna) they would be carried out. Hanafin looked at him with some distaste, evidently, he felt that Paigle was going much too fast and far, even for him. I felt impelled to try again.

"It may be, of course, that Hoxton will want to remove Stella, but they'll be unlikely to do that if we can say we have arranged to tutor for her. They will pay, of course. And I'm sure we can get them to pay for a few other things she needs, as well as things needed for their other children. And Hoxton," I added, "well, they see me as their contact person here."

Paigle's expressive face underwent a change when money was mentioned.

"Now," he said suddenly, "a bit of help with money, for children's clothes and so on—we could all do with that. And she wouldn't be taken away from us, you think, then?"

I said that given the help I'd mentioned, I had no reason to think Stella would be moved from Sladebourne, at least in the short term. Hanafin, who was clearly beginning to cool down, pondered over my words while he fiddled with the blind cord.

"How often do you come here—weekly?"

I told him: sometimes oftener and sometimes less.

"Once a week—very well. Leave it at once a week, but you must ask me first if you want to have dealings with one of my patients in the future. I won't have people arranging things behind my back. This girl is uncontrollable in any school, all that's already been tried, long before you came. She won't be able to live a normal life. Ever." And Hanafin gestured dismissively with his red-knuckled hands.

He had given way. But even now I feel such anger that I can't speak it to anyone—only write it down here. To run someone down at the age Stella is— what in hell gives him the authority to do this? Of course, the real authority is not with Hanafin, and I must not forget that, either.

When they had both gone, Stella slowly came out from the inner room.

"He's like the bad giant," she stated.

Last week I'd read her a story about a bad giant—she had actually remembered!

"Dr Hanafin is not a giant," I said, "he is the doctor who especially looks after you. And everyone is difficult at times."

Stella came over to me, scooping the tiger book off the floor as she did so.

"Can you read it again, Mary? Can you—please?"

Later, as I was leaving, Donna was preparing to take Stella for a walk and sent her to the bedroom to get her shoes. We were standing near each other, when Donna in a rapid furtive whisper said to me: "Miss D., I'm with you." As I must have looked blank, she added: "For standing up to them. They've had it their own way far too long."

I would have liked to think that this surprising remark expresses solidarity. But, on reflection, it sounds more like an expression of hostility towards the management.

Back at the office, there was a call from Hoxton. Tom Grace, Principal Officer in Child Care, wants to come and meet his flock. We fixed a date, and he's bringing a summary of each child's file!

Molly still has not come home. I've asked all the people around where I live, and they have searched their sheds and gardens. I've put up notices in the little local shops and the Post Office. I don't know what more to do.

25 July 1974

Still no sign of Molly. Abstractedly I drove to work today, composing in my own mind endless plaintive notices to put in local papers. I've decided that I cannot bear yet to start door-to-door enquiries. I do miss the creature so much! When at work, I can keep her absence out of my mind, but as soon as I'm on the way home, of course, I can't.

It's hard to go home and be alone there, so I've been spending more time with Nilla, and this is not always a good idea. But there are always distractions. Today, Ray met me on the way in and asked me if I would like some flowers for the office. He said they'd been given a heap for the hospital and he'd pick some out for me.

He has a relative who works in a flower shop just outside our nearby cemetery—she specialises in wreaths—and I can't help relating that fact to Ray's generosity. Still, he's very kind. I'll add a prayer for his well-being to the ones I occasionally say.

A few minutes later, as I was preparing to visit Ivanhoe, there came an agitated rapping on the office door and without waiting for any reply Louise darted in, white-faced, her large eyes larger than ever. All in one movement she came across the room and stood close to me as if seeking protection from some threat of physical injury from outside; she was so out of breath that she couldn't speak for a few seconds.

I was amazed at this, partly because, so far as I know, Louise is still officially away on leave, partly because she's never seemed to be a person liable to panic. I made her sit down, she did so, but kept looking over her shoulder, and twisting the ring she wears—a ring with a tiger's eye stone in it that always looks much too big for her small right hand.

When she got her breath back, Louise said she had to talk to someone, but did not know to whom 'because there's no one here except nurses'. She had thought of me, she remarked obscurely because I wasn't a nurse. Then she told me her story.

Louise lives in a bedsitter which is in the staff block away at the back of the Admin. Building. That block is surrounded by overgrown shrubs and always seems isolated. This morning, Louise got up late and was taking her time to dress when a knock came to the door, and Paigle's voice said he needed to see her urgently.

When she let him in, as she put it: "I was decent, but I just felt his eyes undressing me." Paigle said he had been offered at short notice a place for one staff member on a new course for carers of 'special needs' children. Louise had recently expressed interest in taking such a course: "It would give me another arrow to my bow." So she said again that she would like to go on the course.

Paigle said there was a problem about that—a rival candidate, a care assistant on Kenilworth who had been at Sladebourne longer than Louise. What could Paigle do? He could not second both people, much as he would like to. If he sent Louise, he would of course expect a very high measure of co-operation and loyalty from her in return, not to mention discretion.

Paigle would really like, he said, to do her a good turn. Let her leave the matter in his hands (one of which he placed on Louise's knee at this point) and he would see what could be done. Where there was a will, there was a way.

"Then," said Louise, "I got him to go by saying I was off that day and my boyfriend was coming and due any minute. Mr Paigle never knows the duty rotas. It wasn't until he'd gone that I missed my room key. We all got our own locks put in over there, if you don't then your stuff gets nicked. What do you bet that I'll find that key in a couple of days, lying somewhere I already looked? Sure as anything, he'll have got it copied."

Feeling somewhat at a loss, I suggested an interview with the union rep.

"But it's him, Mary! He's the union rep."

"He can't be, surely. I thought the manager couldn't be!"

"You thought wrong, 'cos he is. All our complaints have to go through him. If he doesn't get what he wants, he'll fire me, he's done it before to people. But he makes my skin crawl."

I share her opinion, for though you're almost sorry for people like Max Paigle, you can't feel that way for long when you think of the trouble they cause. That turnover of young female staff which I'd already noticed is now explained.

And Lucinda's defensiveness, is that explained as well? Perhaps. Anyway, I promised Louise details of the branch secretary of the staff union; their details won't be hard to get, as my own union is affiliated with hers.

Her tale once told, Louise seemed in no hurry to leave the office. She thanked me, went towards the door, then hesitated with one small brown hand on the white-and-gilt China doorknob. I decided to be firm.

"I have to go out now, Louise. But if you really want to stay in here for a while—"

"Oh no, no, I'm all right. You'll let me know about the union, Mary? I feel better now I've talked to someone about it all." But she still looked uneasy, and the whole episode left an impression hard to define or explain. It almost seemed as if Louise had intended to tell me something more, then decided against it and told me something else.

As I went past the porter's lodge, a minute later there seemed to be some sort of commotion inside. Loud sobbing could be heard, and also the voice of Ray expostulating. The group van was parked half-blocking the road because the driver was obviously unwilling to miss whatever might be going on. I looked towards the door and saw Lily, a care assistant from Ivanhoe, standing there completely obstructing my view, but she drew aside as she saw me, and beckoned me into the scene.

Inside the murky lodge Ray bent over a seated young woman. Her fashionable tapestry bag resting on the dirty floor at her feet, she sat and sobbed, bent forward over a paper carrier on her lap. Her hair was most of what could be seen of her, brown, long, and highlighted red, it half-covered the arms she folded around her bent face as if to protect it. Ray saw me and greeted me with obvious relief.

"What's happened?" I said.

"Just picked her up this moment, coming through the gate."

"One look at Ray set her off crying," remarked the driver, and Lily giggled appreciatively. Ignoring them, Ray offered the woman a mug of tea, which she took. Ray looked across at me. "I don't really know what kind of set her off," he said, "maybe if you were to have a word with her—"

A pale, puffy face turned momentarily up to mine, the eyes filling with soundless tears spilling over into the abominable tea. Again, I postponed my visit to Ivanhoe and took Marie Keane into the office, where she began to talk, by degrees.

She is the mother of an epileptic child transferred to Ivanhoe yesterday from a city hospital; this is her first visit to Sladebourne, and since no one told her otherwise she thought it would be much like the place her son had just left. As she came through the gates today, Marie was in time to witness the daily lunchtime procession from Bourne School to the wards.

She saw all those children with their different strangenesses, their different syndromes; children with large heads, children with small heads like birds, children with Down's Syndrome, with quadriplegia, with autism, with varying degrees of disability but all, absolutely all of them, looking poor and shabby, and all with the one invisible identity label: Mentally Handicapped. And amongst them, for the first time, she saw her son.

By the time all the children had gone by, Marie was helpless with grief. She told me over and over again the conclusion she had come to:

"It's not that this is a terrible place. I'm sure it's not. It's just that no parent even if this place was perfect would ever want their child to be here."

And I think that for most people that would about sum it up. Marie feels now she can hope for nothing better for her son. My work is to try to change this way of thinking, but how? I took her to the canteen for coffee and there introduced her to Margaret, who was showing round Gina, a newly appointed speech therapist.

Marie, after meeting them, cheered up considerably, I am glad that she's feeling able to trust someone here. Her eight-year-old son Terry—now on Ivanhoe—is unlikely to need Margaret's skills, but he has no speech and little other communication so the appearance of Gina is timely. I only hope she stays.

Marie Keane is a single parent, as many Sladebourne parents are, from the information I'm gradually collecting. But I don't have time to research the whole subject properly. What I found so distressing about Marie today, has really to do with myself mainly. Her feelings were expressed so vehemently that they triggered off impulses in me that I was barely able to control.

As Marie wept and sobbed, a part of myself wanted to sit down and weep with her, sobbing along with her, completely give way, let go. I had to overcome this impulse and hardly know how I did it. But I do know why I felt like that. Since the break-up with Philip, I haven't cried. Or not openly, and if you only cry inwardly, it can't do you much good.

5 August 1974

"Delightful surroundings," remarked Tom Grace, Hoxton's PO (Children's Services) as we walked to the workshop on a mild, fragrant afternoon, with all the shrubs dripping after a rainy morning. Tom, who is very tall, looked down at me to see what I thought of his remark. Feeling that it was too soon to trust him, I didn't answer, but I was thinking: Did he actually take in what I've just been telling him?

"Although," Tom resumed as though I had spoken, "it does remind me of my time at Fairacres, the private wing of that psychiatric place. A glorious old house, very National Trust. That long drive, bordered by beech trees.

"Conditions in some of the back rooms were diabolical, but you'd never think so, to see loads of daffodils and narcissi in bloom outside the windows. And those windows—they were all arranged so that the residents couldn't see out of them. All meant for show, you see."

My fears were subsiding. At least this man showed awareness of the gap between appearance and reality, which is more than Lillian does. When I was notified, that Hoxton was sending a Principal Officer to Sladebourne to discuss 'their' children with me, I knew I must tell my boss, partly to give her the chance to be involved (though suspecting she would not take it) and partly because she was going to be very annoyed if she heard it from anyone else and thought I was trying to conceal my actions from her.

Lillian is one who prides herself on her openness and honesty. In my swiftly growing experience, most people who are always saying this of themselves are not spectacularly outspoken or unusually honest. They are reluctant to exercise tact with subordinates, so, whenever they feel they can get away with it, they will be rude. On this occasion, Lillian was rude.

"Well, really, Mary, I don't know what you think you'll gain by involving the child's place of origin. Your idea's all hearsay, and not able to be proved."

"Hoxton has a file on Stella's family. And about contacting them—Dr Hanafin makes no objection, nor does Mr Paigle, either."

"And I thought you yourself said the care assistant has no personal knowledge of these alleged visits—"

"That care assistant has not been working with Stella every day of the past six months. It was the other—Donna—who told me."

"This man, now. He could be a perfectly respectable Social Uncle. I know Mr Paigle did try to recruit Social Aunts and Social Uncles for the children. He told me so, Mary, sometime before you came.

"We could have all this fuss for nothing. Anyway, I can't make a meeting with Mr Grace, I've got to be somewhere else. You can write me a short account of what he says, and better put it in memo form."

We were at the workshop now. For an instant, as I knocked, I had the feeling that Stella might no longer be there; might have been spirited away somewhere else. But then she came to the window, as usual, smiling her uncertain smile, until she saw my companion when the smile vanished, Stella left the window, and I could hear her expostulating with Louise before the latter opened the door. When we went in, Stella was not visible.

"She's gone to hide," apologised Louise, and to Tom Grace "it's what she does with strangers, especially men." Her smile took away any edge the remark could have. I asked Louise to coax Stella out for us, and presently Louise succeeded and led Stella from her bedroom by the hand. Stella was tense, her eyes glittered, she looked as if she wanted to break away and run.

A hard blank look I am beginning to recognise had come over her face. When Ted introduced himself and held out his hand to her, she shrank back, as if in dread. The action was theatrical, exaggerated, false in some odd way, yet scarcely deliberate.

The memory came to me of the time when Louise attempted to confide in me, as I thought, but left me again feeling she had not been able to say what she came to say. I spoke to Stella, saying I forget what, and suddenly she turned to me and clung to me, burying her face in my waist as a younger child might do. I felt surprised and embarrassed, but so pathetic was her gesture that I could not think of disengaging myself, and instinctively put both arms around the child.

We have always been cautioned, of course, to avoid as far as possible actual physical contact with a vulnerable person, and it is certainly a liberty one should always hesitate to take. In England, they are more concerned to maintain distance. In Ireland, we were not so preoccupied with this.

Tom surveyed the group we made: Stella and myself clumsily entwined, Louise watching him and watching us with an alert but an otherwise unreadable expression. Tom addressed himself to Stella, asking her rather formally to tell him what her name was. She simply said: "Don't you know already?" without turning around.

"Stella," said Tom, "I do know, but I'd like to hear it from you. My name is Tom Grace and I'm a social worker. I visit Hoxton children living away from home. Mary has told me about you, that's why I'm here to see you."

"So that's what a social worker does. What's Hoxton?"

"Hoxton is the name of the part of London you come from. Don't you remember coming here?" Stella turned to face him and emphatically shook her head.

"No, Mister Tom, I don't remember, and I don't know anything. Except for my name, that's Stella Wilson, and my age, that's ten. I live here, I've been here a long time, years. Anyway, a long time."

Then, in an assumed 'adult' voice, she added: "Louise, you tell Mister Tom: She's disturbed, she's out of control, she's a kid whose been messed about with. That's all."

By this time, we were seated at the table, except for Louise who had gone to fetch another chair from the bedroom, and didn't hear what Stella was saying. Perched uncomfortably on a chair, Stella sucked her thumb energetically in the intervals between speech.

I had wondered earlier if she would say anything at all. Now, she was not only talking but making some kind of sense, and Tom was holding her attention. He had heard, he said, that Stella wanted to go to school. For the first time, she really looked at him. She said: "Yes."

Tom went on to say that it would take time to find a school near Sladebourne for her. But in the meantime, she could have a teacher of her own, who would come to see her in the workshop several days a week, to help her to get ready for going to school.

"Will she take me out?"

"Yes, I think I can say that is one of the things she will do."

Stella said nothing more, but at least, she did not object. I relaxed, feeling better. Tom Grace caught my eye and got up to go. Looking abstractedly towards the middle distance, while she picked at the loose tags of skin around her thumbnail, Stella casually asked:

"Mister Tom, have you got children?"

"I have, Stella. Three children."

"And do you see them?"

There was a momentary silence. Then Tom asked: "What does that mean?"

"You know. Do sex things with them."

"But I don't know, Stella, can you tell us what you think it means?"

"No, Mister, I can't tell you that; it's a secret!"

And abruptly seizing my left hand, which was nearest her, Stella put it to her mouth and bit it hard, sinking her sharp little teeth into the muscle at the base of the thumb. I yelled with surprise as much as pain, and Stella let my hand go.

"You hurt me," I shouted, "what on earth did you want to do that for?"

Stella, laughing wildly, jumped from my lap, fled into the bedroom and banged the door shut. Louise followed her.

"Mary, did she hurt you badly?" Tom removed all the paper hankies from a nearby box and handed them to me.

"She doesn't seem to have drawn blood, but gee, yes, it does hurt. I suppose I asked for it, should have expected something like that, but I didn't—"

"Don't blame yourself. These things happen, and it can be very useful to see her when she's at her worst."

That's fine, I thought, but it wasn't you that got bitten.

Back at my office, Tom Grace told me that he thinks that Stella has been sexually abused.

"We're beginning to recognise that as a cause of disturbed behaviour—it's so much commoner than any of us realised a few years ago. Stella's history, her language, her odd ways—they all suggest it to me, anyway."

"Do you think it's very recent? I am thinking of a man Donna mentioned, a man who came while Donna was on duty, to visit Stella and take her out. After he brought her back to the workshop, Stella was 'hyper and upset' for days and Donna said she could 'get no sense' out of her."

"Who can say? But as to that mysterious visitor, we'll have to put a stop to him. I'll have a word with the Chief Nursing Officer, or whatever they're called here—"

I explained that Hanafin was Stella's consultant and the real power at Sladebourne, that Paigle was currently on holiday in France, and that Terence,

Paigle's nominal deputy, was off duty today. (I did not add that I had deliberately invited Tom for *this* day, in order to minimise interference.) In the end, we decided that a letter to Hanafin, with copies to Paigle and Locke, would be the most appropriate form of action.

The letter, which we drafted, made clear that the London Borough of Hoxton intended to accept full responsibility for the further care of Stella Wilson, including her individual tuition pending appropriate school placement. Details of further plans for Stella would be discussed at a statutory review held at a time and place convenient to all parties.

As present carers of the child, Sladebourne staff could apply for Hoxton's help with the cost of her personal clothing. However, it must be emphasised that Stella was not to leave the hospital with anyone not authorised by Hoxton to take her out.

Tom promised to send this letter, which I felt to be a skilful mixture of carrot (practical help) and stick (threat). Then he retrieved the battered briefcase he had left in the centre recess of my antique desk, heaved it onto the desk top, and opened it.

The bulky files it contained were each decorated with a large sticker forbidding removal from Hoxton Social Services. They were what I had been hoping to see—Volumes One and Two of the Wilson Family File.

"I can't let you hold on to any originals, but if there's a copier—"

I used the one in Lynn's office, which chanced to be empty, while Tom went to see the other Hoxton children, all of whom were by now back in Kenilworth or Midlothian.

The Wilson social records were summarised on a couple of pages at the start of each file and highlighted by the attached reports. Most of what I managed to copy, in fact, were those reports, from many different agencies. The story they told was all too familiar.

The Wilsons were Londoners and poor in every way you can be. Both Stella's parents, Charlie and Sharon, had grown up 'in care', which meant then, in separate orphanages. When they left care, they worked intermittently at unskilled jobs, varied in the case of Charlie Wilson by short prison sentences.

When the two met and started to live together was not a matter of record, but the coming of their children was indicated by a sheaf of Section One forms, representing applications to local Social Services for modest sums of money needed to prevent a child's reception into care. Sometimes these grants did not fulfil their purpose, and as a further collection of forms showed, each of the three Wilson children spent brief periods in foster care.

The family's Health Visitor wrote to the local Director of Social Services that, after consultation with her superiors, she regretfully had to give up visiting the Wilsons, on account of threats made by Mr Wilson to kill her if she ever came near their house again.

A report from Stella's nursery school used the phrase ' like a little wild animal' about her, adding that Stella, then four, spoke little, socialised not at all, and ate voraciously anything she could find that was edible, as well as some things that were not. Reckless and hyperactive, she damaged her surroundings and, occasionally, herself.

The nursery school head understood that home circumstances must account for this behaviour, but due to lack of contact with Stella's parents, it was difficult to be sure. they never responded to invitations to visit the school. A later, very similar communication from a local primary school head summed Stella up as 'ungovernable, possibly ineducable'.

Perhaps it was this report which gave rise to a referral to Hanafin's predecessor at Winterbourne, that Doctor Benson magisterially decided: 'in my opinion this unhappy little girl is mentally handicapped', thereby providing both a diagnosis and, for the time, a long-term solution.

I had only just finished copying to this level when Tom returned to get his files. To my surprise, he sounded quite positive.

"There may even be a possibility of fostering Stella, but we'll first have to get her assessed. (Sure, I remember Dr Benson, he wasn't even a psychiatrist.) I agree with you, she does not really fit in here."

"What happens about parental consent?" I was trying to remember what I had been taught about the law on that subject.

"You've seen the RIC forms. Stella was effectively deserted two or three years ago. Her father, well, he caused the death of the last person he robbed, he's been responsible for a bit of trouble in prison and he's still serving a long sentence. We've no idea where Stella's mother is.

"The two boys were with her, and grandmother told us three years ago they had all emigrated to Australia. I'm not sure I believe that but we have not been able to trace them so far, and I suppose it's as good a guess as any. (Grandmother's dead now, by the way.) You tell me that since she came here to

Sladebourne there's been no record of any parental contact, no letters, 'phone calls—"

"I have to say, the lack of records—that's partly because there's been almost no record-keeping. No one remembers any visits to Stella, but that doesn't mean there couldn't have been some. No one has taken note of anything like that, for any of the children here." I saw Tom's expression and felt defensive: "And they still don't. Some of the people working here with the children cannot read or write well enough to keep records. They probably think it does not matter."

I nearly added because they think the children do not matter, and maybe they don't believe that *they* matter either! But I hope Tom knows what I left unsaid.

We talked a bit about the other Hoxton children, and he was just preparing to leave when Ray appeared at the door with my promised flowers in a tin bucket. They comprise one each of about twenty varieties, with cypress leaves tucked between. I think it's an obvious dismantled wreath, and hope it is not an omen. This is a dismal evening, raining and prematurely dark. Driving has been difficult with my left hand sore in spite of the lovely soft dressing Daroga later put on it.

There's a big Sainsbury's carrier propped outside my door, which I'll leave investigating until I've had supper. Probably something Nilla left.

6 August 1974

Yesterday I couldn't get to work, the hangover was so bad, and the sickness. Drinking on an empty stomach always does that to me, and last night it even brought on a migraine. The whole shock of finding poor Molly stiff and dead and frozen, in that plastic bag outside the door—threw me so entirely that I couldn't think or feel.

Nilla came straight away when I rang. She knows desperation when she hears it, so she didn't waste time, but took me out to the local and resorted to traditional remedies: sympathy and strong drink. The regulars there were so kind and empathetic; they obviously thought I had suddenly lost a near relation. My bandaged hand even, raised concern, though I cannot remember what story Nilla told them to account for it. Now, that my head's better, I can feel grateful to them all.

Losing little Molly is really like losing a friend, she was starting to be one, in her way. One awful thought now is, how did it happen, and the other awful thought is, who knew about it and brought her back here? I must know that. Nilla took Molly away with her in a cool bag because she knows a vet who can check her out and post-mortem her or whatever they do to cats. It could be a death from a road accident, I suppose. But I don't really believe that.

The bite on my hand is healing well, and I'm glad not to have to go to an unknown GP to exhibit an infected human bite, than which there is nothing nastier. Stella has apologised, and in fact keeps on apologising not, I think because she is sorry to have hurt me but because she can use the incident to confirm the low opinion, she already has of herself.

I started trying to get this approach across to her as the really useless one it is; and have decided that the only way she can accept ideas at present is through the medium of stories, which she loves. So that's what we're trying at present.

Tom Grace has written the letter he said he would, and sent me a copy. He says that eventually, Stella will be allocated a social worker who will let us all know the time of the statutory review. So far, so good. But I know she needs more than just a future plan. Stella needs what we all do, and how do you give unconditional love to someone who has never learned to trust anybody?

In the meantime, there are all the other children and plenty to be done for them. We've set a date for the first meeting of the Sladebourne Parents Association. Almost all the parents Gomez and I have seen, averaging two a week, have responded positively to the whole idea once they realise, we are not going to close the whole place here down overnight and return their children to them.

That sounds cynical, but it is not meant to be. What an understandable fear they have! It must have been so painful to most of them to hand over the burden, however, loved, which they carried for years. But it is unthinkably difficult to pick up such a burden again after years free of it. Body and spirit have forgotten the strategies they once knew, and what was only just bearable before, after an interval is overwhelming.

Paul Gomez, back from Italy, is very happy about the responses we've had from the parents.

I know him better now, well enough to know that his warmth is not just manner, but has some real compassion in it. At the same time, he does avoid confrontation like the plague and side steps all difficulties with the greatest ease. Vicky jokes that he's truly a family-centred psychiatrist—centred, that is to say, on his own family.

He loves to talk about his English wife and four beautiful children. But perhaps this is the way he reassures himself about their existence and his own general good fortune. It may be something we all naturally do, to boast a bit when we're surrounded by those less well off.

And Gomez sometimes takes for granted that women are created to wait on him. In my absence, he tried to co-opt Margaret Tobias to sit in and take notes of an interview he was conducting. She protested that she did not know the child the interview concerned; he wasn't on her list for physiotherapy. Gomez replied that this did not matter, adding naively:

"When I interview a parent, somebody must take notes of what is said. It's important for research purposes—I'm writing a paper."

He is always writing papers but does not seem to get any of them to the stage of submission for publication. The notes I take for him are rather sketchy, and he has been disappointed to learn that shorthand is not one of my skills. But I can't help liking Paul Gomez, and I think he likes me, and that's lucky. It could have been so much worse. I could have had to work with someone like Hanafin.

Ah, Hanafin. No wonder he alludes so often to the evil tricks of social workers, to their arrogance, their lack of openness, especially when left to their own dishonest, paltry devices; to their power-seeking concealed beneath spurious benevolence. He hasn't yet forgiven Lillian for slipping me into place at Sladebourne without telling him. She shouldn't have done it, of course, and there, justice is certainly on his side. When one thinks of people like Lillian, much becomes plain.

The first Parent's Meeting is scheduled for a fortnight's time. When I told Lillian, she agreed to come, but quickly reversed her decision when told that the meeting would not start until 8:00 p.m. This is a relief since, if present, she might feel it her duty to interfere.

Here is a sample of the sort of dialogue I have with Lillian.

At supervision, I told her that Hoxton agreed to fund a tutor for Stella. (I did not tell her that the approved tutor is already appointed, and is my friend Nilla.) Also, I quoted the remark of Tom Grace regarding Stella's likely past, and I asked if Lillian could recommend to me any source of information about the care and counselling of sexually abused children.

"Mary, what you really have to do first, is to ask yourself if you are *sure*. I don't see how you can be *sure*. After all, if the child's mentally handicapped—"

"Apparently she's not, Lillian, though even if she were, I don't see that it would—"

"She wouldn't know. That is the thing about these children, isn't it? They don't notice what happens to them because they can't understand it. They don't feel it as a normal child would. Who diagnosed her, anyway? You can't, remember. You can't do that. You're always trying to run before you can walk, Mary."

"Hanafin's admitted that Stella is misplaced at Sladebourne. She's not the only one."

"And there you go again, really, very sweeping and you should be much more careful about what you say. We can't diagnose anybody. We can't set ourselves up as doctors. (Incidentally, we must always be careful to give them their full professional title, doctor or mister or whatever it may be. Not to do it indicates a lack of respect, I always think.) Now, what else was it that you wanted to ask me about?"

"About information, books, courses perhaps; I mean, NSPCC knows about neglect, but there doesn't seem to be much out there about the sort of abuse Stella is indicating happened to her. I feel I don't know how to handle her revelations and don't always react in a way which helps her."

"She could be lying, have you considered that? Children do lie. Mary, I do not want you to become wholly taken up with this. It may be that the girl saw, well, unsuitable films. It may be that her parents were playing with her, and she got the wrong impression. We must be careful not to blow things up, out of all proportion."

Suddenly, and with a wild inarticulate cry, Lillian leapt to her feet and rushed to the window, shouting and then banging on the glass with the flat of her hand. Taken up with keeping out of her way, I had no idea what this was all about until I stood up and glimpsed Frank Fisk, an occasional frequenter of Riverdale's psychiatric wing.

He has a long history as a flasher, and he was now moving in a furtive manner around Lillian's smart new Renault, and adjusting his flies at the same time. That put an end to our session, but I'm still left with the need to find out more about child sexual abuse. I'll ask Celine or Brian at Riverdale—they buy books, they read them, they also hear things.

What occupies my mind idly, in the intervals of planning my further education, is the question of whether Hanafin recalls he has encountered me before. Apart from the one occasion when he lectured to my social work course on brain trauma in very young children, we once met further back in time, in another country and another world. It is unlikely that he remembers it, but I remember it very well.

Autumn 1959

The literal crossing of my path with that of Noel Hanafin took place in rural Tipperary when I was about fourteen. The place where it happened was Mount Alverno, destined to provide in the future a permanent background to my bad dreams.

On a still-warm afternoon in early autumn, with Renee and Fergus Butler I cycled out to the demesne. For a week or so, we had not been to our sanctuary. Curiosity and unease led us to go there now, worried by rumours of the estate being broken up and sold. In fact, there had been an auction held in the town that morning, the result of which we did not yet know.

Fergus and Renee were a little older and much more sensible than I was; so they must have taken in the probable finality of this visit, the possibility that these woods and ruins would after today never again belong to us even in pretence. I must say that I had no such realisation. It was part of my immaturity to be so content with the present that I never looked ahead. My life, which was one of order and conformity at home contrasted with physical freedom outside it, would go on forever, and I truly thought would never change.

On this day, we came to the main gate of our little paradise, and we found it locked, and a new padlock with its chain girdling the shabby ornate bars. After some discussion about it, we made a detour to another gate a half a mile away and little used. But this, too, was padlocked.

The last possibility was the unglazed calf-house window, quite invisible from the road because a hedge grew against it. Leaving our bicycles in full view of the road (no one seemed to steal, in those days,) we scrambled up and dropped one by one through the window onto a heap of damp straw.

Over the years, we had hidden treasure-trove at Mount Alverno, consisting of old fragments of metal such as you could pick up around farm buildings then: horse and pony shoes, hand-forged nails and hooks, harness buckles, and even a pair of iron sheep-shears with the triangular blades. We never brought these things home, for that would have been stealing, but we felt we had some claim to them because we had found them.

We hid them in a well-concealed recess in a corner of the calf-house, through the windows of which we were accustomed to coming and go to our refuge, at times when we felt secrecy was called for. Soon we were making for the wood, far beyond the sheds and the ruins of the house.

Renee said: "I want to say goodbye to the river." She was always expressing her romantic nature by coming out with things like that. She went off to the river terrace with its white flagstones and little broken balustrades; it was a place to daydream, where moorhens could be watched and swans imagined, even a swan-like boat (though we had never heard of Lohengrin) ... while she was meditating, Fergus and I were being greedy.

Once we had collected our bits of metal, dug a hole with one of them and ceremonially buried them all in the haggard, we went looking for crab apples. Fergus could eat these raw. I couldn't, but I knew that Kitty Dunne at home would make them into jelly if I brought enough of them back. The apples had not all fallen yet.

I can remember now, quite well, not just a dream, pure blue sky overhead, the sun still warm but starting to decline, the springy branches we had to hold down to get at their fruit, the few bright leaves we released floating down like feathers and twisting as they fell. The air was filled, not unpleasantly, with the harsh cries of birds. And suddenly, from behind us, came a deliberate human cough.

We both jumped, and I let go of the branch I held. It caught Fergus across the face, and he swore. We looked around. A few yards away in the middle of the grassy drive stood a stranger, a young man who was regarding us in a most unfriendly manner.

He was thin, had straight mousey hair cut rather long, pale eyes set close together, and that kind of narrow face that needs a smile to make it human. And he wasn't smiling now. Over his arm hung the bridle of a heavy brown cob which was busy grabbing mouthfuls of the grass growing thick and juicy along the side of the old drive. The stranger spoke:

"Ye're trespassing here, do you know?" His accent wasn't the local one.

"Ye have no business to be here," he added. Dry-mouthed, I tried to reply.

"We didn't know—"

"There was no notice up anywhere," said Fergus indistinctly, through a mouthful of apple.

"Ye saw the lock on the gate. This whole place has been sold, and my father has it now. He's Richard Hanafin of Clonbrack," he added, as though we had asked, "ye're to clear out now straight away and not come back here again."

His hands were buried to the bony wrists in the pockets of his tweed jacket, he didn't wear proper riding breeches, but grey flannel trousers tucked into socks. His face was red and cold, and I hated every cold inch of him. I remembered stories of the wicked landlords of the past; here, clearly, was their rightful descendant.

But it was difficult to take him seriously all the same, and we stood stupefied for half a minute, wondering if it was all a joke. He had told us who he was, but not his name, so we had nothing to call him by. Somehow, this struck me as sinister and inexplicable.

Clumsily mounting his cob and chucking its head up, the stranger rode straight at us, and we still did not move, partly because Renee had joined us, and *we were waiting for her to say something. Instead of speaking, she started to giggle nervously. Fergal began to expostulate with her, but the stranger, who had suddenly noticed what we were carrying, pulled the cob with difficulty to a halt and interrupted him.*

"Stealing our apples! Empty yeer pockets. And that bag."

Now, no one in our part of the world put much of a value on crab apples. Like blackberries and mushrooms, they were considered lawful plunder by country children. Slowly, Fergal and I emptied our pockets and then the bag, leaving the glowing bright fruit in little piles on the grass. Renee found her tongue while we were doing this, and attempted to argue with the landlord's son.

Young Hanafin looked at her, we could see, in a different way to how he looked at us. Renee, to begin with, was pretty, she was nearer his age, and she was not a robber of apples. So, for a few minutes, he appeared to hesitate and looked undecided, but then it seemed to me that the part he was trying to play, of God in this Garden of Eden, took him over again and strengthened his resolve.

He said no more but followed us to supervise our ignominious departure, one by one, through the calf-house window. Renee came out last, holding her skirt down conscientiously to refuse the tyrant even a glimpse of her pink lock nit knickers.

Afterwards, I heard by degrees through the usual channels—Kitty Dunne and my father—that Mount Alverno was being cleared briar, bush and tree, the buildings bull-dozed, and the site slowly transformed into a golf—course.

Such was my first meeting with Noel Hanafin. The Hanafins as a family were unpopular. In the convoluted and rumour-driven society of South Tipperary, they kept too much to themselves—mother, father and twin sons—to be otherwise.

The father was a vet and also a landowner; one of the sons was a medical student. As Protestants, the boys did not go to our schools, and apart from that, they did not go hare-coursing or beagling, following the local Hunt, playing GAA team sports or attending dances, all activities where young people met each other.

The general impression of Noel Hanafin as a man with a burning need to exercise the power of some kind over others remained with me, buried in memory but still alive when dug up. It came to light after seventeen years when we met as lecturer and student, and I recognised him at once. Though he never acknowledged me even to recognise my unusual surname, I felt he wasn't sure about me and was uneasy on that account.

108

My red hair, the part of me that everyone noticed once, has darkened. My voice has an English overlay partly concealing those flat Tipperary vowel sounds. Dislike may not be potent forever, but while it lasts can certainly help keep a memory alive.

My feeling about this man's physical presence is still keen, fresh, uneasy. And yet, I can't help wondering what brought him here and caused our paths to cross again, so strangely, in another forgotten and neglected place where he is powerful, and I am not.

20 August 1974

This morning I met Locke on the way from the car to the office and thought he looked less pleased with life than usual. His normally neat, clear-cut face had something of a hunted expression. When I greeted him, he stopped and looked at me expectantly, and only then did I remember that I had promised to let him have the date of the Parent's Association meeting, and I hadn't done so yet. So I told him when it is to be.

"Too many new things," he said with feeling, "we need a bit of peace just now, so we can all settle down."

I could have remarked that he has never appeared to me other than settling down, but I thought that in his present depressed state he would not see it as a joke.

"Life is not used to be when I was young," Locke said, "people trusted each other than, or at any rate, they trusted more than they do now."

I made a sympathetic noise and waited.

"I'm taking my annual leave—the wife and I go to the Canaries every year—taking it just as usual, no different to any other time. Sladebourne—well, it runs itself, we're a small enterprise here, and we don't have the turnover the big hospitals have. The job is rated according to patient numbers, as you know."

He paused for sympathy, and I made another non-committal noise.

"Well, now, this time, when I go off for my three weeks, they're putting someone in. Sending a young man from Riverdale. I can't quite make out what they want to do that for, can you? But maybe you already know all about it. Maybe you know why he's been sent, eh?"

I think my blank face convinced him that I did not know, reassured him in fact about me, for he added: "Lynn manages very well when I'm away. And you'll manage, won't you? Mustn't grumble then, I suppose."

When he left me he was looking, I thought, a little less dejected. But the finances of Sladebourne are really in some confusion, and the man sent to take over *pro tem* is no trainee administrator; he is an accountant. Brian Haskins from Riverdale told me this, but I don't want to be the first to tell Locke.

I might have some sympathy for him if it hadn't been for what happened on Ivanhoe last week. It is a dark place, darker still on a cold rainy unseasonable day when everything is chill. I shivered as I went into that gloomy house where no heating will be turned on until October the First. Believing the children to be at school, I had come to look at their notes.

But the children were not at school. Though it was 10 o'clock in the day, some were still in bed, and others sitting listlessly around the walls of the playroom, as I have seen old people sit in the less-stimulating type of retirement home. And everyone was still in night clothes, their shapeless pyjamas or indecently shrunk nighties.

Nobody had even a dressing-gown or a sweater, and they looked at me in such a hopeless, undemanding way! Only Robert, between shivers, said something that I couldn't quite catch. Charge Nurse Sidney looked even more harassed than usual, as he tried to answer my questions.

"We ha-haven't any clean D-day clothes, we r-ran out two days ago, some cock-up at the laundry, but there's only t-two of everything f-for each of the k-kids anyway. I've asked and asked—"

"Who did you ask?"

"Mr Paigle of c-course, and he s-said he'd see to it, but he's g-gone away now on leave, and he never lets us order anything w-without he OKs it first."

"He can't mean to leave you with all of them, like this! They're cold!"

"Well, I know, Miss Delancy, but where he used to work, Mr P. that is, down D-Dorset way, he did tell us they h-hadn't to put any clothes at all on the kids all summer on from May to October, and they were healthy as t-trout. You may say, he does not t-think clothes important."

I rang Locke from the ward; he denied any responsibility at all for the situation. I reminded him that he authorised the ordering of clothes requested by the charge nurses. Then he told me 'That there was something on order but delayed', he added that the cost of clothing was very high, had actually gone up recently, and only the fact that the suppliers were personally known to him kept prices lower than normal.

Moreover, he added, he was not to know any details of the order, but he felt that he should remind me that the order wasn't only for Ivanhoe but for all the wards... so it might not include the clothes I actually wanted... I cut him short and asked him to ring the supplier. "Well, I suppose we could do that. But we would need a special note written to me from the Chief Nursing Officer." (Locke never, if he can help it, mentions Paigle's name.)

"As you know, Mr Paigle's away."

"I do not know the movements of the person you mention, as he has not seen fit to inform me about them. It's very inconvenient." I rang off. The local voluntary organisation for Children with Mental Handicaps employs a part-time welfare officer, Magda Beeton.

When we met recently, she said she would like to visit Sladebourne; well, now was going to be her chance. Magda came over, and I took her on a quick tour around, including Ivanhoe to see the children sitting wrapped in blankets from their beds. (I was glad that Sidney had that much sense.) Sid had also found from somewhere a portable gas heater, so Ivanhoe was warmer than it has been, which does not say much.

The next day, Magda handed Sidney a cash donation from the Society, to buy tracksuits for his flock, and she delivered at the same time a formal complaint to Locke, with a copy to the Area Health Authority. Now, the Ivanhoe children are all back at school, all of them, that is, who have wearable shoes…

So I don't feel sorry for Locke in his troubles. I don't feel sorry for him at all.

27 August 1974

I decided to go home for a break before the Parent's Meeting at 7:30. I was feeling suddenly happy. On the take-off point of this new venture, I am already certain that it will succeed. Late summer is ahead, that time I have always loved better than deceptive Spring. Everything would go well tonight; someone must be praying for me—I felt it, though I don't always feel that sure about prayers.

I went home, ate my slight supper, and changed clothes, dressing with some care to look well but not unapproachable. As I was actually leaving the flat again, the phone started to ring. Some instinct told me to ignore it, but curiosity won.

There was a pause after I gave my name, then the caller hung up. This has happened before, several times in fact. Such things happen; of course, they can happen to anyone. No sensible person worries about them.

That evening was misty and gentle and still, the sky above faintly luminous, and Sladebourne's setting never more enchanting. Cast-iron railings above the wall, newly painted, shone silver in the early evening light. Tufts of pale flowers—stocks, white daisies, pink valerian—disguised the cracked cement paths. Distant vistas looked more promising than I know them really to be. Even the children's houses, lighted within and seen from the outside, looked welcoming.

By the time I reached Sladebourne, Margaret and Vicky were in the biggest room in the school, putting out cups and saucers and plates of biscuits. They had been going to make sandwiches too but were discouraged by the realisation that the guests were likely to have eaten already. An electric urn, on loan from Riverdale, hissed and grumbled on a corner of the largest table.

Ray came in, carrying two tin containers overflowing with the gleanings of grave wreaths. He placed these proudly on the table, one at each end. When he left us, Margaret swiftly removed them to safer positions on the floor. Aitken arrived with Little Fred, both balancing stacks of chairs on loan from the canteen.

Mrs Paigle arrived, and we hadn't really expected her. She is a small, neat self-conscious woman with a pale face and fluffy black hair. She's rarely seen in Sladebourne, and I think, only came now because as she explained in her whispery voice, 'Max is under the weather'. Long before I knew who she was, I've seen Mrs Paigle waiting at the bus stop on the main road outside the gates.

I've never seen her in her husband's Lancia, which seems to be for his sole use. The fact is that they lead separate lives. Mrs P. works at a general hospital in the city, which she gets to by bus. Anyway, she came, which shows interest and may be a good sign!

Other people suddenly started to arrive. Paul Gomez came with his wife. A representative from local Voluntary Services came—don't know her name. Sister Daroga came, elegant in a turquoise sari, Locke came, Sister Irwin came, Sidney came and Duncan came.

At last, the parents came, starting with the Cassatis and Vera Grimshaw's father and mother, who arrived all together. They know each other, as they both have children in Waverley, and they know Daroga and even know me. But I was soon greeting people I have never met before, people who seemed ill at ease and uncertain of a welcome.

Moving forward to greet one such couple, I almost collided with Hanafin, who grinned in a wolfish way at my surprise and explained: "I just want to see how it goes, that's all. But don't start thinking you can include my people without my consent." Forty parents turned up, out of a possible eighty.

An excellent start, Gomez called it. I hope he's right. We gave them twenty minutes for tea and chat, then Gomez called the meeting together and the business part of the evening began—the process of electing a committee and its officers. These are, on the whole, the articulate parents: Peter Cassati is chair, Marie Keane Vice-Chair, Mrs Grimshaw is Secretary, Jim Wills, father of Trevor, is Treasurer.

They want me to attend their meetings, as a Social Services link. They also want Paigle, when he's better. They wanted to have Gomez too, but he's explained he can't make many meetings.

Hanafin had disappeared by then, which is probably just as well because nobody expressed a desire to include him, though several people did ask me who he was.

The agenda is for the next meeting, in two weeks' time. High up on it will be fund-raising, which members feel confident about because most of them have done some of it before. But when we talked and listened to each other, it was plain that the real subject at the top of everyone's list, whether they said it this time or not, is planning for the children's future.

Put another way, nobody wants their child to go to Mount Vervain. Ever. I said this to Margaret, as we walked towards our cars. Margaret just asked if I'd seen Mount Vervain yet. I said I hadn't but had seen a documentary about it. "I wonder what you'll think of it," she said. I said that I imagined it as a bigger Sladebourne. Well, she said, that was true, but not all the truth.

28 August 1974

Nilla rang just as I got into work this morning. It throws me when someone does that, ringing before I've even had time to put my bag down or take my jacket off.

"A couple of things, Mary. First, the post-mortem on Molly. It took so long and I'm truly sorry about that, but don't you see, it wasn't straightforward, I mean—"

"Are you saying she wasn't run over?"

"How did you guess? No, well, she wasn't. Actually, she was poisoned, Mary."

"You mean, deliberately? I can't believe anyone would do that. She must have eaten something she found outside. Molly was free-range, the bathroom window was always left open, she could come and go as she pleased when I wasn't there."

"Now, don't you start to blame yourself? You're always inclined to do that, whatever. But I knew you'd want all the details. And the trouble is, something about the poison seems significant. I don't remember what it was, now, but the girl who did the whole thing, the vet, she said she'd let me have it all in writing anyway."

"You said there was something else. Is Stella all right?"

"Lord, yes. It's actually, you see, that she wants a kitten. Elvis from next door is due to have them, any minute I should think. Stella and I have been doing a bit of work in elementary biology, starting with cats." (Nilla likes to use teaching opportunities drawn from daily life.)

"Is Elvis the name of the owner or the cat?"

"The cat. He's a black long hair, and they'd named him before they had him neutered. And now, though you may not believe it, Elvis is pregnant. He's a hermaphrodite. Susan's very excited, she's going to write him up—"

"Susan is the vet? Who did Molly's PM? You promised her you'd take a kitten off her?"

"Well, yes. But what do you think about Stella having a pet kitten of her own?"

"I don't know. Give me time to think about it."

Like a few months, I thought. Nilla has not known the aggressive side of Stella but I have. There was silence for about two minutes.

"You don't agree with me."

"Well, no. I feel it seems like pushing things. Stella's only had you working with her for the past fortnight, isn't it? Is she ready to take responsibility because it's a lot—"

"I can't see the point of delaying, in all of that. Of course, Stella can learn to look after a kitten. I'll teach her, and she'll get to know it right from its birth. When it's ready to move, say in eight weeks—"

"That's not what worries me. Stella is very rough with people sometimes. And she's not accustomed to animals. She wouldn't understand that you can easily hurt a kitten, indeed, you can kill one pretty easily."

"You're saying no, then?"

"We need to give it a bit of time. Look, I'm under some pressure here at present. Talk about it again next week?"

Nilla never gives up. We ended with a half promise to foster Elvis's as yet unborn kitten in the workshop, with the co-operation of Donna and Louise. I don't feel quite easy about the whole arrangement, and I've been stung into it by the implication that I'm afraid to take any risks. Nilla should know me better than that.

Facing me as I sit at the desk is a new second-hand wooden filing cabinet found, after weeks of search and negotiation, by Lillian's secretary. In one of its two drawers hang fifty orange cardboard slings for Gomez's patients, and in the other a single blue sling for Stella Wilson, the sole Hanafin patient for whom I am officially allowed to do anything.

It is my definite purpose, my ambition, to fill that second drawer with blue files. I imagine Hanafin as a sinister crow perched on top of that cabinet, like something out of Edgar Allen Poe, randomly pecking at these files with a half-open grey beak. First Wednesday in September, he will be coming to my office before the conference so that I can talk about welfare benefits to him.

These will be the tools I'll use, to get involved with his neglected patients. Steve rang—he said there was a message left for me while I was talking to Nilla. The caller left no name, only a number I did not know.

Not that it makes a difference, I've never been able to remember numerals anyhow. I called the number and a breathy voice replied: "Mary, I do need to talk to you—Oh, I'm so silly, you must be wondering who—it's Audrey, from the encounter group." Then I remembered her all right.

5 September 1974

"How are you, Audrey, and how are things?"

"Fine. Actually, I'm married again. He's Ralph, Ralph Harwood, a senior social worker with Kent. And I'm on a teacher training course at Steep hill College, Mary, and guess where they've sent me on placement? Borne School. I didn't know about you being here too and nobody told me until this morning. I've been here a week, and I do need to see you as soon as possible, and could it be today?"

I offered today's lunch break but explained that we'd have to eat in my office, the only private place around here. Audrey agreed to that, she sounds uptight but then, she always did. And I was curious because it's such a completely new departure for Bourne to take a student, and what on earth can they be doing with her? Although my contact with the school is erratic because they seem to find me threatening, I know what goes on there, and change is on its way.

A local Special Needs school, is about to offer ten places to Sladebourne children, or so the Head of Turn well School told me when I contacted her about visiting, last week. I've been wondering ever since how Mrs Bailey and Lucinda will react to the loss of a big tranche of their pupils, and how they'll do the transfer. At last, I managed to put it temporarily out of my mind while drafting a detailed referral of Justin Lyons' deprived family to their local social services area office.

They can't visit their son here or take him home for weekends—something Gomez and I are trying to encourage—because the cost of transport out here is beyond them. I don't have any money to solve that little problem, but perhaps the district office people know a charity that has. When I'd taped the letter, I took it over to Admin. for dispatch to the audio-typist at Riverdale who does all my letters now.

On the way back, I saw Margaret and Vicky, both running. When they saw me, they waited for me to catch up, and unusually for them, neither was smiling.

119

As soon as I was near enough, Margaret said: "Mary, can you come with us? Something's wrong."

"Where?"

"Midlothian." As we turned into Midlothian's enclosure, I recovered enough breath and presence of mind to ask what this was all about. Margaret did not answer straight away. Then she said: "I'm not sure, so I don't want to say anything in case I've got it wrong. It's better if we see things for ourselves…"

Midlothian's front door being as usual wide open, we entered in procession with me last. The customary urine smell met us, topped up with the sweetly disgusting odour I can now identify as coming from the lotion the staff use for their hands. Faint sounds of conversation came from the kitchen and the room next to it, where the children's lunch table was being set out. The children themselves were still at school. And there was no one in the office.

We went swiftly upstairs, the pitch-pine treads creaking under unaccustomed pressure. When we were on the landing, Margaret made for the only half-open door, and without hesitation, we followed her in. Abina, a care assistant, stood at the window of the darkened room, in the act of pulling open one curtain so that enough light would come in to reveal what was there.

Spread-eagled and supine on a tumbled bed lay a small boy. He was naked except for a sheet, his eyes were closed, and he appeared to be asleep until you noticed his head moving slowly, almost mechanically, from side to side as though he was to some extent aware of our presence and disturbed by it. The boy's limbs did not move at all.

His face was difficult to see, but suddenly I recognised him: Mark Shine, one of those who have no visitors, and whose relatives I have so far not been able to trace. When his head turned in my direction I stooped down to look into his face; the eyes were open now, but he was not seeing me.

Margaret conferred in whispers with Abina. I could catch a word here and there. Abina was saying that this had happened last evening when she was bathing several children on her own. She left the bathroom to get something to use for a flannel, and Louis must have turned the hot tap on Mark.

He was screaming, that's how we knew something was wrong. "Where was Terence? Having his half-day off. Where was Sandra? Toileting the other kids."

Margaret lifted the sheet from Mark, whom I now realised to be semi-conscious. Vicky switched on the overhead light, and we could see on the child's thighs and legs several large opaque blisters, some distended, others collapsed and leaking fluid into the sodden bed.

My eyes turned instinctively to where a bedside locker should be, with its load of fluids and charts. It wasn't there. "Why on earth is he still here, and not in the Burns Unit at Riverdale?"

Margaret and Abina answered together: "No one has seen him yet."

"Didn't you call the duty doctor from Paediatrics, Abina? No? Who did you call, then?"

"Abina didn't know to do it, Mary. She's only been working here for two weeks. When she saw Mark was worse today, she called me. Ten minutes ago."

"If Terence was off duty, why didn't you call the Hospital, I mean Riverdale? Mark's been badly scalded, he should have had help from there right away."

Abina now looked terrified. After several attempts to speak, she burst out: "We're not to get anyone from Riverdale, Mr Paigle says, especially not from Paeds. We'd all get into trouble and lose our jobs, he said. They can't do anything to you, Miss, or to you, Mrs Tobias, but they could to me and I've got a young child to think of."

I found myself staring at the neat, circular brooch on the collar of the girl's blue overall. I had taken it at first sight for a State Enrolled Nurse badge. Now, on closer inspection, I saw it carried the logo of a trade union. It was Margaret who found the right kind, tactful words to say to Abina while I went to the downstairs office and made a call to Dr Allen, the Paediatric Registrar.

After doing that, I did not want to wait around, and Margaret, who had sent Vicky back to her work, offered to stay with Mark until the doctor came. There was, of course, something else that I had to do most urgently, and that was to see Paigle, who must be told what I had just done. My plan for this was to make it seem I had merely dropped into Midlothian to read Mark's file, and found him with severe burns, untreated owing to a misunderstanding.

Not a likely story—but Paigle surprisingly heard it without interruption or comment. At the finish, though, he came out with a shrill and passionate denunciation of Dr Morgan, whom he accused of wanting to get people into trouble, but—Paigle concluded venomously—"he had better watch out for himself."

And then Paigle suddenly realised what he had said, and stopped, momentarily shocked at having allowed his feelings full self-expression in front of me. I found myself almost instinctively being sorry for him; soothing him down in fact, and omitting a query as to why the night staff had apparently noticed nothing wrong. The genuine rage I still felt was all directed against poor Abina, not at all at Max Paigle, and I am still not quite sure why.

As I emerged from admin., I saw the little blue car of Dr Primrose Allen, coming in slowly over the gate-lodge ramps, and was cheered by the sight. Even the discovery that the only sandwiches the canteen had left, were doorsteps packed with grated onion and strong cheese, leftover from the order lovingly prepared for decorators working on Kenilworth, could not cancel out the relief I felt.

Audrey arrived at the door of my office almost as soon as I was there myself to open it. A dark whirlwind of a person, intelligent and impatient, she is the sort who in earlier centuries might have been accused of witchcraft, mainly because she found it hard to keep her mouth shut, and had a habit of being right. Re-marriage hasn't altered her much. After a brief exchange of greetings, we got down to business.

"Do you know what Bourne School is like?"

"You tell me," I said.

"They don't do any work. *Nobody* does any teaching. It's unbelievable. You know that lassie who takes the children with cerebral palsy? The one with the plummy voice? Mrs Nugent? She sits all day long crocheting lace collars for the School Fete. She's not being paid to do that! While she's doing it, her assistant puts toys in front of the children.

"Just puts them there, and walks away. Anyone knows disabled kids need to be shown how to play with toys. And there's no plan for anybody"—Audrey's prominent brown eyes glared at the memory, and before I was able to divert her, she began again:

"They sit, those kids, like that all morning. The ward staff collect them for lunch. Back they come, after that, and go into the playground if it isn't raining. Then back to the same old toys in the same old room, where Mrs Nugent is still crocheting, until the stroke of three when she packs up and goes home."

"I can imagine. Audrey, are you attached to this lady's class?"

"No, thank God, I'm with Vincent Snape."

"And he's better?"

"Well—marginally. But he does the same things over and over again. I've been there a week now. And I've been keeping a diary of what happens or doesn't happen. It's for my supervisor; otherwise, she might not believe me. And

Vincent—he never takes those children out of the school door. *Never*. D'you know why? Because he can't. He's agoraphobic."

"He can't be! He travels to work here, five days a week. From the outer world of-of-Bromley."

"He is agoraphobic. A pal brings him to work by car and collects him too and takes him home. Door to door. He just told me."

I reflected that Audrey had at least been able to gain Vincent's confidence.

Audrey's expression became still more intense.

"Mary, you must be able to do something. They're all just using the system. The only two people in the whole school actually trained as teachers are the Head and the Deputy, and they don't teach. It's ludicrous. Nothing ever starts, nothing develops—they're simply childminding!"

And you, I thought, are simply letting off steam and using me to do it. Whatever I say will sound feeble, but here goes:

"Oh I believe you," I said, "but there's little I personally can do. Bourne are only prepared to involve me in connection with fundraising, and I'm not part of the education system, I'm part of the local social services' hospital division. But what you're saying has given me some ideas."

Your diary—why can't you use it, not alone for supervision issues but to record whatever happens that *you* think is wrong? What about using it to enlighten the inspectorate? I'm sure they've already got suspicions they'll be grateful to have confirmed. Anyway, see what your tutor thinks of that. And you've given me another idea.

Sladebourne parents rarely see the school in action—just the school building, when they come for a social event. Now, we've got a Parent's Association, it can negotiate for parents to visit Bourne School during the working day, and visit other schools as well so that they have something to compare it with. Why not? Parent Power!"

And to emphasise, I jumped to my feet and punched the air. Then I saw the startled look on Audrey's face was not all due to my sudden gesture. She was looking past me, and through the window. "Someone is spying on us!"

"Who—where is it?" For there was no sign of anybody when I looked out.

"A man—a short, John Bullish type. He could only just see in over your window box."

"That, Audrey, would be our Chief Nursing Officer, Mr Paigle. He probably thought I'm beating you up, but I don't care, if it means he'll leave us in peace for a while. Now, what about a super-strong cheese-and-onion sandwich, to go with your coffee?"

Soon Audrey was telling me about poor Wilfrid, the second male teacher at Bourne School. Wilfrid recently attempted to restrain a hyperactive teenage boy by pinioning his wrists to an adjacent wall, the way NYPD do it according to current TV dramas. The boy resisted in the only way he could, by bringing one knee up.

Two days have now passed by, and Wilfrid is still 'off sick'. I suppose we are really cruel, but that incident struck us both as funny.

20 September 1974

This afternoon, I went to visit Stella. At first, she did not seem to hear Louise open the door to me. Louise put her finger to her lip, enjoining silence. Stella was working at the table with her back to us. A surprise was being prepared, about which I was not supposed to know.

Standing behind her, I studied my client. Her hair is longer and thicker now, the tended blond wings of it sweep across her shoulders. Donna and I have succeeded in throwing out all her shapeless second-hand clothes and bought new with the money Hoxton gave us. The Stella of today wears jeans, and a cotton sweater in that clear red so flattering to blondes.

She chose it herself, to match her red sandals. Even from behind, she is a different creature from the neglected being of five months ago. If I were asked to put down the difference between Stella then and Stella now, I'd say that she looks today as if she belongs to somebody. But legally, it seems, she still does not.

"It's finished, Louise, come and look!" Then Stella turned around and saw me.

"Oh hide it quick, she mustn't see, hide it for me, Louise." And she thrust the treasure at her carer, who, coughing, placed it in a folder beside her bag on the shelf.

"And what do you say to Mary?"

"Oh hello how do you do Mary!" gabbled Stella as she went hopping around the room like an overwound clockwork toy.

"You seem to have plenty of energy left after school," I said, "how did it go today?"

"All right. I did a few things. But I can't go out now because poor Louise has a bad chest. She's coughing. I don't know what her chest's done that's bad, do you? But I do *really* want to go out now."

It almost seemed as though she was making an attempt at a joke and I've never heard her try anything like that before!

Louise, between coughs, explained that she has bronchitis and really does not feel very well. I told her she should not be here at all, but Louise said she thought it would be alright as long as she kept warm. Donna is on holiday, but back tomorrow. I was thinking.

"When you take Stella for a walk, do you go around the grounds by the railings, out along the road outside the railings, or into the woods?"

"When she's good, like now, we go into the woods. It can be harder, she's more likely to run for it. But you could take her, Mary, she'd go with you. She wouldn't run away from you. I'll tell her to behave."

Now, I had never before this taken Stella anywhere on my own, doubting my ability to control her if she did not want to be controlled. When she realised that we were going out, she jumped about more than ever, seized her anorak from its peg and tossed it in the air, and kicked her new lace-up shoes across the floor.

Getting Stella ready was like fitting tackle on a restive pony, and like a pony's her eyes had a gleam of energetic mischief. At once, I had to leave Louise's flattery out of reckoning, it wasn't connected to reality. Yet the same Louise, helpful to the last, was telling us where we could walk.

"Down by the side of the maintenance hut over there there's a track to the bed of the bourne. Of course, it won't be running yet, we've had no rain to speak of, have we. Over across the bed, you'll see another path going up the bank opposite, and that comes out near the school."

We left her standing at the door, looking after us, perhaps having doubts. With her fringed coat and dress and her high suede boots Louise looked, I thought, like a character from a romantic novel about dispossessed Native Americans. And no sooner were we out of Louise's sight than Stella, who had been walking very slowly and dragging her feet, whirled around and jumped away from me in one movement, then disappeared into an adjoining thicket.

Half prepared for something like this, I followed her promptly but not too closely. We were in a laurel plantation fringing the main woods, and those woods are not really very large, a couple of acres, no more. When I could see the movement of the bushes ahead of me, I stood still and called her name: "Stella!" and again "Stella!"

There was no answer, no discoverable sound, but in the silence a sense of anticipation. Then suddenly, leaves rustled, and fifty yards away a magpie flew to a new tree. I caught sight of Stella's blue anorak and followed it.

The way was downhill, and we could not have been far from the path described by Louise. Stella ran like any escaped wild young creature, headlong, careless, jumping some obstacles, falling over others, getting up and running again, hooting with laughter until too breathless to laugh anymore. It was hazardous to run there, for leaf-mould lay deep in hollows of the ground, concealing them; and roots and brambles set tripwires for unwary feet.

Above our heads, beeches still kept some of their leaves, hanging dark against the pale blue sky, but tawny brown in the shade. Soon I was at the bottom of the little valley of the bourne. I could not see anyone, and saw no path either, just the stream's present bed of dry stones half-concealed in lank dying grasses and weeds.

Crossing this bed, I walked forward, then suddenly through a parting of the trees saw a ferny clearing, and saw Stella lying sprawled across the roots of a small tree.

For one horrible instant, I thought her injured, perhaps dead, so quickly do we anticipate the worst. But as I came nearer, I felt sure that she was watching me through narrowed eyes, her mouth smiled, and she didn't look a bit distressed—Stella was pretending and this was all a game. If I did not get the next move right, Stella would be off again, and I did not want to spend the rest of the day organising a search party, as people have had to do more than once in the past.

Guardian Angel, I prayed, give me a break, right now. Inspire me.

"Stella, look, the apples! You've found an apple tree!"

She sprang to her feet shouting: "Where, where, show me, Mary!"

"Look up there, just over your head!"

She saw the high yellow apples, tried to climb the tree, and fell back crying with annoyance. A swift runner, Stella is an inept, impatient climber. But by now I had caught up with her.

"We can get some apples if we shake the tree. If we both do it, they'll come down."

Together we clung to the gnarled little tree, the sole survivor of a forgotten orchard. Together we shook it until we had a dozen or so of golden yellow, slightly wrinkled fruit. Stella was entranced, evidently, she had not previously connected fruit with trees. Now, she bit into one of the apples, removing it abruptly as it twisted her lips with its sourness.

"They're no good."

"Yes, they are. They're cooking apples. You take them to school and Nilla will show you how to make a cake with them."

Stella pondered this for a moment, then began frantically stuffing apples into the pockets of her anorak. The pockets once filled, she came to me with her arms full of the surplus apples and dropped them at my feet. Unsure what I would do with them, nevertheless she did not ask me. I managed to pick them all up. Stella came nearer me, fixed me with her green stare, and said abruptly:

"Nilla lives in a big house. Have you got a house?"

I said I had a flat.

"Nilla isn't married," she remarked, "are you?"

"Yes," I said before I thought, then realised I did not know the answer.

"What is it—what is 'married'?"

Oh, Gee. How did we get into this? "Well, it's when a woman and a man promise to love each other for the whole of their lives."

It was difficult to say that. I don't know if I believe it or not. And I knew what was coming next.

"Do they do sex things together, like with me?"

"No, no, not like you, Stella, what was done to you was wrong. With grown people, it's different; it's not like it was with you; it's meant to be a way to show love. The way you were treated had nothing to do with love."

I do not even know what sense Stella made of what I was saying, or trying to say. I've never had much practice talking to kids. And I cannot know how far she understood or believed me, either. We had got back to the path by now, and mercifully there were no more questions.

But I know there will be when Stella has thought them up. She has started something and will go on with it the next time she has a chance. For me, of course, her explorations open wounds.

I left Stella with Louise and got back to the office as soon as I decently could, but then, as soon as I got there felt the need to go home to the flat. On the way, I stopped off to get food. It hasn't been possible lately, to shop during lunch break.

There were queues in the supermarket halfway down each aisle. Seeking mineral water, I came to the pet-food gondola with its displays of food for birds, and dogs—and cats. As I deliberately remembered that cat food was no longer something I had to buy, the curious pain of losing Molly came spreading through my consciousness like a stain through the cloth. It spread and spread.

I couldn't have believed that the death of a pet animal could make me feel like that. It almost seemed to me that I was being punished in some way, and for doing what? Probably, for being alone. At the checkout, I wasn't thinking. I joined an untidy queue and on purpose let a woman with a basket go ahead of me.

I was only trying to be generous, and I spoke to her. She didn't answer but perhaps she was deaf. When I started putting my trolley's contents onto the moving belt, a man behind me, clearly irritated by my slowness, started to help me unload.

Now, I hate when anyone does this. Ordinarily, I don't say anything, but this time I glared at him, said: 'No thank you, I don't need help' quite loudly and turned away from him. Now, much later, I can still recall his look of bewilderment, and I still feel angry, but this time with myself. A patient, humble person, like Louise for instance, would never act like that. If only I could have some of her patience!

25 September 1974

Today dawned a fair Autumn Day of almost Canadian splendour, coloured as bright as a good memory. On such days, when I was very young and still living in Ireland, we tried if possible to get out into the country.

Still thinking of those times, and of the people close to me who were alive then, I got into my car this morning, started it, and then suddenly became aware of someone hovering at the nearest window. It was a thin old man, wearing a peaked cap that did not look right on him somehow; it exaggerated his shallow forehead and long nose. But he was trying to speak to me, and I put down the window.

"Good morning, Miss, I heard your car door early this morning."

I must have looked as puzzled as I felt.

"Your door," he explained helpfully, "you were banging it. Woke me up, it did. At 5:00."

"I didn't bang any door," I said.

"I said to Sarah—that's the wife's name—Sarah, I said, the noise, that'll be that young woman over the way, the one with the Irish accent and the little Fiat."

"But I'm only just up and going out now. It wasn't me you heard. It wasn't my car door."

"Just like rifle shots, it was. Like in Norn Ireland. I'm a light sleeper, see, and always have been. Once awake, I stay awake."

"Not guilty," I yelled, having decided he must be crazy. He stepped back, and I drove off feeling harsh and aggrieved at the one time. It was not a promising start to the morning.

And as so often and so dangerously I have tended to do while driving any distance under stress, I let the past in on me through one of those gaps in attention that open up when the mind tires.

In that past, I am sixteen again, and it is a Sunday afternoon in Autumn, out in the fields far from the town. Below the light luminous mist only grass is visible all around us, long grass disordered and silvered wet with moisture drops. It is slow to walk through such grass, the tangles snare one's feet. But we are all dressed for the fields and for the day, with trousers tucked into boots, old coats, scarves, and woollen gloves.

From ahead of us and from either side of us come the noises of people and dogs half-seen in the mist. The cold echoing horn calls of the beagle pack's huntsman pursue us also, as we stumble among grass-tufts, struggle across dykes, or climb precariously over locked gates. Nilla, as always, is ahead of me, and able to see best what is going on.

I'm among the stragglers in the last rank. I can't see much, and my fingers and toes are numb, but these minor discomforts do not matter because I am near Declan, with whom I am in love. We don't speak very much to each other, he and I. When others are within earshot we talk to them enthusiastically, in fact, we make a point of doing it.

We know we live in a society where every word, gesture and expression is observed, reported to others, and used as the foundation for the main popular recreation—the construction of rumour. There is always a sense of dismay about the making of rumours. However unreal and inaccurate, they are essentially ill-natured, with just enough realism left in to be believed.

Between us, we carry an ashplant, each holding one end. It's Declan's ashplant, which he used to steady and pull me over a particularly awkward ditch. We stayed holding it. If there hadn't been so many people there to see, we would have held hands.

I have forgotten what it was like, to live safe and ignorant in that muted and restricted world. Forgotten how Declan's mother collected us in her car, drove it with one hand, dispensed cut-up fruitcake with the other, and talked non-stop so that I don't have much to say to her except Thank You. When we get to my home, Dec gets out and opens the car door for me, and we touch hands when we think his mother does not see. Then I go in home, light-headed with the sense of how wonderful it is, a life that offers such experiences!

Now, fourteen years on, I turn into Sladebourne's open silver gate, to meet the inescapable present. Today it is Steve in the porter's lodge, saying Good Morning by gesture only; just noting that I have put in an appearance. Somewhat later, having dismissed the past, as I begin drafting notes for the weekly case review, make phone calls, and deal with posts, I am aware of putting off the need to think seriously about what Hanafin and myself are going to say to each other in this room early this afternoon.

Hanafin is in some ways what my father would have called a blackguard and a chancer. Hanafin seems unaware of the impression he makes on others; or else he's only concerned to having his own approval. If it suits him, he'll be gracious, and if it suits better, he'll bully you. He appears to enjoy bullying women—I've seen him bring Margaret to the verge of tears—and this leads me to speculate on his family life.

I don't think it likely that Hanafin will try to intimidate me today. His type likes to have an audience for their displays of power. No, the question I have is quite different. Does Hanafin remember the past as I do—does he recognise me as the girl he ordered off his father's newly bought property fourteen years ago? I have to ask what difference it would make to my life if he did remember.

Well, it would make this difference, that he wouldn't be able to claim so easily the airs and graces he has now, and maybe some Irish paranoia about the happening being used as a joke against him would turn him more conciliatory and easier to deal with.

On the other hand, if it never gets mentioned at all, my fear is that he'll go on thinking that there is something about me that he can't trust, can't stand, and equally can't fathom. That wouldn't be to anyone's benefit, would it? Shall I play it by ear?

And yet this man has agreed, perhaps from curiosity, to meet me on my own territory. Looking around that territory, I thought it must be made as threat-free as possible.

The desk! Nothing could be done about moving it. It did not yield to any amount of pushing; it would have to stay where it was. I pulled the two armchairs to face each other before the gas fire, which was comfortably hissing, its appearance, as I have discovered, much better than its performance.

Swiftly, I snatched and binned the sprays of yew from Ray's latest flower offering. I filled the kettle, to be ready should the occasion call for tea. I put out pens and paper within reach. I even asked Aitken, who was on telephone duty, to hold any calls. I said some prayers. I was ready.

And now I heard a voice shouting at Steve, who shouted something equally indistinct back. Footsteps approached the door. A pause, then a knock.

"Come in, Doctor Hanafin, good afternoon!"

"Your clock is fast," he said, "it's still morning."

I asked him wouldn't he sit down but, ignoring the offered chair, he sat instead on the edge of my desk so that I had to take the chair myself to avoid having him loom over me.

"Well now, doctor, there are a few matters to discuss, Stella Wilson to start with—"

"Stella Wilson. Well, what?"

"I've had a call from Hoxton social services. They want to discuss plans for her—"

"Then 'They' should—whoever 'They' are—have spoken to me and *not* to you. She is in *my* care, as she is *my* patient."

"The person who spoke to me was the Principal Officer for Children's Services, Tom Grace. As you know, he has seen Stella. I have told you about that. He gave me some of her past histories. She was admitted when Dr Benson was in sole charge here, but Hoxton kept the legal responsibility for her." I was getting tensed up already, but so was the doctor.

"Look here, if this is all you've got to say, you can't expect me to spend time listening to it. If those people want to see anyone about that child, they'll have to see me!"

"And that was in fact what I told them. They know they must see you. They want me to organise a meeting. I told them I would need to ask you if it could be held here."

Hanafin paused; this was evidently unexpected, so I pressed my advantage.

"They normally have these meetings—statutory reviews—in one of the district offices or the Town Hall complex. I explained that you and Mr Paigle were both very busy people, and I asked if to make things easier the meeting could be held here. In this room, for instance. They will supply a minute-taker. And," I added, "Mr Paigle doesn't know about this yet, I'll tell him later today."

"You already know," said Hanafin reluctantly, "that I'm here every second Wednesday afternoon. You can ring my secretary to make an appointment for one of them. And can't you do something about that big fellow, that porter at the main gate? He's damned rude."

"Dr Hanafin, I'm not employed by NHS so I don't have any responsibility for the porters. Mr Locke would—"

"And a fat lot of use that would be. Listen to me, Miss Delancy, listen to me, if you please. I've told you before, I won't have you interfering. You are not a doctor; you are not a psychologist. And I want—" here he took a folded paper from his jacket pocket, "I want to know the meaning of this."

Uneasy, not to say anxious, I took the paper and unfolded it. I saw an application form for a place in a private residential home for children with autism. It was partially completed in neat block letters, and from the box for 'Social Worker' my own name, handprinted, stared out at me.

I turned over the form, and saw right at the end the place for the signature of the applicant as 'person with the main responsibility of care for the child.' There was a big flowery signature, quite indecipherable and entirely unknown to me.

Hanafin sat on the edge of the desk, in judgement on me and obviously comfortable about it. He had been waiting to catch me out and was fairly sure now that he had done so.

Compassion, the most unexpected of emotions, awakened in me like a flower opening. My dread of Hanafin's anger went away, and something of the respect I had had for his authority went with it.

"I don't know anything at all about this form. And I don't know this signature either."

"But your name is here! Louis Davies is my patient. Nothing to do with you."

"Dr Hanafin, I still don't know anything about this, but it seems to me that Mrs Davis could have got it herself and filled it all in by herself. She could get my name from anyone, staff perhaps, or another parent. Actually, that is something else we should talk about.

"The parents ask why Dr Gomez's patients have access to a social worker, and yours haven't. Some of them ring me up to ask me things, mainly to do with welfare entitlements. I can't very well hang upon them. Then, there's the money—"

"What money?"

"Mobility Allowance. Children here could be getting it, if we can convince DHSS they'd benefit from outings, from the sort of trips to the seaside Mr Paigle organises sometimes. The money would be useful for those. But of course, we need your backing."

I had nearly said 'permission', but just stopped myself in time. There was silence, apart from the soporific hissing of the gas fire. Outside the window, a bird started to sing, stopped, then suddenly began again with a different tune.

Hanafin was staring at the fire as if seeing it for the first time. I looked cautiously at him, at his thin fair hair, his bony lantern-jawed face, his bony hands and large feet protruding awkwardly from the expensive suit.

"And you're sure you know nothing about this form? Terence thought you did."

"I've never seen it before, but Terence sent me a message last evening which I haven't followed up on yet. Perhaps it had something to do with this."

"Perhaps, indeed. Well, I don't object at present to your giving benefits advice. But that's where it stops. No home visits, no letters, no interviews with any of my patient's families. Mr Paigle can do whatever in that line I think is necessary. Is that clear?" Turning he saw, must have seen, the question I was about to ask him in my whole expression, the indignation in my eyes.

"These children are here because—they cannot live at home. Only here can they be safely contained" (the voice rose, the accent altered now to flat Tipperary).

"It is cruel," said Noel Hanafin with feeling, "deeply cruel, to raise false hopes in people, hopes that their child could ever become normal and lead a normal life. Ever heard of therapeutic optimism, Miss Delancy?" I shook my head.

"No, I rather thought you hadn't. And it applies to social workers just as much as, perhaps even more than to psychiatrists. Don't you forget that? Now, if you'll excuse me, it's almost time for our Case Review."

And he left before I'd even had the presence of mind to say: that treating people positively does not always signify a denial of their limitations.

This time, the Hanafin I have encountered is not so much arrogant as defensive, vulnerable and hard to be feared at all.

Yes, it was almost time for the review, but there I still sat, my mind circling the revelation until Margaret called to collect me a few minutes later.

Louis Davies, one of the children down for review this afternoon, is a 'born runner'. Graceful, handsome and healthy, he is also, according to Gomez, profoundly autistic, restless as a wild creature, and lives only to escape. According to Duncan the staff nurse, Louis if he could spend all his days and nights ranging from Sladebourne woods, and never come indoors at all.

Duncan understands Louis, but not quite how to manage, much less how to train him. Louis's parents lead separate lives, and their son seems to be all they still have in common. Whenever they meet, it is solely to discuss his future. I know that one such meeting took place recently, Mrs Davies told me about it when she came to my office to help collate the first edition of the parents' newsletter.

I had already heard that possible placements for Louis's future had been discussed, and wasn't surprised when my advice was directly asked. I decided for once to be prudent. However, I feel about Sladebourne, it cannot help criticise it to parents. So I suggested that Mrs Davies ring Hanafin's secretary to make an appointment to see him. Mrs D. stared at me and laughed, but without amusement.

"You can't really mean that. One interview with that man was quite enough!"

"He finds it difficult to see parents—" I began, intending to point out the stressful, crowded nature of the doctor's life. Mrs Davies took it another way.

"Too right he does. Then why do this job? He does not have to do it. There must be other things he could do."

And Mrs D. went on to tell me, by way of contrast, how delightful a certain famous children's specialist she'd met socially had been to her. He had made her feel at ease by telling her a dirty story, and then he'd given her his home telephone number to ring if she felt she wanted to talk to him at any time out-of-hours.

"Not that I ever have rung him, mind you, but still."

No, I thought, Hanafin certainly won't treat you like that. And moreover, he has no charm, nothing to deliver to others except, I suppose, bad news. Almost at once, I felt compunction at my lukewarm excuse for him, more insulting in its way than any direct criticism would be. But perhaps Mrs D is really on to something. Why on earth did Hanafin choose a speciality he could only be negative about?

I've actually felt upset recently at the readiness of Terence to attach responsibility to me about that form of Louis's, and the readiness of Hanafin to believe him. Clearly, Terence dislikes me and has come to find me a threat. And it's all my own foolish fault. A few days after my introductory tour, I went to see Terence about one of his charges and mentioned my own nursing background thinking that would ingratiate me, but it did the very opposite.

Despite his charge-nurse status, Terence never completed any course of training, and the presence here of a person who did may be a constant reminder of that, and hardly welcome. As far as Terence is concerned, I'm a great menace and a possible spy, useful at times but never to be trusted.

He will be likely to use any weapon that chance puts into his hands, he would even (and I feel chilled at the thought) try to get me out of Sladebourne. Hard as life is here at times, I don't really want to leave, at least while there's so much to be done. And of course, there is Stella.

Sitting through the Case Review this afternoon in the barren surroundings of Midlothian, conscious of Terence's unfriendly eye on me, I felt trapped and constrained. Terence is a plausible bespectacled rogue I think, a nasty and dishonest person. But Paigle knows this, so does Hanafin; why take on someone like that and hold on to him as if he were the best person they could possibly get for the job? There must be some hidden reason, which I may never know.

Otherwise, the review was interesting. Ivor Smith was down to share the afternoon with Louis. Ivor was presented first, and Gomez and I had prepared a surprise. We persuaded Ivor's mother to come to a special review of her son's progress.

Elegant Mrs Smith sat in the front row beside Gomez, and when everyone else had said their piece, Gomez introduced her, and she told the assembly how we fixed up for Ivor and herself to meet a psychiatrist skilled in communication with the deaf.

On the basis of that interview, plus our reports, Ivor has just been offered a place in the rehab. unit Dr Ghent is opening in Surrey next month for deaf-mute teenagers. Today, please God, is the last time Ivor will enter the circus ring!

I have to say, it was enjoyable to see the astonished faces of Hanafin, Locke and Paigle, the surprised faces of the rest of the audience, and the tearful triumph of Amanda Smith, experiencing hope for the first time in years. And Ivor? He suddenly looks taller, and less scared than before.

The second part of the review was to have been about Louis Davies, and I was not looking forward to being interrogated in public about him by Hanafin. What actually happened was that a phone message came for the doctor, Paigle went out with him, then came back to announce that Hanafin had been called away. Mrs Davies, perhaps, fortunately, was not present either, so Louis's review was a very low-key affair, conducted by Paigle as a sort of duet with Duncan, and there were no revelations of any kind.

Those came later when Sister Lewis dropped in to see me. Bertha Lewis is Sister Daroga's deputy and a pale shadow of that energetic creature; a shy woman, who rarely expresses an opinion unless she has to. When Bertha does say what is in her mind it makes a disproportionate impression. What she had originally come to see me about, was to find out if Hanafin would back our applications for Mobility Allowance for some of the children. Over a cup of tea, I told her the good news.

"Dr Hanafin and Mr Paigle really will support it. It'll take a while to actually get the money, of course, but we need to do some advance planning anyway, maybe to recruit voluntary helpers for the outings. I have sounded out a couple of the local associations, but somehow, they just don't appear very keen."

Bertha wrinkled her forehead. Her hand, with its short fingernail innocent of varnish, played uneasily with her teaspoon.

"That's good about the doctor and Mr P; that's really good news. Only— we'll need volunteers, I'm sure. We had some, only they gave up coming to a wee while before you came."

Before I could stop myself, I asked: "Why? What happened, then?"

"They were nice young girls, the volunteers; helping on Waverley, playing with the children, but there wasn't the right place for them. They were only fifteen or sixteen. You don't want anything to happen to them when they're giving up their time to help others. It's all wrong!"

She went on to tell me: 'in the strictest confidence' that Terence had seduced one of the volunteers, a sixteen-year-old from the local High School. Following a divorce, he married her, but his first wife and children continue to live in the council estate just over the road, while Terence with his new bride occupies a rent-free staff flat at Sladebourne. There aren't many staff flats, and they usually go to single people, who resent a couple having one.

Paigle, who is, apparently, very taken with Terence's teenage wife, wanted to employ her on the site, but she got work elsewhere and turned his offer down. All this explains a good deal, including the reaction of the volunteer associations. Bertha is a friend of Terence's first wife and the present situation seems terribly wrong to her.

She is also aware that any opinion of hers expressed openly will be put down to ill-will or sexual frustration. Bertha did not actually say this to me—such expressions are neither of her time nor of her nature—but we share a negative opinion of Terence and Paigle.

"It must be hard for Mrs Paigle," I found myself saying.

"A poor thing, Mary, a poor creature. Believe me, even if that man beat her, she'd never leave him. Though God alone knows how she puts up with him."

Bertha recollected herself; she should not be gossiping like this with me. She changed the subject, got up and took her to leave. She doesn't really like Sladebourne, I thought, probably only the work with the children keeps her here, as I saw the trim corseted figure making its determined way back towards Waverley.

Over the next few days, no more was heard of Louis's application form, nor did Terence mention it again. And I was busy, trying to get three of Waverley's adult residents into a local day centre, and organising a Welfare Rights information session for parents plus Sladebourne staff, having first managed to persuade Lillian that this was an essential part of my job. Lillian belongs in spirit to those proud days, not so long departed when hospital social workers were Lady Almoners.

True, Lillian no longer wears the starched, skimpy white coat with the Institute of Almoners badge on one lapel, but she does carry herself with a ladylike self-assurance perhaps not out of place in a teaching hospital, but totally foreign to the district office, and to the duty desk with its rising tide of bewildered, angry or plain distressed humanity.

Lillian, it is clear, has never checked anybody's welfare entitlements, and sees no reason for me or for any other social worker to be able to do so. I wonder what she would do if she knew the whole truth, that with Celine's help I have even begun to extract money from Riverdale's Hospital Amenities Fund for the child patients in Sladebourne, none of whom had any toothbrushes. Eventually, I hope to get these sorts of things from other sources, but it all takes time.

That time is actually coming nearer every day. My approaches to London social services departments now bring responses. Some boroughs send social workers to our case reviews of their children. They tell us about small group homes which they are setting up for children like ours. I am even invited to come and see them.

Peace reigns in private also. The disturbing silent phone calls have stopped. No more letters come from Philip. Stella likes her tutorial classes, according to what Nilla says—proof, if we needed it, that she does not have an abnormally low IQ.

Then why are my nights filled with such terrifying, foreboding dreams? Dreams in which Hanafin's asymmetric face appears, now as leader of a company of ghosts, now as sneering keeper of a prison from which I try hopelessly to find a way out? All nonsense. Put it out of my mind. Tomorrow

I'm going to learn something real; Deptford College is hosting a seminar and discussion on Child Sexual Abuse, and I will certainly be there.

1 October 1974

The room in Deptford College was small, airless and crowded—with furniture, not people—and situated at the top of a Victorian city building trying to re-invent itself as a seat of learning. The absence of lifts made the room impossible of access for anybody who couldn't climb five flights of stairs; maybe this was why most of the people making up the audience were thin, athletic-looking, and young. Apart from Celine and myself, there didn't seem to be anyone else from a hospital.

It was pretty stuffy when we came, and my attempts to open windows were helped by a blonde girl who introduced herself as Adrienne Shorter from Camberwell's Area Four. I'm not sure where that is. It's probably near the South Circular—Adrienne said it had a lot of council housing estates.

Adrienne, who seemed to be partly responsible for organising the seminar, introduced the speaker: Pauline James, a psychotherapist who works only with children. She is Liverpool Irish—now, that was somehow a surprise—and small, and neat and unobtrusive. This made more shocking by contrast what she was telling us, about the damage done to children by sexual abuse.

They feel worthless, used, dirty, irrationally guilty and blameworthy, and these feelings can obviously lead to behavioural difficulties which don't exactly make them easier to help. Briefly, the harm that's been done to them skews the whole of their relations with other people. They can't trust anyone because, insofar as they know, all men abuse, all women collude with them, and nobody protects children.

Pauline outlined some of her cases, clients she is actually working with. One of those children sounds very like Stella. Pauline sees this girl for a forty-minute session three times a week. At first, the girl wouldn't stay in the therapy room with Pauline for longer than a couple of minutes.

Gradually, things changed, and now she stays full time. It took months, to get this far. What Pauline seems to be doing, is encouraging the child to talk about what happened to her. Once Pauline gets this far, she can set further goals.

Some of what Pauline was telling us I have already heard from Tom Grace. He's even quoted stats—wasted on me, as I never can remember them. But the general drift, I can remember.

Tom said—and Pauline confirmed this—that most instances of child sexual abuse take place within the family, and are perpetrated, colluded with, and concealed by family members. In fact, however unready we are to use the term, these are crimes of incest, and God knows how many there really are because we only get to seeing the tip of the iceberg.

The sensational, tabloid-worthy cases one reads about, the Stranger-Danger tales starting with a child abducted and ending with a child dead, are actually very few—no more than a couple in Britain in any one year. Incest is far commoner, but is a secret crime, and keeps its secrets.

What really shook me, though, was not so much the accounts of the physical abuse, although God knows they were bad enough. It was the reaction of most of her hearers to Pauline's conclusions. The younger women—we were all women there—were so incredulous, so totally dismayed—as if nothing in life up to then had prepared them for the shattering disappointment of what Pauline was trying to tell them.

They simply could not credit that sexual activity could damage anyone so as to affect their whole future life in a negative way. It just could not be true! They had, I suppose, been accustomed to see moral absolutes as dreadfully outdated. But here was a therapist, a woman from their own age group, saying that something causing the greatest pleasure to one individual can actually do terrible harm to another, and be, like, cruel and criminal. They could hardly take it in.

It reminds me of the way people react if they're told that recreational drugs, cannabis, for instance, can activate schizophrenia, an incurable illness with distressing and dangerous psychotic episodes. How can it be true? When do all the big stars and celebs use it? When everyone who's famous smokes hash? How can she expect me to believe that? She sounds like a fifties woman!

God, there are times when at twenty-nine you feel really old.

Nilla asks me to write her something about Hanafin's background. Because she was away at boarding school when we were all young, she never got to meet him, and she says she's been offered Louis Davis as a one-to-one pupil, and she wants to study his psychiatrist as well! I wish her joy. She has promised to keep what I write for her absolutely confidential.

Report on Noel Hanafin. (Strictly Confidential.)

Long ago, it was always assumed that people who converted to another religion did so for reasons to do with material gain. In the case of this branch of the Hanafin family, their change of faith happened very long ago, and it certainly gained for them a toe-hold in the upper ranks of the Irish middle classes.

Grandfather James Hanafin, a tenant farmer's son, became land agent to the Duke of Barsetshire who owned half Tipperary. Richard, James's eldest son, trained as a veterinary surgeon and married the daughter of a local solicitor known to have 'acted for' the Duke in several matters. They had twin sons, John and Noel.

At some stage during the boys' early childhood, their parents separated legally. This was an unusual event in Ireland at the time, and the whole business, of course, was surrounded with secrecy. Noel remained with his father and paternal grandparents, but John left the locality with his mother, and so far as neighbours' knowledge went, they both moved to England where she had relatives. Nothing more was known of the mother and son for some time.

Noel at the age of twelve was dispatched to a boarding school, one of a kind founded to foster a sense of identity in the Irish Protestant community of the time. It was run on the lines of an English public school only much smaller of course, and less expensive. Did he like it? No one knows.

Anyway, Noel seems to have justified the expense of his education, going to Trinity on a scholarship and choosing to study medicine. (It would have been at about this time that my first encounter with him took place.) Noel followed graduation with a spell in the RAMC. Then, he went for psychiatric training at a London hospital, and by coincidence, it was the one where I was working 'on placement' as a student nurse.

I have to say he was unpopular there. One medical secretary was heard to say of Hanafin: 'Nothing ever goes right where that man is', which about summed it up. Hanafin's patients were always the ones who failed to show up for appointments. If they did appear and were not seen immediately, they had an inclination to disappear again.

If they stayed, disputes broke out between them and Hanafin, needing the intervention of administrators which the latter much resented having to make. Hanafin's correspondence went adrift regularly, his patient files were always the ones to get lost, and his was the consulting room most likely to get double-booked.

It might be all pure bad luck, but Hanafin also contributed to his own misfortunes by a general lack of attention to what he was doing. People took this as indicating a deep lack of motivation, and maybe they were right.

Now, as I say, I was working in the same hospital, but mercifully, not in the same department, so we didn't meet during a couple of months that I was there. We did meet some years later when as a social work student, I opted to take a module concerning NHS psychiatric services for children. Hanafin was one of the four lecturers involved. By the end of the short course, he did know me as an adversary if nothing else.

How or when Hanafin chose to specialise in work with children, no one seems to know. There were rumours about a relative of his, a child, being treated badly by the system. Whatever the truth of the story, it did not make Hanafin sympathetic to the feelings of their parents. He had always tended to give families short shrift, and he went right on doing that.

The few absolutely unavoidable encounters with parents were always carefully structured, almost stage-managed, to give them the least say possible. I felt, he wanted anyway to keep an unbridgeable distance between himself and most other people. There are various ways to do this, and Hanafin did not try to employ the 'English Class System' one—to do that effectively, I think you need to be English yourself—he used the 'Power of Professional Status' method, to keep distance and enforce respect.

I am a doctor, says Hanafin in effect, so I know what is happening to you, and understand it much better than you can. I will tell you all that is necessary for you to know, but don't question me, for if you do, you question my authority. If you want to see me privately, this must be only on my terms, not yours, since my time is always more valuable than yours. In fact, it's far too valuable to be wasted on people like you.

7 October 1974

At Sladebourne, the season for summer holidays being over, Locke and Paigle are omnipresent. Everywhere I look I see one or other of them, never, of course, both together. They keep to separate territories, and Locke hangs around the building containing my office. Today, he appeared at my door and handed me my stationery order, so long-awaited, with a degree of the ceremony that I felt was meant to kill the suspicion that he had received it weeks ago and forgotten to hand it over.

Last evening, as I was going to the car with two sackfuls of papers for the Riverdale shredder, Paigle approached me, carrying a large white cardboard box. Suddenly, silently he tried to hand it to me, but I could not take it without dropping what I already carried. When he realised this, we were both embarrassed.

He tucked the box, with some difficulty, under his oxter, and then quickly pulled it out again when he saw that I had managed to put down the plastic sacks. I said first: 'What' and then 'Thanks', as I took the box. Paigle only smiled and departed grinning with satisfaction.

I connect the presentation of that box to the major event of that morning when Paigle and Daroga were both invited by the supervisor of a local authority Day Centre to come and see what that could offer to some Waverley patients. I was responsible for arranging this event, which seems to have been at the least a social success.

But gratitude takes so many forms, that I still felt apprehensive about what might be inside that box. It was: a very big milk chocolate Easter egg, decorated with green satin ribbon and pink marzipan roses. I am left with the mystery of where, in the month of October, Paigle managed to find it.

On reflection: our local sweet shop, encouraged by Daroga, is disposing of all its out-of-date confectionery to her, and free of charge of course.

I considered at first giving the egg to Stella. But we—that's Donna, Louise, Nilla and myself—are seriously trying to keep her away from junk food, and we reckon the brand of chocolate in this egg comes pretty near to that. After a lot of discussions, Donna accepted it for her ten-year-old nephew. He seems to be a tough little boy, with none of the problems of our girl.

Yet, there is hope for Stella. Even Nilla thinks so, going by what she told me the other day:

'That child is really coming on! Hasn't kicked or bitten anyone for nearly three weeks now'.

We plan to have a specially good Christmas for her. But we dare not mention it yet, in case Tom Grace comes up with foster parents and knocks all our plans sideways.

I've got to know most of the Sladebourne children, and some really well. But there is a kind of special link between Stella and myself. It's not a simple attraction, she is really and painfully present to me in a way the others are not. I think of her as the one for whom I've got most direct responsibility because she is so misplaced and should not be here. That responsibility involves: disappointment, suffering, and also pride in her progress and hope for more of it.

But the future for her is so dreadfully uncertain!

I've given up the half-hearted attempt to do Life Story work with Stella, and that was (I can't even say it to Nilla, only write it, and only here) because it is so upsetting to hear that rather flat, childish voice recite the course and catalogue of her past neglect and sexual abuse, or even worse, to see, in a horrible parody of the way little girls play at being women, Stella putting on what I suppose is the manner of a prostitute coaxing a customer.

Over the past six months, at different times and in different ways, Stella has offered herself to Nilla, to Paul Gomez, to Tom and to myself. She evidently thinks that anyone, female or male, who shows any interest in her, must want her body for sexual gratification. She responds to adults with a sad coquetry, a resigned and charmless travesty of love.

'This is what I must do to get your attention and maybe a bit of your affection? Very well then, this is what I must do, it is, after all, the way life is for me.' Written down like this, it seems easy, obvious in fact, to know how to counter what she implies. Find some way to demonstrate to her a love that asks for no return.

But one of the main obstacles to doing this lies with Stella herself, her inability to believe us when we see any value in her. We all appear incomprehensible to her. She can never take anything we do for granted.

It will take years to overcome that state, I said to Nilla, years upon years upon years. How is it possible to help people like this? I ask as I read the few books there seem to be on this topic, and realise there are no easy answers.

Yet there's Pauline, and she believes that some help exists. Maybe not from me, but from someone else—someone uncomplicated, imaginative, outgoing, accustomed to working with children, able to give them love. Someone, for instance, rather like Louise.

Long ago in that life that's over, my life with Philip, I began by wanting our child. As the reality of my husband's illness slowly got through to me, I prayed not to conceive, and something heard me, for conceiving I never did. As his illness progressed, Philip lost interest in sex.

I could not compete with whatever was going on in his head, with his fantasies that soaked up all his attention. The physicality of love ceased to attract him. Yet consciously or not, he had married me with a plan in mind. He had not hoped that he could escape from his illness, he knew there was no escape from that.

But he had taken for granted that I would be able and willing to give him all the help he needed to continue to exist; that it was to be my sole purpose in life, my vocation, what I was for. That I would need to be told about this plan in order to commit to it, that it should not be imposed on anyone without their consent, never occurred to my husband at all. My realisation, slow as it was incoming, that this nightmare state we were in was in fact something which Philip had intended from the start, almost turned me against him as nothing else could have done.

If he had been a cruel or a callous person, maybe such a discovery would have had less power to shock. But Philip was—is—a gentle creature. The revelation of how he really saw our future and my part in it convinces me that I never really knew him—or knew myself—in any sense that matters.

Now, thinking of the pain and failure so recent still, I realise I cannot respond to other people as I once could. I have looked open-eyed and helpless at the devastation of my life as if it were the view over a whole country changed and damaged by an unpredictable storm, and the conditions causing the devastation are still raging within hearing distance. When all I thought I had was swept away, my confidence in some areas of life went as well.

I doubt and question everything now, including everything I believed in before. It is this fragile and uneasy state that makes me helpless in the face of need like Stella's.

What she should have, I tell myself, is a strong and confident mother, with a warm and generous heart. Someone like this, able to save her, she will be able to trust absolutely, and then her healing will begin.

13 October 1974

At weekends, I never get up early, and my friends all know this. So it was with a sense of unbelief that I became aware of earliness, of dull light coming through the slatted blinds, of the sounds of birds and yes, the sound of the telephone—which I delayed to answer, sure that it must be a wrong number. There seemed no reason, at 7:30 a.m. on a Sunday, to think otherwise. At the last possible moment, I snatched up the receiver, to hear Donna's voice.

"Mary, the gentleman, he's come!"

"Hello, what—"

"Maybe I shouldn't be calling you up—"

"I'm awake now anyway. What gentleman?"

"The one you talked about. He's here now and he, he wants to take Stella out for the day."

"He can't. Mr Paigle, he knows all about it too, can't you get him?" Responsibility for Stella's care surely could not possibly be all mine!

"They can't find him. He should be on duty still, but Fred thinks he went out. Maybe collecting for the therapy pool. We can't find out where he is. And night staff's gone off duty too." Donna's voice was starting to get high and squeaky with panic.

"Donna, listen. Tell this man he's got to wait until I come. I'll be coming right now. What did you say was his name?"

"I don't know. Just that he's been here before, and he says they all know him. He said he's got left to take Stella out whenever he wants. When I told him you said—?"

"Listen, it's not only me or what I say. Whatever used to happen before, now we can't just let anyone come in and take a child out. There's a law against it."

"But it's the weekend. And I can't stop him, can I? And he says Terence told him it was OK."

"If you let her go, I will have to get the police to get her back, and there'll be even more trouble!"

"Oh, it's no use taking it out on me, Miss Delancy. It's not my fault, and I can't prevent people from doing what they want to."

I swore to myself and at myself as I got out of bed and groped for clothes with one hand, talking to Donna meanwhile, telling her I was sorry; of course, it wasn't her fault, but please could she keep him 'til I came, and not let Stella go with him on any account. Five minutes later I was on the way to Sladebourne, bleary-eyed and shivering in the cold car, and full up with resentment as well.

Where was that lazy slob? Where was Paigle?

Sladebourne's gates were open as I sped through them in disregard of all speed limits. I glimpsed Steve's big unshaven face at the lodge window, gawping as if he saw a thunderbolt. Outside the workshop, an old green MG was parked facing towards the gates.

I stopped my own car and got out. Running fingers through uncombed hair, blinking still-sleepy eyes, licking dry lips, I knocked on the closed workshop door. As I did so, I heard, like a reminder, church bells across the wooded valley calling to prayer.

The door opened very suddenly to my knock. Stepping into the room, I took in the tableau at one comprehensive glance. Donna, who had opened the door to me, was standing in the corner nearest it. Her face showed all her anxiety, but still a welcome relief.

Stella, in her new blue dressing-gown, sat at the table, opposite the door. One thin little hand kept twisting a lock of hair, yet her face was without expression, and she gave no sign of recognising me. Opposite Stella so that I could not see him properly against the light through the window, sat a tall thin man who got up and turned around to face me.

When he did, I could only stare, speechless because all of the words I had been ready to say were gone. My face and eyes must have displayed the shock of a confrontation with the totally unexpected.

"I apologise," said the intruder, "I've startled you, I see. And what a pity," he added, now looking at me with a kind of polite contempt, "that we disturbed you, and all about nothing."

By then, of course, I had realised that he was not Hanafin. My bewilderment and shock, on the way to anger, were still considerable. Who was this man, anyway? What was he doing here? And how did he come to look so like our senior consultant? The voice, as he went on apologising, gave me some clues.

It wasn't exactly like the doctor's; with this man, the original accent of provincial Ireland was entirely overlaid with middle-class English vowels. It's the identical twin, I thought, the brother who went to England with his mother when the parents split up. It must be he; it can't be anyone else. The other Hanafin.

I said who I was and that I was there in default of the management. Then I asked the stranger's name.

"I'm an old, old friend of this young lady," and he smiled, indicating Stella, "you may call me John."

"John?" I said, waiting for the rest of it.

"Just John," he repeated, but this time a muscle jumped at the side of his jaw. Stella slid out of her chair, apparently casually, and took up a position behind me.

"I did not know," I said, "that Stella had any old friends."

John Hanafin laughed, in a way that sounded forced. "Dear God, she has friends, many friends. Haven't you, pet?"

But Stella was no longer facing him and did not reply. I could feel where she was, behind my back where he couldn't see her, attached to my sweater with a twisting grip.

"Listen, John," I said, "Donna here rang me because I'm the social worker for Sladebourne. All the children here are now in the care of the local authorities they came from. Stella is in the care of Hoxton. No one is allowed to take her off these premises unless they have permission—it's the law. I can give you details of the person to apply to—"

"Really? Now, look, Miss Delancy, I've been coming here regularly, Max Paigle will tell you that, to take this little thing out, give her a spin in the car, show her a bit of the world, buy her an ice cream. It's my bit of social service, the only thing I do for others. Stella knows me, she likes me, she's telling fibs if she says she doesn't.

"They all know me, Max, Terence, all of them. All those good people in charge. Ask any one of them, if it isn't all right? Sure, what harm is there? What harm could I do her, yes, you tell me? You tell me, what harm?"

I did not answer him, what would have been the use? Did he think to persuade me that Stella was playing games? That uncomfortable grip on my sweater was telling me otherwise. My path was, anyway, quite clear. I could not let this man take the child away, whatever he said to justify himself. So I attempted to explain, angry, hungry and headachy as I felt right then.

And John ceased being polite and ingratiating. He asked how I proposed to stop him? What would I do if he just drove away with Stella? I told him that I would ring the police, tell them he had abducted a child, and give them the registration number of his car. He told me that I had no authority to do that.

"Enough to do this," I said, reaching suddenly for the internal phone. My hands shook as I dialled the two-figure lodge extension and asked Steve to come at once. Then John Hanafin swore at me, using the words men like him use for women who resist them, words traditionally intended to hurt.

The polite veneer was all gone now, and any plausibility he had gone with it. Confronted by Steve, who arrived almost as I hung up, John fled from the workshop. As Donna instinctively locked the door behind him, we heard the roar of the MG's defective engine disturbing the Sunday morning peace of Sladebourne.

With any luck, Steve said, he'd get pinched going down Bourne Hill, where they had speed traps. I don't recall much more of what Steve said; only that for him he said plenty, and most of it concerned silly young women who thought they could do everything on their own.

Stella, who still kept a hold of my sweater, suddenly let it go. Shaking, I sat down. Donna, relieved and grinning, prepared to make tea. I began to take in the presence of Stella close to me; her unbrushed fair hair tickling my face, her wide-apart green eyes staring myopically into mine. She was saying something to me: "You're bigger than him," that's what it sounded like.

Later, back at the flat and thinking of everything that has happened and not happened, I begin to feel not relieved, but uneasy and I'm not ashamed to say, afraid. A situation which at first, I hardly took in, now swells large and alarming as a dark cloud overhead. At some time that cloud will break, thunder will sound and the rain will fall in torrents, it will descend on me, and where is my protection? I feel suddenly completely alone.

There is Tom Grace. Tom is all very well in his way, but he's available for only one purpose, to protect Stella. Lillian, I can't even consider it as a help, she will want to distance herself from me, as she would from anyone in trouble. Nilla is a friend, but not a colleague. She has no real idea of what working here is like, and I don't know that I can even try to tell her.

All I am is a shivering representative of a semi-profession so new as to have only recently decided what its basic training is to be. If the conservative structure of the English local government took decades to accept the need to employ trained engineers to service the air-conditioning safely, why should it hurry to back the efforts of half-trained people like myself to change the way disabled children have to live?

Something answers that. We are dispensers of hope. We haven't anything else to give. Together with the rest of humanity, we climb a terrifying stone mountain, ledge by ledge. On the ledges below ours, we sometimes perceive creatures even worse off than we like to think we are.

If we can share our ledges with them, their lives improve. Ours, on the other hand, might not always. I suppose what we do about *that,* is the test of our belief if we have one. What I've done, is to start praying again.

14 October 1974

This morning I spent with Daroga, in Waverley. I've now collected the original addresses at the admission of ten out of her twenty patients. These addresses are all in London and somehow look to be old. They won't be on the new maps, but some of them may be known to the new local authorities. I hope they're better at record-keeping than the staff here!

At 2:00, Steve dealt a blow on my door—his way of announcing guests. Celine and her student Joan greatly admired my office, which of course contrasts with their sanitised working spaces at Riverdale. Then we set out for Midlothian, to start our tour.

Celine suddenly stopped, made a sign for silence, and ran back to a corner of the canteen building which we had just passed. She cautiously looked around the far corner of it, then rejoined us, walking rather deliberately on her tip-toes. Joan looked at her with some surprise, and also with apprehension.

"You won't believe it, we are being followed!" Celine said, grinning.

"I'll believe anything can happen here," I said, "what does the follower look like?"

"It's a short man with a red face. He keeps dodging into places, like doorways. Could he be a leprechaun, perhaps? But he's got a bicycle with him, a woman's bicycle too. What is the significance of that? Come on, Joan, you're up to date on psychoanalytic theory."

Joan appeared unwilling to commit herself, so I intervened.

"For God's sake, keep your voices down. That's Max Paigle, Chief Nursing Officer and resident womaniser. Whatever about his bicycle's gender, he's following us because he thinks you are spies from Riverdale. It's a Cold War situation here; he and Ben don't see eye to eye—"

"You sound as if you don't either, Mary. Handy with the women, is he?"

"He's not the greatest problem."

And I told them a bit about Hanafin. Celine was bewildered but intrigued. An Anglo-French urban upbringing has not prepared her for communities where, even if not actually blood-related, everyone knows everyone else's business all too well. Joan, on the other hand, had no difficulty believing this. She is a Scot, and they are more like us.

"Do you think," she asked, "that this Doctor Hanafin knows all about you, then?"

"I'm not sure. If he does, he never shows it. But if he ever does, he must remember that I would know a lot about him, too."

"You could blackmail each other," suggested Celine.

I shuddered. The sound of that word frightens me. Joan saw the shudder, and she suddenly began to mimic Lillian. She actually 'does' our manager very well. After we'd all had a go at imitating our manager, I felt much better. It's wonderful what a bit of cattiness does for the morale of the workers.

Much later, as I saw the girls off at the door of my office, we had a brief glimpse of Paigle's head and shoulders appearing round the corner of the porter's lodge—like a gargoyle but lower down than they usually are. Even later, as I went on an errand to Admin, Paigle passed me by, cycling for dear life in the direction of Kenilworth. I gave him a smile, but he stared dead ahead, pretending not to see.

I've confirmed that my suspicions about Paigle's suspicions are correct. He sees my colleagues as spies, and it took some trouble to convince him that it was not so—that they simply wanted to see where I worked. Clearly, I blundered by not including Paigle in the tour.

In an attempt to make up for it, I told him how impressed my guests were to see builders at work on the new lavatory annex in Midlothian. This did not help me either, since welfare worker Magda from the local Mencap society, whom I took around at short notice a few weeks ago, is apparently responsible for getting that bit of renovation started. But I was wrong and should have been wiser and more tactful in my dealings with Paigle, and more aware of his feelings towards the Paediatric Unit and its staff. I must try not to make those mistakes again.

Weeks before the date of Stella's review, which is the day after tomorrow, I sent out invitations: to Stella, who will attend part of the meeting, to Louise, Donna, Nilla, Paigle, Locke *("Do I really have to come, Miss Delancy, are you sure you need me?")* Lillian, Ben Morgan, Hanafin, Tom, myself and the minute-taker—about a dozen people, so my room is not going to be big enough, and

155

anyway it was a good move to suggest to Paigle that we use his. We have had many discussions about this, and he even seems pleased with the idea.

I did not think we need a minute-taker, but Tom said we had to have one, and Lynn's agreed to do that part. Tom also has been helping Donna and Louise with their reports; a great load off me, as I don't think adult education is my strong point. But I did help Stella make a report for herself.

It's really a letter to the meeting. As Stella cannot yet read or write very well, I have offered to read it for her. It's pretty ordinary stuff, mostly about wanting to go to school, but nothing in it to give anyone a shock. The shock will come when Tom Grace puts his foot down about Stella's uninvited visitor.

21 October 1974

The review commenced this afternoon at 3 o'clock. A quarter of an hour earlier, Lynn, Nilla and I assembled in Paigle's office. Paigle joined us, going first to sit as usual behind his desk.

Suddenly, realising it would not look right, he got up, pushed his desk right back to the wall, and moved his seat around to the front of it. I felt this action, unexpected as it was, to be in some way symbolic and important, although no one said anything about it at the time.

As the afternoon was dark, all the lights were on, their reflections swimming in the polished floor and the beautiful panelling. We brought in more chairs, fitting them into a circle. The chill of an already declining autumn day was gradually replaced by heat from the antique squib-shaped radiators attached to opposite walls.

Tom came in, and sat beside me, Louise came and sat on my other side, her tapestry hold-all against my foot, her sweet, earthy scent in my nostrils. More formally dressed than I'd ever seen her before, in a long homespun skirt and tunic, with her hair plaited and tied, Louise kept moistening her lips and glancing at Tom as if awaiting a prompt from him.

I knew he had rehearsed her in what she was going to say, a printed copy of which she held but, as I suspected, could not read. Stella was sitting outside in the hall with Donna. Gomez and Hanafin were both with Locke in his office, Ben was—somewhere about, and we were all awaiting Lillian, who was to chair the review, and who was late.

I had momentarily the sense of being part of a staged performance; with the shadowed edges of that luxurious room concealing an audience of ghosts from Sladebourne's military past, come back to see if the world they had known might, possibly, be different now.

The room door suddenly, silently opened, to reveal no ghost, but the substantial Lillian. She paused momentarily in the doorway, shrugging her silver-grey shawl off the shoulders of her dark-blue dress. Lillian knows how to look at a group of people, without letting her eye rest on any single one, unless it is the most important one present. She surveyed the scene with one powerful glance.

"Apologies, apologies to everyone. I'm so sorry to be late."

Paigle and Tom Grace, the only men present, rose to their feet and simultaneously indicated to Lillian the most comfortable of the chairs, while I introduced them to her. I then went to collect the rest of the meeting.

When we were all assembled (all, that is, without Stella) Lillian suggested we begin by each one introducing themselves. This practice is just coming into fashion, and I could see that the doctors did not like it. Gomez has described it to me already as pretentious and timewasting.

However, they sat up and took notice when Tom Grace introduced himself, and they all followed his example without protest. They kept quiet when Lillian went on to explain the purpose of the review as arranging a formal transfer of Stella's care from NHS to her local authority. The only one who seemed inattentive was Hanafin, who sat next to the door and kept looking at his watch.

Sitting opposite him, I was sharply aware of his impatience, and also of a general sense of unease about him. Tom Grace, meanwhile, at Lillian's suggestion, was briefly outlining the Child Care Review's historical background for the benefit of those present who had not attended one before. He came down to the present day, to explain that Stella Wilson seemed to be inappropriately placed at Sladebourne, an institution for the intellectually impaired.

Transfer of care, said Tom, could be, and in this case, must be, a gradual process because of the need to first find a suitable foster placement for Stella. Tom finished speaking and looked apologetically at Lillian, who smiled sweetly upon him. "I think, Mr Grace, you should really be chairing this review instead of me."

"No thanks, Mrs Saye. I have to complete these forms as well; and you know, it's not really possible to do both at once."

Lillian accepted her responsibility, turned to Ben Morgan and asked him to describe Stella from the paediatric viewpoint.

"Stella was examined last week by my registrar, who found nothing *physically* the matter with her, but that she's under-stimulated, over-active and heedless. Normally intelligent, and as I said, neglected. I do have a question for management, about this little girl. How came she here in the first place?"

And Ben looked directly at Hanafin, who seemed annoyed, and snapped: "Girl's psychotic, that's why."

"I think," Ben interposed swiftly, "we'd like some illustration of what you mean."

Hanafin opened and shut his mouth twice before replying: "She has a history of bizarre behaviour. Attacking people. Screaming Shouting. Is out of control at times." He stopped. He had finished. Paigle, sitting near him, nodded vigorous agreement.

"But what exactly does the girl do that's so bizarre?" came from Ben Morgan, who added under his breath, "and what the hell does 'bizarre' mean anyway?"

"Ask the care staff what she does. They are here."

Louise thought it was her prompt, and began to speak, but was quenched by Lillian who evidently thought that to use one of her favourite expressions, '*things were becoming sensitive*' and interrupted her. Lillian asked Ben if he couldn't add to his comment questioning Stella's placement.

"I've not actually examined the child myself, as I already said, but Dr Allen my registrar did and found no evidence of any serious intellectual disability. We now have the services of a child psychologist at Riverdale. Shall we ask *her* to assess Stella Wilson, if we are all agreed?" And Ben smiled his foxy smile.

Hanafin seemed to come back to himself then, nodding agreement to the referral. But he was also clearly distracted, not attending fully to what was going on, possibly, I thought, listening out for something else, something threatening, something coming from outside of that room.

Perched uneasily on a chair that looked too small for him, Hanafin looked very uncomfortable, and his bony hands hung clasping and unclasping between his knees. Knowing his dislike of being observed, I removed my gaze, unwilling to meet his even by accident.

"Psychologists, now. They don't know *anything* about children like ours," muttered Paigle.

"Think you'll find otherwise, Maximilian," Ben only calls Paigle by his full first name when Ben is angry.

Lillian cut in: "Miss Mowler, I'm sorry we had to interrupt you. Please continue with your report."

159

'Miss Mowler' is Louise. Surprised by the Dickensian name, it took a few seconds before I recognised it as hers, and by then I was already finding her report selective and strange, even though she had memorised every word of it:

"Stella's far more settled now than she was a while back. She's not hit anyone for ever so long, and since she's been going out to Nilla she's been another girl. She'll talk to you now. You can have a conversation with her.

"She plays little games like draughts and that with Mary. And Mary's got her new clothes, so she looks different now from what she did. Stella's starting to get interested in her looks, more like an ordinary little ten-year-old girl."

Louise stopped. Lillian thanked her. There were no questions, but I saw Ben raise and tilt his head, the fox hearing a suspicious noise, and I did wonder at Louise leaving out Stella's revelations about her past. Hasn't Stella told her *anything*?

But perhaps Tom decided it better for the two main carers to present such differing views of their charge. Yes, that must have been it. He has his reasons. Louise went out to summon Donna, still with Stella in the hall. As she left, Tom raised a hand.

"Apart from her two carers, and the hospital social worker Mary Delancy and myself, no one here today has actually heard Stella mention abusive experiences while at Sladebourne House."

As if in response to this, Donna came in and sat as near as she could to Lillian, who asked her to report. Looking first at Lillian, then at me, Donna plunged into her story:

"Well, there was this visitor come, every couple of months since I bin here, and that's two years near enough. It was this man, and he's been coming with a car and wanting to take Stella out. She'd get all wound up, excited and laughing, but not happy if you see what I mean.

"More hysterical, flinging herself about. She'd say she didn't want to go with him, and she'd run away and try to hide, only there is no place to hide in the workshop. Well, he'd take her out, and in two hours or so he'd bring her back. Would she have been missed? No, Mister Grace, she wouldn't have been missed.

"She doesn't go to school, so no one there missed her, and no one else would know she was out, excepting us. What was she like after she come back? Carrying on and throwing around the sweets he'd just given her. When she'd calm down, she wouldn't talk to anyone, just go off by herself.

"Oh, and the wetting. She'd wet herself always when she was back. When I'd try to get her to put on dry panties, she'd hit me and sometimes try to kick me. That's what you want to know about, isn't it, Mr Grace? Mrs Lillian?

"But as to what Stella says to me *now*, she'll tell me how he did things to her, touched her up, he did, and more. But of course, all that's been stopped since Mary Delancy sent Mr Priestly away."

"So you know his name?" came from Ben Morgan.

"Sent him away?" from Paigle.

Their remarks collided with each other. Lillian wasn't clear what either had said, and Lynn abandoned her shorthand notes to check with Tom; there was a minute's distraction and confusion, under cover of which Hanafin silently stood up and left the room. I half-rose to go after him, then came to my senses and sat down again.

Tom's cool voice called us all back to task:

"At this stage, perhaps I should say that when I met Stella Wilson for the first time recently, she indicated to Mary Delancy and myself that she had been sexually abused. It is evidently something she has come to expect from men."

Nobody said anything at first. Then Ben Morgan, turning his eager fox face towards Paigle, remarked: "Well, and all this going on unbeknown to you, Maximilian. Extraordinary! But I interrupt, Mrs Saye, forgive me, and please continue."

Lillian and Tom exchanged glances, and it was Tom who continued: "Of course, we'd have great difficulty in establishing the proof element here. Police won't act unless they have enough evidence to charge the alleged abuser, and I do not think Stella could yet provide this in a convincing way.

"We have, as well, to think of the possible harmful effect on her of criminal proceedings, cross-examination and so on. But we are legally obliged to protect her now and, in the future, and this is what Miss Delancy was doing when she sent the unwelcome and possibly dangerous visitor away."

Everybody looked at me, and then at Paigle. I don't know how I looked, but he looked terrible, his normal florid colour replaced by a livid appearance, with his cheeks sagging and purplish. It occurred to me that he will look like that when he is dead. I turned my eyes away from him.

Meanwhile, Tom's relentless, smooth voice went on: "Questions arise as to how this man came to be admitted here in the first place. I don't suppose for a moment that (here he looked straight at Paigle and from him to Locke) that just about anyone could take a child away for hours and no questions asked. Perhaps this is not the time or place to go into these circumstances in detail. We must now concentrate on protecting Stella Wilson for the future."

Lillian found her voice: "What do you suggest?"

"As soon as we can find a suitable foster placement for her, to remove Stella altogether from Sladebourne. In the meantime, to operate the guidelines which I have already suggested, in writing, to the Hospital Secretary and Chief Nursing Officer. Also, to carry out a complete reassessment of Stella as she now is, using the facilities of the Paediatric Department at Riverdale."

"Surely that's an extreme reaction. After all, we don't know that any lasting harm was done to her. We don't..." Locke's voice dwindled into silence as he met Tom's gaze, which was cold indeed. He tried again:

"I mean, if no harm was done, she could remain here as long as she wants. Dr Hanafin will need to be consulted anyway. We can't decide without him. She's, his patient. And she's so young. Maybe she did not understand whatever happened—"

His voice faded out as he began to realise that his remarks were having a result he had not foreseen. Several people, Gomez, Nilla, Ben, Paigle—were now addressing Lillian simultaneously, and no one was listening to Locke. Lillian gestured towards Gomez, who responded:

"Dr Hanafin has been called away, but in his absence, I can safely say that he will support the plan outlined by Mr Grace."

"Thank you, doctor. Now, Miss Ryan."

Nilla jumped slightly—I think she had momentarily forgotten that she was taking part.

"I work with Stella at the local tutorial unit, where I've been teaching her on an individual basis over the past eight weeks. Occasionally we go to my home as well—to give her the experience of a different setting. Stella's attention span, to begin with, was very short. It has improved recently, and she is now able to complete some tasks without interrupting them.

"She is erratic in her behaviour, and her restlessness can make life difficult for both of us. Her self-esteem is very poor, you know, and she is aware of her deficiencies to some extent. But Stella wants to learn, and she responds to attention helping her to do so. She would still have difficulty in sharing attention with others, and this factor must be borne in mind when a placement comes up— she needs ideally to be the only child in the foster home."

As I knew already what was in this report, I did not react to it. But the others were impressed. Ben said something in an undertone to Tom, then to Gomez, who nodded agreement. Lillian, a witness of this, turned around to face me and asked for my contribution.

I said I could only agree with everything Nilla had said about Stella. But I would like to stress her vulnerability, made apparent by the incidents described by Donna Vincent and by our shared experience of the unwelcome visitor. I explained that he had refused to give me his name and that I would like to know how it came to light, as Donna had mentioned it.

This request caused some discussion. At last, Paigle admitted that he *had* spoken to 'Mr Priestly' on one occasion. He denied giving him permission to visit Stella or take her out. Asked by Tom if anyone else could have given this, Paigle hedged.

He said that there had been a lot of changes in the care system, and he felt shocked at the notion that children in a long-stay hospital could be assumed to be at risk from anyone who took them off-site even for a couple of hours out of pure goodwill. He was not the only person, he said, who felt this way. But some people (he looked straight at me here) who had no real authority, though they could change everything overnight.

Gradually, the realisation seemed to come to him that no one was likely to agree with what he was saying, and he started to slow down then like a clockwork machine someone's forgotten to the wind. When at last he stopped, Lillian asked Nilla, who was nearest the door, to fetch Stella in.

Nilla opened the door and left it open, as is her habit with doors. I was near the door. I heard Nilla talking, but I could also hear someone else very loudly and excitedly laying down the law on the phone in Locke's office just across the hall. I could swear that the voice I was hearing was Hanafin's voice.

He had not been 'called away'; it seemed he had deliberately withdrawn from the meeting in order to contact someone. *To warn them, perhaps?* The door closed after Stella came in with her escorts. A subdued little figure, Stella made the only unobtrusive entrance I have ever seen her make. Holding Donna's hand, she sat between her carer and her teacher.

There was a silence of about half a minute, while the child looked about her anxiously. Lillian made a vague gesture towards Tom, indicating—I think—that she wanted him to 'tie things up'. He did this in the form of an address to Stella, whom he welcomed formally. I can't see why he had to do that.

He said that the meeting was held simply to make plans for Stella to have a family to live with, outside of the big substitute family provided by Sladebourne. To arrange this would take some time, but Mary Delancy would keep Stella in touch with everything that went on. *How, I wonder, will I do that?* Stella would have plenty of time to get used to the changes coming in her life. Tom then asked Stella what she thought about what he had just said.

"You said I could go to school. When I go away from here, can I go to a school?"

"Can she?" mouthed Lillian to Nilla, who nodded. Tom said he was sure they could find a school for Stella, even if it took some time. Nobody asked my opinion, and that was just as well, for I would not have felt able to answer so confidently. There are boarding schools for maladjusted children, and I have visited some of them, but I have not heard of one day school for children like Stella in the whole of London.

When the review was over, and we left the room, I looked around for Hanafin, but he was not there, and all anyone knew about him was that he had been called away.

22 October 1974

Jaded and depressed I got up this morning. Things looked better, if only just, after a shower and a cup of coffee. Now, post never comes before nine, which is the time I officially start work and feeling as I did, the temptation was very strong to do one of two things—wait for the post, or wait a bit later still, and call Fr. Dwyer on the Marriage Tribunal number.

I haven't heard from him for what seems a long time, and he did say he thought it would be straightforward. About a year, he thought, before the Process (he always called it that) was complete and the marriage was officially annulled. Was the year past yet? Well, I suppose it must be. Uneasily I rehearsed to myself the troubled recent past. Grounds for annulment to me seem relatively distinct, at least in our case.

Just as I finished my call to Lynn, to say that I'd be half an hour late, a swishing noise announced the arrival of mail. There was the usual selection of advertising junk, but today underneath it all was a letter with a typewritten address. The envelope was thick, white, official. My heart rose with relief as if my anxiety had called a response into existence, and I said a mute prayer of thanks.

This must be the letter from the Marriage Tribunal, my own personal Letter of Freedom! Carefully I placed it on the mantelpiece, and suddenly feeling hungry made an omelette and ate it quickly. When I'd finished, I turned my attention to the letter.

But it wasn't about the annulment. It did look official, being typewritten on a hospital's headed notepaper, but it came from Philip. I was so shocked and disappointed that tears came into my eyes, and for some seconds I could not read any words, only the signature. Philip has been transferred to another hospital several months ago, he wrote from there, he has received treatment there and is much better. He wants to see me, and the letter is simply to arrange this.

At first, I could not think of how to answer it. Philip knows, of course, that I am seeking annulment he was told all about it during a lucid interval eighteen months ago, told not only by me but also by his mother, who was angry with me and did not soften her language. But does he remember being told? We have not met, he and I, for just over a year. Both of us moved at around that time: Phil to a different hospital, myself to the new job.

Then I thought, well, why don't I ring up and find out how to get there, and when visitors can come, and things like that. Leave the heavy stuff until we meet. This afternoon: I could ring and arrange it this afternoon.

Meanwhile, on the way to work, I try to think about yesterday's review. A fostering placement—how long to arrange that? I know nothing about fostering. What sort of people foster? Nilla might sound as if she knows all about it, but the reality is different—she gave it up after one trial placement went wrong.

She never wants to be reminded about that. I'll have to ask Tom Grace, and I suppose he'll give me a whole lot of stuff before I get an ounce of really valuable information.

Sladebourne this morning is full of rumours about the review. My late arrival at work kept the pot on the boil, as it was hoped that when I came I could confirm or deny reports that both Locke and Paigle are about to get into serious trouble. There seems to be no detail of that so-called confidential statutory review which has not got out and been discussed by all! Professional confidentiality as such does not appear ever to have existed at Sladebourne.

Even the porters want to know if Stella is really leaving the institution, and marvel at the whole idea of her doing so. It's clear that, within memory, no child has ever left Sladebourne, except by death. As Daroga put it, the notion that a disabled child (Stella is seen as that) might be eligible for fostering, perhaps even adoption, is as extraordinary as if they had inherited a fortune.

In little groups, in corridors and kitchens and store-rooms where Paigle could not hear or see them, or in places like the canteen, so public that it did not matter whether he did or not; even on the external phone to me, people wanted to talk about the wonderful brand-new idea that somebody extraordinary in that outer world beyond the silver railings could want to take on a Sladebourne child.

The sub-story, of John Priestly, was hardly mentioned. No one would readily admit that they had ever spoken to him. No one mentioned Hanafin's abrupt departure from the review either. The more I thought about it, the stronger became my conviction that Hanafin didn't leave to avoid answering awkward questions from Tom or Ben, he left for one purpose only—to warn his brother, so the latter would not endanger himself by coming here again.

I have felt sorry for Hanafin recently, but how can I go soft on happenings like this one, where he can't bring himself to protect a child? I'm going to walk warily from now on and be less confident about assessing the motives of others.

Stella met me at the door of the workshop. She actually reached out and took my hand, she was excited and her eyes shone, but she also seemed rather nervous. Her reaction to the discussion of plans for her future showed up her almost total ignorance of any life except the abusive one she has already experienced and the bleak confinement at Sladebourne for the past three years.

"No, I can't tell you where you'll be living because I don't know myself. And I can't say if there'll be any pets. Not every family has pets." I did not get the impression that Stella believed me.

"If I was a little cat," she cried, letting go of my hand, "you'd care what happens to me. You don't care. You'd let me die and people do all horrible things to me." Louise appeared shocked at this outburst. She corrected Stella, who took little notice, then she tried to call her to account.

How could Stella be so ungrateful to me? And Louise began to call attention to my virtues in a manner to embarrass me as well as sounding really insincere. My impressions of Louise seem to be faulty. I must find out why Tom let her off so lightly at the review. Tom really should tell me more. After all, I'm virtually managing the workshop now, as Terence seems to have given up on it.

Day after tomorrow, I have arranged to take the day off to go to see Philip.

24 October 1974

The corridor was wide, and down the length of its floor ran broad stripes in primary colours.

"Follow the red until you see the sign for Pinel Ward," the young man at reception said nonchalantly. He had never asked my name, much less checked whether or not I was expected—so I could have been anyone, about to do anything.

The red stripe went on and on, and I followed it, ignoring a momentary obsessional desire to place all my steps within its boundaries. Shining and pale, the ceiling and walls reflected whatever daylight filtered into through frosted glass windows. The few people I saw looked shabby and submissive as they crept by, keeping close to the walls and away from me, the stranger as if even the right to walk there was something I could take away from them.

When the sign for Pinel Ward appeared, I saw that it was up a short flight of stairs to the left. I tried to turn the knob of its heavy door, but it slipped in my hands and did not yield to pushing or to pulling. Through patterned glass panels could just be seen a vista of beds, with indistinct moving figures in the background.

I was about to bang on the door, when a white-coated man with a flat gentle face came up silently behind me, causing me to jump as he did so. Detaching a bunch of keys from his belt, he unlocked the door, opened it, and motioned me to come in.

I told him who I was. He hesitated, then led the way to the ward office, where he gave me a seat and perched himself on the cluttered desk. He introduced himself as the charge nurse of Pinel Ward and said his name was William Mackay.

"Mrs Parry, I think you haven't seen your husband for some time." A statement, rather than a question.

"We're separated. I haven't seen Philip—we haven't seen each other for about six months."

"Yes. You don't know, then, how he's been since?" I shook my head.

"Your husband has not been so well recently. But he's better now than when he was readmitted to Pinel a couple of months ago. Less withdrawn."

William extracted a folder with Philip's name on it from a nearby cupboard. A few grey minutes went by while he opened and studied it. At last, he put it down and spoke to me.

"But though he's better, Philip's treatment has only been partly successful. You know we can't cure schizophrenia—only try to control it."

Yes, I said, I knew this.

"Dr Schuler thinks that your husband would react badly to any involvement with divorce proceedings, for instance. Any kind of stress—"

William spoke looking, I thought, rather severely at me. I explained about Philip's letter asking me to visit, and William looked surprised.

"Typed, you say? Now, I don't see how—but stop, perhaps I do. One of our volunteers' types letters for patients. They dictate to her, then they sign the letter if they want to, and stamp it. It goes out with the hospital post, it's part of the rehab programme, encouraging patients to keep in touch with the outer world."

"I see. Perhaps it was my mistake to come. Phil may not want to see me after all. He may have changed his mind about it."

"I shall ask him." And William paused, evidently wanting to hear why, after as long as six months without contact, Philip should want to see me right now.

"It's probably about the annulment of our marriage. You see, when we married, we had a Catholic wedding, all OK but nobody, nobody ever said anything to me about the schizophrenia. Perhaps they thought: it won't ever happen again.

"When it started happening again, they may be thought that I'd somehow cope with it. But I couldn't. So I applied on my own to have the marriage annulled. For that process, the people who deal with it will need to contact Philip's psychiatrist. They may have done this already—I don't know yet. So—"

William said that he saw. But his face didn't give much away, and I was not sure if he'd understood or, more important if he believed me. Anyway, he got off the desk and went out, then in a couple of minutes came back and beckoned me to follow him.

I could not really take in much about that dayroom because of the noise. The TV was on loud, positioned on a shelf so high that no one of ordinary height could reach the controls. This was in one section of the L shaped room.

In the other section, a music system discoursed loud, rhythmic music. The few patients were all sitting down, some appeared to be asleep. No one even looked up when we came in.

Noise has always had a confusing effect on me. I could not, at first, identify Philip, then I saw he was there all right, facing the TV that was now showing a trailer of a comic programme for children. When William called him, Philip got to his feet and came over, a smile briefly visiting his face as he recognised me. I put out my arms instinctively, and Philip leaned forward into them, placing a pale, bristly cheek against mine. Unexpected tears pricked the edges of my eyelids.

We could not talk there, indeed with the noise level, no one could. We were shown into a small, cold side room used for private interviews. There were no curtains at the one window, to frame the red and purple of a stormy London sky. We sat on plastic-covered fireside chairs with wooden arms scarred where people had stubbed cigarettes on them. An empty, dirty large ashtray rested on the floor; it was the only moveable object.

"How are you, Phil?" I began, then timidly, when he didn't answer, "I got your letter, but it wasn't clear to me why you…" And my voice died on me.

Philip was fatter than I remembered him, fuller in the face too. He was still smiling faintly. I did not feel certain that he had understood me.

"You got a new job," he said at last, "do you like it?"

"It's OK," I said.

"I heard about it from Mam. She comes twice a week. She got your new address for me."

"It looked very official, your letter."

"I had an official letter too, Mary. About you want to get our marriage cancelled."

There was a pause, during which Philip's smile faded slowly, slowly.

"I thought Catholics didn't believe in divorce. But now you want to divorce me."

I had not thought ahead of what I'd say if Phil reacted like this, but then suddenly words came to me without any delay at all.

"Phil, do you remember what it was like when we lived together? Do you remember how it was, after the first months, when you started having the breakdown?"

"It was all right, Mary, that's what I remember."

"It wasn't all right. You couldn't talk to me, or to anyone else. You couldn't work, or do anything; however, you tried; however, we tried. You didn't seem to know what was happening around you. I couldn't leave you alone, even to go to the corner shop. When I did... you set fire to the kitchenette, making toast.

"You'd forgotten what to do, to put it out, to turn the gas off. If someone hadn't come to the door from Jehovah's Witnesses and helped, you could've been killed. It got so you just sat and rocked yourself most of the time and were unhappy and no one could reach you. When Mam and I got the doctor, at last, you barricaded yourself into the bedroom. Don't you remember the police coming?"

"Something about a door."

"They had to break it to get to you. But it's even not just that. It's more."

His eyes no longer met mine but I did not allow myself to feel how cruel I was.

"Phil, you remember when you asked me to marry you, and I said yes when we told people, told your Mam, when we got engaged, when we bought things for the flat when I bought a dress to get married in when we got married? When we made love? All of that time, all of it, you knew about your illness and you never told me. You knew the breakdown could happen again because it had happened several times before.

"And I knew nothing, and how could I know, when you never said anything whatsoever about your illness. It's not about divorce. Our marriage wasn't real anyway from the first because we couldn't share the real way you were, we couldn't get through to each other, and I need something that states that."

Phil was already halfway to the door. When I got back to the ward, he wasn't visible. Instead, I saw William.

"I've blown it," was what I said to William, "really blown it now."

After a while, I remember him telling me, quite gently, that he thought it would be best if I did not stay there longer. Phil was easily upset at present and might become aggressive... I had not thought of that.

Philip was in the office now, William said, and we could see each other there if we wanted. When I spoke to Phil, to try to apologise, he did not look at me or answer me. When I took hold of his hand, it was cold and limp in mine. So I went away.

I've never wanted so much to cry, but could not find a church to cry in. The only one that was anyway near, had a notice up to say it was closed outside the times of services because it had recently been vandalised.

28 October 1974

Today, walking up the chilly drive from the workshop, where I had just made peace with Stella by reading her the story of *Chicken Licken* which I've always liked myself, I found Locke walking beside me.

"About that meeting you arranged," he began, and then went on to demonstrate how little he had taken in about the plans for Stella and the whole John Priestly episode. Although he asked me occasional questions, Locke seemed distrait and did not take in the answers I gave him. *Ducky Lucky*, I thought, would have done better. At last, he got to the point.

"I suppose you'll be putting in a report, then?"

"What about?"

"Well, if you don't know, who will? I'm referring to the remarks made about letting in undesirable visitors. Critical comments."

"I haven't given it much thought. Anyway, if anyone reported anywhere, it would be Mrs Saye as the person who chaired the meeting, wouldn't it? Not me."

"Oh," said Locke, "of course. That's true. Mrs Saye has always impressed me as a real gentlewoman. One who would never take advantage of others, of those momentary lapses we all have."

After this glowing tribute to my boss, it took me some time to pick up my cue, but at last, I said: "I go to Mrs Saye for supervision pretty regularly. I would be able to let you know what she was thinking of doing about, well, carrying this matter any further."

"I would be—I mean, it would be very kind of you if you were to do just that," Locke said. I had answered him impulsively but now started to realise that I should find out what, if anything, Lillian intended to do. As a naturally indolent person, she was unlikely to take on extra work herself but might, if she felt it necessary, get me to write a report which she would then edit and sign—a bureaucratic process which I find infuriating although in some ways it makes sense.

Seen from Locke's position, the review and its possible consequences for him would be the crisis point reached in a long uphill struggle which he seems to think he is bound to lose. Well, I thought brutally, there is nothing much I can be expected to do about that. I felt more than a trace of contempt for Locke, his curls, his white shirt with the showy cuff-links, his tears.

For the next hour, I chased Lillian by phone all-round Riverdale Hospital. She was on A Ward—no, she had just left. She was on B Ward—no, she had not yet arrived. She could not be found. She was found but she was interviewing a client.

Now, she was busy but she would call me back later. At last, I heard the familiar dulcet voice and was able to ask its owner if she wanted a report from me, referring to the John Priestly incident.

"Oh, well Mary, I'm quite surprised that you should find you needed to contact me about this. When I was told you wanted to speak with me, I expected something urgent and important. No. I have been asked for no report. It's all so vague, that whole story, and all of it resting on that little girl's word.

"A most peculiar little girl, I have to say; something of the little actress there, no doubt. But no, it's really up to Leonard Locke or that Paigle man to investigate what their staff do or don't do, and it's no part of *our* responsibility to call either of them to account. We are Welfare, Mary, they are Health. You must learn to see the difference."

I tried to say that Dr Morgan had seemed to think everyone at Sladebourne had some responsibility for whatever happened to a Sladebourne child.

Dr Morgan, said Lillian, was A Law Unto Himself. His ideas were impossible—too grandiose. Everything he wanted for the Paediatric Unit cost about a million pounds. Dr Morgan was not a good example to follow.

I wonder if Lillian knows that Ben Morgan has invited me to lunch with him at Riverdale. I would not be surprised to find out that he has actually told her.

Ben Morgan combines his post as a paediatric consultant at Riverdale with an extensive private practice in North London, where he lives. His junior colleagues speak of him with awe as one of the richest doctors in the country, a glowing example of material success. But that is not the whole story about him. Even those who enjoy Ben's company, relishing his wit and sense of humour, regard him also with some wariness because they cannot predict what he will do or say next.

Ben is, I am sure, genuinely fond of children, and really concerned for them. Perhaps his more than passing resemblance to a well-known character on children's television contributes to the way *they* see him—I don't know. I know him as a likeable, capricious creature with the power to defend, but also to wound. And at this particular time, he is carrying on a sort of intermittent war with Max Paigle, whom he apparently cannot abide.

"I almost wish, Mary," he will say to me, *just* within range of Paigle's hearing, "that something will go badly wrong in this place. Some scandal, something of that kind. Some good reason to close it all down *quickly.*"

And Paigle, overhearing, colours with fury. He is not Ben's equal in verbal exchange, and he knows it. Ben has even been known to refer, in Paigle's presence, to Midlothian as 'the concentration camp', and to the workshop as 'that bin'.

Margaret Tobias says it is Ben's sense of justice at work overtime. I think it is rather Ben's sense of mischief. He can be a vengeful enemy and a dangerous friend—a provocative and tempting friend. It is as a friend that I am going to lunch with him tomorrow.

29 October 1974

Built in the expansive sixties, Riverdale Hospital lacks the antique and dignified shabbiness of most of the London hospitals I already know. Its atmosphere and indeed its layout rather bring to mind a small-scale international airport, with the same impression of echoing confusion, questionable efficiency, and of expectancy slowly wilting into boredom.

Everything is carpeted that could be, the big potted plants look plastic even when they are real, and once you are on the inside of those automatic doors, the air seems dead. I threaded my way through a packed outpatient department, then rose by lift to the Senior Staff restaurant on the fifth floor.

I had summoned up all of my social courage. I was wearing my clingy Italian wool dress and was no more than five minutes late. When we met, Ben's slightly quizzical upward glance made me feel that something in my appearance was wrong. Maybe it was the hairstyle—I had thought to suggest Gina Lollobrigida, but probably it just looked as if I'd forgotten to use a hairbrush.

Ben's manner—his greeting of me without mentioning my name, and his quick circular survey of the dining room before we entered it—gave me some clues. This was real cloak and dagger stuff, and we were not out to attract attention.

We took an inconspicuous table—I had dreaded to find Lillian among the diners, but need not have worried; the few other people present were male, serious-looking and somehow, not Lillian's kind. I accepted a sherry, and over the reconstituted celery soup Ben got down to business.

He has a plan, which is nothing less than to achieve the swift removal of Paigle from the nursing management of Sladebourne. "You've no idea—oh, but you obviously do have *some* idea—what he's like. He's just got rid over the years, of anyone working in this place who had any intelligence, or conscience either. Anyone who tried to change the status quo. Nothing positive can happen at Sladebourne until he goes, retires, gets knocked on the head, or something."

"And what do you think will do that?"

"Political pressure, my dear." Ben poured out the wine, lowering his voice dramatically. He did not want anyone else to hear his treason. "Dr Fermatt's paying a state visit next month to all the hospitals in this group. Including Sladebourne. A trad thing to do before Christmas puts him in credit with the public."

Dr Fermatt is Minister for Health.

"So you're going to tell him?"

"No, dear, you are. Or at least, we are. You and me both."

The Minister's visit is likely to be very brief but is absolutely certain to take place, Ben said because of all the fuss over That Book. I know about That Book—a recently published, widely reviewed account by a writer with hands-on knowledge of her subject: the impoverished lives of disabled children growing up in closed institutions.

Descriptions of what life is like for the hundreds of child patients in these places shocked the British public deeply, and, according to Ben, 'all sorts of people' are putting pressure on the government to speed up the availability of more appropriate forms of care. Questions have been asked 'in the House' as to why there is no satisfactory system of inspection for long-stay NHS institutions for children. Letters and articles have appeared on the subject, and not only in professional journals, but also in the *Guardian* and the *Times*.

Ben's plan is, on the face of it, quite dishonest. He, first of all, intends to keep Paigle ignorant, so far as possible, of the date of the Minister's impending visit. Faced with the shock when it suddenly happens, Paigle can hopefully be shown up as that main obstacle to progress Ben considers him to be. With Paigle out of the road, according to Ben, it will be easier to speed up the assessment of children and their preparation for placement in more suitable surroundings.

"Lock'll know, of course, about the visit, but they don't talk, do they?"

"They don't, but they share a secretary."

"Well, we'll just have to fix her, somehow. We'll see how."

"But Dr Hanafin and Dr Gomez—they'll know, won't they? How—"

"Gomez, I'll talk to you. As for Noel Hanafin, we can't expect much from him at present, the tortured soul!"

"I didn't know. How is—I mean, what's torturing him?"

177

"I would have thought you might have already known, seeing he's quite thick with you, isn't he? No? Really? Well, his wife's left him. Perhaps he didn't want to tell you *that,* or not just yet."

I winced, and Ben saw me do it.

"I heard that they had a disabled child," I said.

"Had is the word. A son died some time ago. No, no, I don't think we need to bother my colleague with all this just now." From which I understand that Hanafin is not a party to Ben's plan, nor does Ben intend that he should be.

Ben was keeping my glass topped up, but drinking little himself. This did not occur to me straight away because I was so preoccupied with trying to take in the details of the battle plan. It seems to be in two sections, one part consisting in supplying the Minister, ahead of his visit, with a fact-list about Sladebourne— a list to suggest questions Paigle or Locke would have difficulty in answering; e.g. why no records of visitors to the children have ever been kept—questions like that.

Ben wants me to help him with the fact-list. I didn't say anything, so he went on to the second part of the plan. Ben will contrive for me to have a few minutes alone with the Minister.

Then, I can tell him what is really wrong with Sladebourne and what can be done to set things right. A major recommendation would, naturally, have to be the replacement of the present Chief Nursing Officer by someone much more in tune with current child care practice.

And so on, through the roast chicken with its soggy, flavourless stuffing, the creamed synthetic potato, the anonymous greens. We were facing the Black Forest Gateau—a little frozen still, in spite of the overheated room—when the warm alcoholic haze I was in started to lift slightly, and by the time our coffee came I was beginning to feel the unease that had little to do with the quality of the food.

And now Ben Morgan had finished what he wanted to say. The green eyes in the foxy face held mine as he waited for my reply. My mind was busy digging up and surveying some of the warnings it had given me earlier about getting involved in Ben's schemes.

"I'd love to help," I said, meaning it, "but I can't see how I can do anything like this. I mean, the report, present it all on my own. Oh, I can write it, but Mrs Saye will have to OK it even before *you* see it. If she thinks it's alright, you may have it for the Minister, if not, well—"

"And you'll see Fermatt?"

"I have to think about that. You see, it's not really clear to me why yourself or Dr Gomez, for instance—"

"With my commitments, I can't ever count on being available here to meet the Minister. Should be, should be of course, but can't be sure until the day. No. What will happen will happen in the therapy department, plenty of little rooms there. Margaret Tobias will take the Minister on a tour of her department and you will be in one of the little rooms, with your report. Now, do you see?"

I saw, all right, and after some more discussion felt unable to do anything but agree. I am terrified of meeting Dr Fermatt, a figure looming in every sense large, and am by no means sure about the wisdom of waylaying him to suggest how the closure of Sladebourne could be better managed.

Yet, it is so tempting, to anyone like myself, given to seizing opportunities! Such a chance is this that I really feel I cannot let it go. All I could think of to do right away was to extract a promise from Ben that we would meet some days before the official visit, so I can rehearse what I am going to say.

The rest of the lunch, I don't remember very well. Ben tried to find out more about me, quite amicably, but for some reason, I didn't want to tell him much. He said he couldn't place my accent. Was it, perhaps, South African?

Later on in the same day, Margaret, Vicky and I were standing right up on the top floor of Midlothian, under the roof. It was cold because for some reason central heating does not work properly there, in spite of which this loft it is being used as at present as a bedroom for three disabled teenage boys.

Facing us were Derek and Frank—residential care officers from a North London borough, and between us sat Matthew French-looking, as he might well do, somewhat anxious. Staring bleary-eyed from one face to another, the speechless Matthew made noises that sounded uncommonly like questions. Both visitors smiled; the older one, Derek, began to talk to Matthew. Nervously, I interrupted them.

"Can you tell us a bit more about Hazeldene? You mentioned speech therapy—"

"First of all," said Margaret firmly, "Matthew will show you how he walks."

I'd forgotten that she had had to put off other things to be here. It had been short notice for all of us; the visitors, to whom I had written after spending a day viewing their new group home, had arrived here at only half an hour's notice.

"Well, Matthew, anxious to show us your walking?" The boy looked at Derek, almost as if he knew how much might depend on this interview—for that is really what it was. Breathing noisily, Matthew pressed both hands onto the wooden arms of his chair. Bracing his arms, he stood suddenly upright, swaying a little, then he caught the hands held out to him by Margaret and facing her slid first one, then the other plimsole foot across the grimy floor.

Margaret retreated before him, leading him until he had crossed the large room with her, then turning him, brought him steadily back to his chair, into which he sat rather heavily. As he did so, the attic door opened and Terence was suddenly among us, apologising for being late, excusing himself and also Paigle for the latter's absence.

I introduced Derek and Frank to Terence, explaining to him carefully that because Matthew's parents lived near Archway, they were anxious to have their son considered for a place in the new home there. Terence's expression did not change, but something else about him did. He evidently felt the short notice given him to be deliberate, arranged by me to steal a march on him and his superior, and I knew that any attempt to soften this view could only make things worse.

Before leaving, Derek took us aside to say the final decision wasn't his, but from what they'd seen of Matthew today he and Frank both thought he would be suitable for Hazeldene. He had potential to improve, they felt, and they could offer him more individual help than possible at Sladebourne. Terence had already started to discuss something else with Margaret—just as well. Time to spread the news when we have a formal offer, in writing!

29 October 1974

Matthew, of course, is Hanafin's patient. He is the first fruits of my early encounters with Hanafin, long ago as it seems now. My feeling about Hanafin has really changed in the last weeks. I still hate some of the things he does and says, but can no longer hate what he is.

When he publicly bullies and storms, it does not upset me anymore. When he calls to see me in the office—and he has got into the habit of doing that before the start of each review he attends—Hanafin does not bully. Perhaps this is because he has my undivided attention; perhaps because he is not having to compete with anyone. He is even starting to consult me.

One day last month, for example, inconveniently close to the starting time of a review, Hanafin came to my office, and when I opened the door to him, he pulled a bundle of paper from his coat pocket and thrust it at me.

"Read that, see what you think, and tell me!"

I couldn't read it then, there was no time. So I kept it for later and finally took it home in the evening to read there. The bundle was a long, long letter, written on expensive paper in that neat legible script which used to be called a Civil Service Hand. And it was very nasty, for all that.

Phyllis Nagle was writing about her grandson Michael, who seems to be nine or ten years old, in some undefined way physically and intellectually disabled, and living for most of his past life in the annex of a local children's hospital which is, by degrees, closing down. She visits Michael often and occasionally, with the help of a local charity, takes him home for the day.

Phyllis, as the sole family member involved, is extremely angry about what she has been told of plans to place all the children from the hospital in group homes in, so far as possible, the communities they came from. Her grandson, she writes, is a sick child. Hospitals are for sick children to live in, she says.

They need to stay in bed and not go to school—what's the use of the school, when they won't ever be going out to work? All they need is to be kept happy, not be moved around and so on. And what's all this about Children's Homes? They are dreadful places, no one in her family ever had to go into one of those! (Here followed a long rant, copied from a popular tabloid, about scandals in Victorian orphanages.)

Phyllis says she heard about Sladebourne House from a friend who works there. Phyllis has been to see it—or at least, to see Waverley. She thinks it would be perfect for Michael and that is where she wants him to go when the hospital where he is at present closes down. That is her wish, and she is prepared to fight for her right to make decisions for her grandchild. If anyone opposes her, they will see what she can do! And so on, for eight or nine pages.

Phyllis has spoken to the Chief Nursing Officer at Sladebourne, and Mr Paigle apparently told her she would need to write to Hanafin about her grandchild. This then is her letter. When Hanafin called to my office the week following, I handed it back to him.

"What do you think of it?"

"It's nasty, and there's almost an attempt at blackmail. But after all, what can she do? And what made her think of Sladebourne?"

"God knows. But we can't take that boy here, even temporarily. We have no places for long-term children now. We can't help her. And anyway, she has no right to tell me what to do."

"Of course not. Look, how would it be if I refer her formally to her local Social Services? I can have a word with them first. That's if Mrs Nagle agrees, of course, I'll ring her first—maybe she can be talked round."

So I rang Mrs Nagle, who proved to be the possessor of an unctuous voice I had heard some weeks before, ringing to ask me if she could speak to Hanafin. Oily she might be, but in no way flexible, in fact, very set in her ideas. If anybody laid a finger on her grandchild, they would see what she could do.

I suggested that a local social worker could advise her how to put her case stronger, and after all, she needed to know about everything actually on offer, didn't she? At length, reluctantly, she agreed to give it a try. I referred Mrs Nagle to Camberwell, to the Children's Team there, and thought no more about it.

This incident might be, I hoped, the first plank in a bridge between Noel Hanafin and myself. That bridge was not going to be elegant nor would it be quickly built. But it could be strong enough to last for as long as it was needed.

Gradually, as Hanafin became less anxious and suspicious, the barriers to my work with his patients would disappear. I had confirmed that his bullying manner was a front, but was not yet sure what it covered up, or why any cover-up should be necessary.

In public, Hanafin's behaviour has hardly changed at all. He is still dismissive and overbearing to me and to everyone, but now with an added glint in the eye as if to say that he knows that I know that he is putting up a pretence but he doesn't care, he's enjoying doing it.

As for me, I do not react to these exhibitions but stay calm. It was, then, a shock to me that Ben picked up a change in the atmosphere between us, and misunderstood the cause. Hanafin has never revealed any private stresses to me, and in a strange way, that hurts.

For the rest of that week of Stella's review, and the whole of the week after, Noel Hanafin has been absent from Sladebourne. I rang his secretary at Mount Vervain, to be told he was on leave, and his date of return uncertain. The secretary, speaking calmly against a background of crashing and shrieking, suggested Dr Gomez (who hasn't been seen here this week either), might know more.

I hesitated about what to do, for Archway has confirmed their offer of a place for Matthew French in their new project, copies have gone to Hanafin and to Matthew's parents, and the latter understandably, having seen the set-up, want their son to move there as soon as Hanafin authorises this. How can we get a formal discharge from Hanafin if we don't know where he is? At last, I tracked down Paul Gomez, who just arrived, back here, chatting to Sid in the Ivanhoe office. He listened with some surprise to my news about Matthew.

"But Mary, that's marvellous, I didn't think we'd get a response so soon. Would this project take any more, do you think?" I explained that Matthew alone has a residence claim on Archway.

"We can't hold everything for Dr Hanafin. But not to worry, I'll sign the discharge note."

"Is he likely to be away weeks, months? You see, there are other matters coming up."

"He hasn't taken any leave for years, so how much can we say he will take now, maybe we won't see him until New Year! No, just my joke, he did say he'll be back for the end of November."

Sidney, who had left the office when I came in, returned carrying a newspaper. Placing it on the desk before us, he said: "I think you b-both need to see this."

183

I KILLED MY GRANDSON OUT OF LOVE said the big black letters. Just underneath were fuzzy head-and-shoulders photos, one of a solemn toddler, the other of a smiling middle-aged woman. Neither one was familiar, but further down the page were names we knew: Phyllis Nagle and her grandson Michael White; Dr Noel Hanafin, consultant psychiatrist at Sladebourne House.

Gomez took up the paper, and I read it over his shoulder. On the previous morning, Mrs Nagle, as was her occasional custom, took her grandchild out for the day from the hospital where he had spent all his life so far. She gave him a spoonful of jam into which she had inserted a lethal dose of her own sleeping tablets, crushed.

She waited for these to take full effect before calling the police and giving herself up. Mrs Nagle attached all responsibility for what she had done to Hanafin, whom she accuses of driving her to a desperate act by refusing to help her and her sick grandchild.

"This is terrible," said Gomez, "do you know who is this lady?"

Yes, it is awful, and Gomez, Margaret, and later Nilla, in their various ways have tried to comfort me. Mainly, they ask why I should keep thinking of myself as responsible for the crime of a person I've never actually met or even seen. At first, I did not want any of their comfort but during the day, and by slow degrees, I've come partly to accept it, remembering the relentless quality in that unctuous voice.

I do not think that anything I could have said or done would have checked Mrs Nagle. Gomez said he feels that the idea of killing Michael if things did not turn out for him as she wanted, must have been in the grandmother's mind long before she wrote that letter to Hanafin.

She saw the child as a possession she was not ever going to share with anyone else. And what has happened to the referral I made? I checked—Camberwell Team have not yet been able to get around to seeing Mrs Nagle, due to the pressure of work.

Gomez and I also feel sorry for Hanafin; especially Gomez who realises he could have been easily caught in the trap himself; his name could have been the one adorning the front page of the *Daily Scream*. We wonder if, wherever he is, Hanafin yet knows about the tragedy—Gomez seems to have as little idea of his senior's whereabouts as the rest of us have.

Could any legal action to avoid more publicity be possible—is there a way to silence Mrs Nagle? Hardly. Her action will probably be seen by the press as motivated by mercy and altogether guiltless, I think, but she could continue to accuse other people. Gomez consulted a solicitor friend of his, who thought any attempt to stop her would only make things worse.

I was relieved to hear this, and think it would be foolish of Hanafin to react publicly unless he has to. He should not have to take all this responsibility on himself. But when I said this to Margaret, she reacted with unexpected fury:

"You don't know what he's like sometimes, he deserves all the blame he gets! He asked me for a report on Lucy Meadows, on her walking ability. I thought: he's putting in for an orthopaedic surgeon's opinion on her. Not before time, she needs to have something done as soon as poss. about those tendons— a poor child can hardly walk! I gave him the report, got it to him double-quick.

"Then, the next day his secretary told me what he did with it. Sent it to the legal people dealing with the Meadows' divorce settlement. Geoffrey Meadows is a rich man, his wife wants a large settlement and their disabled child is part of her case. But she never takes Lucy home, and you may be sure nobody will, once they're separated. Who's going to bother about a little disabled girl? I hope stupid Dr Hanafin gets any comeback going!"

I wonder if Margaret's anger will keep hot until Hanafin's return?

30 October 1974

Paul Gomez now conducts the weekly reviews at Sladebourne, and he has made some changes. No longer can just anybody come to them who fancies a bit of diversion, attendance is now limited to those with something to say about the case. Gomez deals with Paigle's wilder comments by ignoring them.

It doesn't always work, but it makes the atmosphere far more peaceful. People begin to relax; to discuss and ask questions instead of challenging all the time. Social workers from the outside world come more readily for knowing that no one here will seek to scapegoat them.

More and more parents come, supported and informed by Gomez and the rest of us through the Parent's Association. The calm, organised and effective life I dreamed of in the recent past seems just around the corner and within reach.

I wrote my report for Ben Morgan, and yesterday I sent it to Lillian to read. She rang me today and said she was horrified. If anyone but herself had seen it, it would have ended on the desk of the Director of Social Services! Or so she said.

What have I been thinking of, to write such dreadful things? She feels concerned about my state of mind. Why am I so angry? But perhaps I need a break. Am I intending to take extra leave over Christmas? Personally, she thinks that would be a good idea. As to the report—she will rewrite it herself.

"I don't think Dr Morgan will want it, so," I said before I could stop myself. But then, of course, Lillian got angry, and I had to apologise to her, and finally agree to let her edit what I had written.

Stella is still making clear progress with Nilla. With me, on the other hand, it's of the two steps forward, one step back variety. I can take her on short walks without her trying to run away. She no longer gnaws at her hands.

I took her to a charity fete last Saturday, held at a local primary school. Stella behaved almost normally, apart from imposing her will on other children by interrupting them persistently and trying to take over their games.

When I explained afterwards to her what she was doing, she did seem to listen for a few precious seconds. Did she really take it in? I cannot be sure. But she seems to understand more. I never doubt the hope we have for her future.

Stella's future, of course, rests not with Nilla or with myself, but with Tom Grace. Every two weeks I find myself ringing Tom, ostensibly to report some new bit of progress, but actually to jog his elbow, so he won't forget her. Recently, Tom's answering voice sounds a shade too patient, too full of effort, pretty exhausted if the truth were known.

Perhaps he is getting tired of my nagging, but if I did not push, who would do it? From regular contact with parents, I am learning that the greatest advantage a needy child can have is a bloody-minded adult as their advocate. I have to accept that, from the day we met, the yoke of Stella's advocacy seems to have settled itself on my shoulders. It is Fate, I suppose. Or God, if you prefer a positive option.

One evening last week, Nilla and I were having supper in my flat. A home-made pizza was in the oven and beginning to smell good, and I mixed the salad while Nilla wrestled with the wine bottle and my ancient corkscrew. She had just been saying how quiet, how civilised everything is in the Close where I live, compared with the rackety place on the main road where she lives when we both became aware of a whole lot of shouting and banging taking place just across the road.

When we looked out of all the windows, it was the one in the sitting room that gave a grandstand view of No. 12 opposite, where everything was going on. It is the home of Mr Lewis, my deaf neighbour with hallucinations. In the gentle gathering autumn dusk, three vehicles stood outside his house: a police squad car, an elderly Rover, and a little yellow Citroen which I recognised as the property of Liam Flynn, a mental health specialist based in the local Social Services office.

He was the one doing the shouting and the knocking, and now we could see his lanky form conferring with Dr Braithwaite, a local GP, at the closed door of No. 12. The two seemed to be arguing. As we watched, two policemen emerged from their car and took over from Liam at the door. Simultaneously, Mr Lewis appeared at a first-floor window, opened it, and shouted down at them. He was, so far as could be seen, naked, and he was telling them all to go back to Belfast and stop murdering innocent decent people.

By now, lights were on in several neighbouring houses. The shorter of the two policemen borrowed a ladder from people in one of those houses. He put it against the sidewall of No. 12 where a high-up window looked to be open, and he began laboriously to climb the ladder.

As he did so, Mr Lewis, who had been shouting continuously for ten minutes, banged *his* window shut with such force that a chunk of cement dropped from the sill, narrowly missing Dr Braithwaite's bald skull. The GP moved for safety beneath the porch, produced some forms clipped to a board, and with Liam's assistance began to fill them in.

We could not tear ourselves away from these events (though we did remember to turn down the oven on the pizza.) It occurred to me that of Mrs Lewis, whom I know by sight, there was rather ominously no sign. I remembered that the part of the Lewis's Garden behind the house, lacking a back gate, is bounded instead by a breeze-block wall crowned with barbed wire. No route of escape for anybody could lie there.

Liam, now on his knees, seemed to be holding a dialogue through the letterbox. Who was he talking to, and where was Mrs Lewis?

Then several things happened all at once. The policeman on the ladder reached the window, opened it, and disappeared through it. The front door of No. 10 next door opened to disclose a middle-aged couple, supporting Mrs Lewis between them.

She wore a coat over her nightie and clasped a large blue handbag to her chest. She was shouting—they all were, but with excitement rather than fear. Talking loudly, the second policeman, the doctor, and Liam followed her back into No.10.

"They've probably gone there to phone for the ambulance," I told Nilla, "that'll take at least half an hour to come. We may as well eat, they won't hurry for a mental health admission."

I set the table while Nilla took over the commentary:

"The doctor has come out again. Oh, that's very funny. The copper is leaning out the window—he wants the doc to come up the ladder and join him above—but the GP won't. He wants to go in by the front door. Now, the copper's disappeared and lights are going on all over the house. Look! Yes! The front door opens, Liam and the doc go in."

We started to eat, and about twenty minutes later the door of No. 12 reopened. Tripping slightly over the doorstep, Mr Lewis emerged. He wore his overcoat, his boots and apparently nothing whatever else, and he carried a large plastic carrier bag with the Union Jack on it.

He snatched his arm back from the grasp of the policeman who was trying to help him, and he started shouting, something about the SAS and someone he wanted them to Give What For To. Dr Braithwaite emerged and tried to engage Mr Lewis in conversation, but Mr Lewis pushed past him, still shouting.

The doctor persevered for a few more minutes, then suddenly gave up, wrote a bit on the form, handed it to Liam, got into his Rover and drove away very fast. Liam helped Mr Lewis into the ambulance, which left as unobtrusively as it had come. The show was over, and all the neighbours drew their curtains.

Knowing that Liam would be coming back later to collect his car, I went out and left a note under the windscreen wiper. We might as well offer him supper, we had enough for another one. Liam turned up at ten, having been given the customary lift back to his car by another ambulance.

Between mouthfuls of slightly overdone pizza, he told us Fred Lewis had a long history of paranoid behaviour, which had only come to Liam's notice recently with the complaints of a couple living further up the Close—a building contractor and his wife, both from Coleraine. They have been getting threatening phone calls, coinciding with the visible presence of Fred in the phone box opposite their house. When they contacted the police, their pet cat suddenly disappeared. Nilla looked at me. I began to feel sick.

"That plastic bag," said Nilla, "the one he was holding on to, and carried out of the house, was it—"

"Now, how did you know that? Yes, indeed, it was the missing moggy, dead and frozen stiff as aboard. As I say, everything gets explained in time. The staff nurse at the bin—sorry, I mean Lakelands—took it off him, though it was personal belongings, yes? Got a hell of a shock, when he opened it."

"Do you lot ever find out why people behave like that?" from Nilla.

"Well, in a way, in a sort of way. Fred *is* truly paranoid *and* a bit demented with it, but what I'd call the aggressive phase started when the grandson was killed serving with the British Army in the North. Bomb disposal. Fred took it personally."

Trouble is, when you hear something like that, it leaves you nowhere to put the responsibility.

31 October 1974

Now, that I'm trying to talk to Him again, I ask God from time to time to have the annulment settled. Not always, and not desperately. It would be a lot more urgent if I were involved with somebody. But I am not.

No, you can't count Hanafin, although I have sometimes felt for him, in a way. Yes, I have to say it now, I have felt drawn to him, but then he'll do something, or say something, which I simply can't ignore because of what it seems to reveal about him. I've been trapped once, by needing someone to need me.

I am not going to be trapped again in the same way. But at times like this, well, I suppose I do rather miss Noel Hanafin when he isn't around. But not too much, and not all of the time.

Work has doubled in the last few weeks with the unforeseen sudden addition of all of Hanafin's patients to my caseload. At present, there are ninety-seven children here! It overwhelms me, and in some ways, it is useful because it keeps me from thinking about anything else.

When Lillian spoke about all the leave owing to me, she was actually right. Since starting here, I've only taken five or six days off and really need a longer break. Exiles together, Nilla and I have together concocted a plan for this Christmas holiday. We both feel we must include Stella, but we want to avoid giving her any ideas about us being permanent in her life.

We're just her guides back to the world of the living, Nilla says, and I agree about that. For that and other reasons, we've decided against a family type Christmas. We don't want to bring her to either of our flats; Nilla's is over the Centre where she teaches Stella, and to use my flat would be, I think, to risk confusing her about my role. I am not her future parent, and I want to avoid any confusion in Stella's mind about that.

On the other hand, there seems no reason why we should not bring Christmas to the workshop and involve Donna, who will be on duty then and will share it all with us. We need to start planning—early in November. Nothing must go wrong and nothing must be left to chance.

Nilla will be on holiday from mid-December, so I've booked two weeks' leave, starting from Christmas Eve. We've tickets for the local panto early in the New Year. What will our girl make of it? Stella's never seen any stage performance. I'm looking forward already to seeing it with her.

Lillian sent me back the draft of my report transmogrified, there's no other word for it She's rewritten it by removing every phrase with teeth and substituting honeyed phrases of her own. This gives such a curious effect that Lillian actually noticed it, and then she cut out whole paragraphs more. The final draft reads frankly odd.

I sent it back to her with a note saying that it was no longer mine and that I could not send it to Dr Morgan as my own. Lillian was: 'Surprised at my response.' She seemed to have thought that Ben can be placated with any sort of old rubbish anyone chooses to give him, but after some argument, she accepted that I possibly knew Ben better than she did.

I rang Ben on the personal number he's given me and told him what had happened. He sounded disappointed as if realising for the first time what a powerless tool I really am, but he did remind me about the Minister's visit in December.

My voice shook as I assured him that I had not forgotten (how could I), and that I will be there as arranged, with something prepared to say to Dr Fermatt. When I outlined to him what I intend to say, I wasn't sure if Ben was listening to me or not; he seemed rather distracted as if something else was going on where he was.

Tom Grace, when I formally asked permission to take Stella out of the workshop a few times over Christmas, was not enthusiastic.

"Umm, well, you know the situation on the ground, but I just hope it doesn't arouse false expectations."

"When Stella is fostered, it's anyway going to be such a total change for her, having to adapt so much, that if we can begin now, in a small way—" my voice trailed off.

"Mary, there's been no response yet to the ads, and I don't see the girl lasting long with any of our existing FPs."

"What about trying something like one of those projects Parents for Children have?"

"Do you know how much that costs? How much do they charge? I don't see *our* Case Review Committee passing that kind of expenditure. There's our time, too, placing those children, with the huge shortfall of social workers Hoxton has—we've fewer than any other Greater London borough, and that includes adoption officers!"

Tom must have felt he should make something up to me then, for he added:

"Tell you what, before I forget I'll give you the contact number for the new Out of Hours team—we've just set it up, but everywhere will have to have them soon… and if it helps, I'll be covering Christmas with them this year."

And no doubt getting well paid for it, I thought, as I took down the number Tom gave me. The Mary I was six months ago would have been angry with Tom, and would have let it show. Now, I realise that getting angry only makes everything a long way more difficult.

Very shortly after this conversation, I had a visit from Lynn—a Lynn I've never seen before—subdued, pale and puffy-eyed.

"Mr Locke would like to see you," she said, "if you can spare the time, at twelve tomorrow he'll be in his office, if not convenient then can you ring him and fix another time. Please."

I stared; the last word had been a sob. "You look flaked out, here, sit down," and I pushed what I tend to think of as the client's chair (the velvet one) in her direction. Lynn broke down. She sat for several minutes, weeping silently with the tears dripping onto her cream satin blouse. I put the box of paper hankies within easy reach and began to listen.

"I've been wanting to talk to someone about it, only it's not very easy." After a while, Lynn got 'it' out. Her older sister Annie had frequent epileptic fits, was a slow learner, needed a good deal of looking after.

At 10:00, she went to special boarding school and following that, to a Home down the country, which her family assumed offered lifelong care. The costs of both school and Home were paid by a Forces charity, for Annie and Lynn were soldier's children, whose father died in his country's service in World War II.

"They had all kinds of things for them to do, for all of the girls; cooking and gardening and washing and shopping, and they kept that big place clean as well. Always busy, they were. There was one particular nurse there, Annie liked—Mrs Callan could get her to do anything!

"We used to visit Annie of course, mum and I did, but we never took her out much in case she'd have one of the fits. Mum passed away last year, so there's only Mum's sister Agnes and me left now."

The Home was managed by a charity, and everything changed recently when the manager they'd known for years retired. Lynn got a phone call asking her to attend a meeting with the Home's new Management Team. Lynn and Agnes both went, and Agnes said to Lynn beforehand, she'd somehow got a suspicion that the home wanted Annie out, and so indeed it proved to be.

They were told that since her favourite Mrs Callan had recently taken early retirement, Annie had not been happy. The new managers regretted having to say it, but clearly, the Home was no longer the place for her, and she would have to move on: 'everyone has to be prepared to take change'.

They explained that the charity which owned the Home was 'updating its function in the light of today's requirements, by converting to a Residential College for teenagers with moderate intellectual disabilities'. The existing inmates, mostly over forty, obviously did not fit that description so other placements were being sought for them, with the help of their families and 'other agencies'. The meeting attended by Lynn and Agnes did not include, so far as they could see, any other agencies.

Feeling under definite pressure, Lynn and Agnes arranged a date to collect Annie. She was pleased to see them and to be going with them, but her relatives were upset to see Annie's few possessions assembled for her, not in a suitcase or a travel bag, but jumbled together in a plastic sack. Lynn asked the care worker in charge about her sister's personal papers, birth cert., medical records—

"If we can find anything," she was told, "we'll send it on." Medical cover, it seemed, had been provided to the Home by a retired doctor and friend of the former manager, who did not want further involvement. Dental care? Annie seemed never to have had any.

Transported to South London, Annie was naturally very confused by the new environment. Then she discovered Television, apparently for the first time, and could hardly be dragged away from it. After a couple of days, Lynn thought it would be safe to leave Annie viewing while she went shopping for an hour.

Returning, she opened the hall door to a powerful smell of paint. Then she looked down. Annie, wishing to improve the hall's dark tiled floor, had painted the entire area with the contents of a tin of white gloss discovered in the garage.

And that was only the beginning. Annie was not aggressive and indeed in ways could be charming, but she was also a mischievous, unpredictable sprite, a plump *poltergeist.*

Keys went missing, ornaments were mysteriously broken, newspapers were torn up before they could be read, unfamiliar food was sent plate and all into the rubbish bin, and everything that came into the house through the hall letterbox was posted a second time—down a crack in the sitting-room floor. Windows and outside doors were left open, lights left on all night. Most difficult of all, the smiling Annie did not seem to comprehend more than a tiny part of anything that her sister said to her.

The local GP appealed to, could only sympathise, couldn't help at all except to prescribe for Annie's fits. Lynn knew Annie to be too old for admission to any place like Sladebourne. But she thought of asking Gomez about Mount Vervain. Then, as a second last resort, she thought of me.

Just occasionally, everything works the way it is supposed to. This time, within days of my referral, a social worker from the district where Lynn lives took Annie to see a local day-centre and arranged for her to attend it. Consulted on the subject of residential care, Annie showed a preference for a return to something like the institution she had left—but with the addition of TV and more outings!

She said she found it 'always lonely' when she was at home and Lynn was at work. I think she will accept a place on offer in a newly opened group home for vulnerable women, where a few of the local day centre attendees already live. Mount Vervain is no longer an option—admissions there will cease from the start of next year and, according to Paigle, the institution's senior staff are all being offered early retirement on especially advantageous terms.

Now, whereas Annie seems untouched by her recent experiences, Lynn has been completely altered by hers. I have, apparently, driven her nightmare away, and delivered her from chaos. She has become grateful, approachable, confiding even. No longer are there any difficulties with typing, postage, message-taking and the transfer of information.

Now, I have disclosed to me, with far more detail than I want to have, all the intricacies of Lynn's relations with Locke and Paigle. Locke, it seems, loves her truly but cannot leave his depressed wife. Paigle's sexual adventures are condoned by Mrs Paigle who does not, on any account, want a marriage break-up.

Lynn despises both men, and feels she has them both in her power; and that she can, any time she wants to, bring a case against either for sexual harassment. More intelligent than either of her admirers, Lynn apparently enjoys something of the authority of the ringmaster, that ruler of beasts who can put them through their paces with the flourish of a whip.

1 November 1974

At midday when I went to see Locke he was, unusually for him, not seated at his desk but standing before the bay window with his back to it. The day was dark, and at first, I could not see the expression on the face he half-turned toward me, as if he did not feel like facing anybody just now. The recent meeting, and the tears I had then seen in Locke's eyes, came to my mind. Apart from greeting him, I kept quiet and waited.

Locke began by telling me of events I already know about, having been involved in setting them up. Local social services are now, to Sister Daroga's great relief, offering Day Centre places to all of the Waverley residents over eighteen. Places have been offered at a local special school for ten Sladebourne children, to be chosen by Mrs Bailey.

Both of these offers are to come into force early in January. I could not display the surprise Locke evidently expected from me, so he gradually realised that I must already have heard his news, and then he became hesitant, trying to read my expression as he went along.

"I understand there's a move on foot, to transfer children from here permanently?"

"Well, there's only been one transfer so far."

"But there are others, aren't there? Coming up, I mean, in the pipeline?"

"The Cassattis are moving to Manchester soon, and they've found a voluntary home prepared to take the two boys. We got reports on it from the local agencies—it seems OK. Louis Davies, so his mother told me, is being tried out for the Chess borough Community at the end of next week. His parents arranged that, and we helped.

"Then, Trevor Philips—Brixton Education Authority has agreed to fund a place for him in a specialist boarding school for children with speech and language difficulties; in the holidays he would join the fostering scheme connected with the school. Oh, and Vera, Vera Black. She is to have a trial stay at the new Spastics Society place near Shoreham."

When I'd said it all, it really did not sound too bad. But it was plain that Locke did not share my pleasure.

"And new entrants, new patients for here, you don't say anything about those." I was silent.

"Children are leaving here, and no more coming in. What are they going to do with the ones that can't be looked after at home?" I stayed silent.

"The truth is, isn't it, the numbers are coming down. Now, you must see, that if this goes on, we'll be threatened with closure. No longer viable—that's the term. It doesn't make any sense to me, all these people, high-ups, council officials from everywhere, all over London (from outside London, even, I don't understand why we have to involve them), calling us to account when we've always done a good job here on our own."

I made as if to answer but Locke, usually passive, responded with a rejecting gesture of the arms, and a raising of the voice, indicating such feeling that I stayed silent.

"I came here after the War, when it was an orphanage, a place for unwanted children they'd evacuated, from London mainly. It was dilapidated, all of it. All the buildings were. We got in nice stuff, good furniture, carpets, curtains. The gardens were all neglected, they needed a lot doing to them, and my wife took an interest, she could do, then. We had garden fetes, we raised funds. Thousands. The mayor used to come."

I imagined photos in the local papers, a younger, happier Locke receiving cheques, his wife smiling discreetly in the background. They'd have kept scrapbooks possibly, to record his success. For success is what it really was for Locke.

"I could have transferred, gone to Riverdale when they finished that, fifteen years ago. Was asked to put in for it, but I said no, I'd rather help the kiddies, maybe that was because it turned out we couldn't have any of our own. Nobody ever complained then! Everyone pulled together, one for all, all for one, loyalty like in the War. But since you came, everything's changed, and nothing that we do seems to be right anymore."

I tried to tell him why I did try. I said that it wasn't only occasional new people like myself who brought change. The last war itself had brought change.

More was expected now, simply because more was known; standards had altered because the borders of the possible had shifted. It was positive, I said.

But the more I spoke, the less he listened v. He stood there with his faded good looks, staring into the middle distance from the past, seeing his career going west and *that* was all down to me and other people like me. He was fifty-five, only that; he'd ten, maybe fifteen years to go to retirement. But now they would close Sladebourne down if the numbers went on dropping.

More, they could actually redeploy Locke, and he had thought that could never happen, though the unending stream of rejected disabled children would flow for decades to come—now, it looked ready to disappear into the ground. I could hear the very place, hear Sladebourne itself, justify its existence through his mouth.

"We do a good job here, we take the ones other places won't have. You're critical of us, Mary, but wait 'til you see some of the other places. When you see them, you'll realise how good the children have it here. Yes, we do a good job here. We take youngsters other places won't touch, and they settle down with us, it's the homely atmosphere that does it.

"And most of the kids are much better off here than they were at home, I can tell you that! All of our staff are people who really know about mental handicaps. Why it's marvellous what they can get the kids to do. Just the other day I saw that little boy whose name you just said, Tommy, Tommy—"

"Trevor."

"Trevor. Well, Trevor was cleaning a row of shoes. Staff members taught him to clean and polish all the shoes on the ward. Now, that's what I call being really useful. Music therapy and art therapy and speech therapy is wasted on those boys. But they can be made to be really useful. A boy here—some years back—I used to let him clean my car, every week."

Seated as I was opposite the window, concentrating on trying to express positive empathy without an element of the actual agreement, Eugene suddenly crossed my line of vision. He was standing in a reverential attitude before Paigle's Lancia, admiring it from all angles, then he passed on to Locke's Rover, running spatulate fingers gently over the bonnet, caressing the smooth green metal, then tracing the chrome trim which must have been just about visible to his damaged sight. Eugene would never injure the objects of his reverence: he seems content to worship.

"And there's another thing," said Locke irritably, "now I know what it means when they start moving children away from here for schooling. I've always found Lucinda Grant and Carol Bailey decent women. They've given years of service between them to this hospital.

"Oh. I know they'll be offered other jobs. But they won't get anything like they've got here because they haven't the certificates, the bits o' paper and so on that people want today. Out on the streets! They'll be out on the streets!"

It was hard to keep my face straight while I tried to explain that my actions were not mischievous, no, no, I was not trying to have *anyone* set up or sacked. Even as I said this, I felt amazed at anybody fearing the powerless person I truly know myself to be.

I wondered also how Locke would react if he could see Eugene and what he was doing right then. But I thought I knew already what he would do and say, and felt depressed by the knowledge. So often, in the last six months, I have heard the same messages, from Locke, from Paigle, even from Terence (when that careful person shows emotion,) from Mrs Bailey and from Lucinda as well.

Their main commitment is not to the children here, I think, but to the system which rates NHS employees above *all* patients—the latter existing simply in order to generate work for the former. A system like this one only survives for as long as no change in public attitudes ever takes place. The Sladebourne staff are like passengers in an overladen boat, where nobody can move, without risking the upset of the whole.

What they don't observe is that the boat is already leaking, pierced by ideas outside the institution. Weight and balance alike are altering, dark skies prepare a storm, and if passengers ignore this, as Locke would wish, their boat is certainly bound to sink!

On the way back to my office, Ray came to meet me, full of a desire to help.

"A lady bin ringing for you, three, four times. She give me a number but I didn't get it. She said she's Head Teacher at the Tunnel School."

We all know by now that Ray can't be expected to record messages, so why is he ever left on duty by himself? Head Teacher Kay Lukin, of Turnwell School, sounded annoyed when I spoke to her.

"Miss Delancy, the person who answered your telephone seemed to have little idea of your whereabouts," I explained, apologised.

"Miss Delancy, ten Sladebourne children are due to come to us next Monday, for one day as a preliminary visit before the end of term. They start here all together in January. I've been unable to contact Mrs Bailey, and I really need more information about these children."

"Yes, I see, but I have no details about the children's educational history, as I'm a social worker for the residential side, not the school—"

"The children—have you their medical histories, next-of-kin, home addresses, that sort of thing?"

"Well, yes, but—" (and I thought, but only for a moment, of sending her to Lillian).

"So can you please possibly give me any information about them?"

"Look, may I come and see you about this? So we can discuss what you really need. Quicker to do that than having to put it in writing and send it by post."

4 November 1974

I saw Miss Lukin this morning. Her round pink face flushed as she handed me the sheet of paper extracted from a file on her desk. The paper held ten typewritten names, nothing more.

"When I heard officially that we could have ten, I rang Bourne Hill and spoke to the Deputy Head. This is what she sent me. I assume reports will follow, but I do need more than this to start with. I haven't been able to visit Bourne Hill for myself; when I ring there doesn't ever seem to be anyone there who can sanction a visit."

Again, I said my piece, stressing that I held no responsibility for Bourne School and its affairs since my role was limited to working with parents on plans for the children's futures.

"Well, and what do the parents think of their children coming here?"

"I don't believe they know yet. I don't know who would have been likely to have told them."

"Don't believe. Not told. Oh, Miss Delancy, this is too ridiculous!"

So I explained that Sladebourne parents were considered for years to have handed away all responsibility for their children to the NHS for life: an idea which is only now being contested. I added that we—that is, the care staff, therapists and myself, heard rumours about school transfers only days ago, but naturally could not discuss them with parents until we knew more.

"*We* didn't even get a list of names!"

Miss Lukin's face now showed disbelief in addition to plain shock. I said that I would gladly share with her any useful information about her prospective pupils, but feared that to put it in written form could be seen as a serious breach of confidence on my part. Speechless at first, she quickly seized on the main point: I could give her some of what she needed.

Out came her notebook, for which I supplied dates of birth and if we had them, the family addresses of the Turn well Ten. I added names and contact phone numbers of their wards, their charge nurses, and the doctors. At the finish, I added some details about each pupil which would be useful for the Head Teacher to know.

"Verity Long is registered blind, has no recorded visitors or enquiries about her. I am trying to locate her family in the Deptford area but so far with no luck...

"Mary Leahy has Down's Syndrome. Father's dead, mother's remarried and has other children, but takes Mary home regularly. Mary speaks, but only to her family...

"Richard White is autistic, at least, I think so, but he's never had an assessment. He was adopted at three, has no speech or sign language, but his adoptive parents visit often and are involved with the Parent's Association..."

I think all the parents will be pleased to hear about this offer. They'll see it as a step forward for their children, going to a real school.

I'd said the last bit without meaning to—it just slipped out. Miss Lukin's round grey eyes widened at me, but all she said was a dry 'Thank you!' and we went on with the list.

Even in the short time I've spent there, I can see and feel that Turn well is a very different place from Bourne School. Squeezed onto a triangular piece of ground not quite good enough for council housing, cluttered inside by a maze of folding partitions, there is still an air of warmth, energy and purpose about Turnwell that makes me realise what's missing at Bourne. Maybe it's just the colour and the noise, but yes, Turn well is a real school.

Parent's Association members reacted more positively to the school transfers than I ever dared to hope. Nesta's mother (although Nesta, over eighteen, is not on the Turnwell list) has already begun organising a programme of visits to the school so that all parents, as she says, 'Can get an idea of what there is around.' The Parent's Association secretary is Richard White's adoptive father, Phil.

While pleased about Richard, he still sent a stiff letter to ILEA complaining that they failed to tell him of his son's transfer *before* informing Mrs Bailey. All known parents of the 'transfers' want their children to attend Turn well. Nobody with a choice wants their child to stay at Bourne.

I suspect that Audrey's work diary must have contributed to this happening. Even allowing for excessive drama in her presentation style, it was a good piece of work and the effect on her practice supervisor seems to have been marked. He had no hesitation in sending his views on her conclusions up the line to County Hall.

Bourne Hill School has just the other day been inspected, for the first time, and evidently by someone impervious to Lucinda's charms. There is now a floating rumour that Bourne will be closed even sooner than had been planned. Locke's intuition was right, but will it make him any happier?

The wonder is to me, not that parents abandoned children at Sladebourne in the past, but that so many did not. Most still visit (tolerating occasional rudeness from staff), still bring clothes and toys (which disappear), still come to money-raising events, and to reviews where they are alternately harangued and patronised. The lives of some of these parents could be described as endurance for love; what we used to hear called, at our convent school, a 'white martyrdom'—lacking the glamour of the bloodstained version, but very painful for all that.

After she had finished tapping me for information, Miss Lukin did say, when I was praising the parents to her: "You understand, I'm not in the business of knocking them either!" And of course, she is not. We are both in the far more difficult business of giving out free hope.

11 November 1974

Christmas is weeks away, and already the run-up has started. We're all busy, but visits to Stella at least twice a week have to be fitted in. They are a necessity. Yesterday when I came, Stella was just back from Nilla's tutorial class, which she is beginning to call 'school'.

She was happily unwrapping an untidy parcel, apparently consisting of plastic bags, and eventually, she took out from it structures of tinsel and wire and a bundle of coloured paper. "Nilla said I could take these home and put them up. They're decorations, look! This is a lantern to put around a light. That one's a star. That's paper chains, for the walls. I said I'd take them here because it's my home here, isn't it?"

I ignored all the silent questions: *Why am I still here? What is to happen to me? When?*

"It's your home just at present, Stella."

She went to the window and stood for a moment, with her hands on the sill, looking out. The view was not exciting, being mostly the back wall of Ivanhoe and a bit of Midlothian's well-trodden garden, but I do not think Stella cared. She was, probably, looking back to the events of the day at the tutorial centre.

I know of what happens there not from Stella, but from Nilla who reports an uneasy peace between Stella and the other pupils. Now, that Stella is sometimes with a small group instead of being tutored one to one, she sees the other children coming and going with parents, while no one apart from Louise or Donna ever collects her. There have been a few bullying episodes recently, in which Stella was the aggressor.

And there have been other signs, denoting depression to Gomez, and to myself. Stella's been seen to cry when there was no obvious reason for doing so. As I stood there yesterday, I suddenly felt moved by pity to go and put my arms around her, to give her a good hug, to share her isolation with her.

And of course, I could not do that. With someone who has been maltreated and abused in the way Stella has, you leave the initiative to them. But I could be wrong about this. I don't want her to think me as I must sometimes appear, cold and remote.

Now, no one could possibly think of Louise as cold. She is not remote either, she is warm and ingratiating. People, I tell myself, are as they are. I don't have to copy Louise, or copy anyone. Do I really feel jealous of her? However, that is, my visits to the workshop are somehow more comfortable when Donna is in charge there.

On this particular evening, Stella does not want to talk or be read to. Instead, she wants to watch TV with me, preferring an early-evening programme intended for much younger children. Hunched in her chair, sucking her fingers for all she is worth, Stella finds something yet wanting.

As I sit beside her she suddenly, clumsily catches at my right arm, lifts it as though it were an object, and re-arranges it like a collar around her neck as far as possible, then she leans back on it. I am tethered, she has made sure that I cannot move without her knowing. This gesture, both uncomfortable and pathetic, takes me unawares, but not Donna, who smiles at us. I have not noticed before, how pretty Donna's smile is.

We sit like that, tethered together, for about twenty minutes. Then, I notice something lying on the floor near the TV monitor.

"That's a video film, isn't it? Where did it come from?"

"Oh, that's Louise's," said Donna, "she brings them in for Stella, you know."

A pile of similar little packets reveals itself when Donna turns on the overhead light and draws the curtain across the window. I think: how good of Louise, to get those for Stella. Cartoon films, I suppose. Louise is far more up to date than I am. I say something like this to Donna, but she doesn't respond. I pick up one of the packets and put it in my pocket to investigate later.

On the screen, there is showing, not a cartoon but a feature film with very self-conscious actors playing one of Grimm's fairy tales. A miller's daughter with huge, round eyes sobs between her plaits because someone expects her to spin a whole roomful of straw into gold. Donna says suddenly: "That chap, that Minister, will he be calling in here?"

"I don't think so, why?"

"Well, it's just, like, maybe somebody ought to tell him about the parties in Midlothian."

"Donna, I've got to go now, can you come with me to the door and tell me what parties? I've never heard about them before."

Gently I unwrap my arm from Stella's neck and, surprised at her lack of reaction, find her to be asleep.

What Donna had to tell, was soon told. Last Christmas Day, when all visitors had gone, the Midlothian children were somehow squeezed into Kenilworth, doubling up and using a supply of camp beds. This was uncomfortable for all but had the advantage for the staff of leaving Midlothian empty and at their disposal.

A bar was set up there, complete with amplified music, drink and, I suspect, recreational drugs supplied by contacts of the staff. A good time was had by all those on and off duty until the morning of Boxing Day when the place was all cleaned up and the children swiftly moved back.

I thought rapidly. What staff do when off duty is none of my affairs. But some of these staff *were* supposed to be on duty, caring for the children. And the drugs? I know nothing about drugs of the sort Donna meant. During my nursing career, I encountered pathetic, middle-aged addicts abusing morphine derivatives prescribed to them for pain relief.

But Donna means the mood-altering drugs now widely used, and tolerated as 'harmless' and 'recreational'. I thought fleetingly of the possibility of Terence, for example, experimenting on his charges with them.... I could not put it past him, the idea was not impossible at all. But how prevent it? And why?

In reality, did we have to do anything? Last year's party was last year, and surely opportunistic, probably a one-off. Locke, Paigle and the medical staff would all be at home with their families, having put in a morning appearance helping to serve Christmas lunch. Almost half Midlothian children, those whose families visit, go home for that day anyhow. So we're talking about a small number—

"I don't see any point in telling Dr Fermatt about this. He'd expect the hospital management to deal with anything like that themselves. An internal matter. And I've not actually seen it happen, Donna, and who could say it did—"

"I could, Mary. I was at it."

"You'd be prepared to speak up? They'd kill you!"

"I don't care. I'm leaving anyway in January, my boyfriend got me a job at Riverside, he does maintenance there, I'd meant to tell you. Look, while the party went on, nobody fed those Midlothian kids or changed them, either staff were stoned or they didn't give a toss. Then there was a kid died—"

"Are you serious? That's… just tell me what happened."

"It was when we were all having a laugh, like, so we didn't see anything. We'd just moved the stuff back, it was early Boxing Day. Luke Reddie, that was his name, fell down the stairs in Midlothian. Well, but he had a fit first."

"But if that was an accident, it could happen anywhere—"

"He got knocked out. See, he fell the whole flight down, hitting off stairs. He was laying down their ages before the ambulance come. Linda couldn't find the number to ring; it was the porters who got it for her at the end when they saw Luke. She couldn't ring Riverside—"

"Because Mr Paigle said not to call out anyone from Dr Morgan's team?"

"Yes. So you see."

"I do. But I still don't think Dr Fermatt will want to know about this. There must have been an enquiry and an inquest at the time. Weren't there any relatives?"

"There was something Linda had to go to, alright. But she didn't get into trouble over it, 'cos they didn't know how long she took, getting help. I dunno about any family—didn't see or hear about them at the Court or wherever Linda had to go."

I went thoughtfully back to the office. It was dark enough now for all the lights to be on in the houses, giving Kenilworth, Midlothian and Ivanhoe an illusion of comfort. Their windows have been sprayed with a white substance meant to look like drifting snow, which conceals to some extent the bleakness within.

Only in Daroga's enclave is anything to be seen which might attach a meaning to Christmas. As the thought came to me, I actually saw Daroga leaving the porch of Ivanhoe, her sharp face outlined against the lighted door. At once she noticed me and came to meet me, an archaic and appealing picture in her Sister's cloak and white veil.

"Going home now, Miss Delancy?" We are always formal with each other's names.

"I think so, Sister. How are things?"

"No worse. Congratulate me, I got some money from Mr Paigle. The first time!"

"Have you all the older children at Day Centre now?"

"Just starting. They go to a party there, next Monday evening. They say: You don't have to send food, but we'll send some. Laura will make the samosa, I'm showing her how. Christmas Day, we do the party here. Home from Home. You going to be with us for Christmas? I invite you to come!"

I thanked her and explained that I would be on leave. Even to her, I don't want to talk about the plans for Stella's Christmas. A superstition of mine, I think.

"Nothing is perfect," said Sister Daroga, "nothing in this life. But Miss Delancy, it is different here now than before. Wait a moment! I know, we cannot always agree with what happens. However, people need to be given time. Pushing them won't make them better. And change is very hard for some to take. We all need to remember this. Goodnight, Miss Delancy."

Out of shadows beyond the main gate, I saw the huge car glide forward, stop, and I saw the front passenger door open. Daroga, slipping between half-closed silver gates, entered the car and was silently gone. Not for the first time I wondered about her other life—and how she knows of my meeting with Dr Fermatt, scheduled for tomorrow.

She would have least to fear any sweeping judgement, least of all that of the Minister. Indeed, she has just warned me, I am certain, that management complaints would be very imprudent to make at present.

Yesterday, Ben Morgan and I consulted briefly, sitting in his car in Riverdale car park in the few minutes he had to spare between other engagements. We rehearsed what I shall say to the Minister. I will not be expected to say much. The Minister is busy, or as Ben says, has a full schedule. The thought occurs to me—will he let me speak at all? Is he expecting me to speak? Do politicians listen to the people who elected them?

Harsh Northern light through Ben's windscreen made his face look strangely bleak and worn. I found him distrait, tired, showing his age for the first time since I've known him. Ben's Corgi dog, on the rear seat, shifted uneasily and growled, it did not like my being there.

"Is he in the car all day?" I asked Ben.

"I take him out for a run whenever I can."

"But do you really have to take him with you everywhere?"

"Yes. There isn't anyone at home."

Some people with dogs keep them entirely for their own needs, and Ben is not the only one I know who brings a dog to work.

As I was leaving the car, Ben noticed a book I was carrying, Peter Marris' *Loss and Change*—and asked if he could borrow it. Surprised, I handed it over, and later remembered that the author and Ben both come from the same place: maybe they even know each other. I still feel surprised at this incident, having never put down Ben as a student of philosophy. Anyway, I told him he could have the book for as long as he wanted.

"And, do you mind if I ask you something?" (He looked at me warily now.)

"Are you still absolutely sure that what we are doing—about Dr Fermatt—is right? That we should be doing it, I mean? You see, I don't think I'm really very good at this. I may get it all wrong and make things worse." Fleeting exasperation on Ben's face gave way to an odd, resigned smile.

"Of course, you can do it, Mary. Look, I wouldn't have asked you if I thought you weren't able. But I suppose, really, that I ask a lot. It's no way to treat a lady!"

Now, he was acting again. The mask was back in place with that last catchphrase, and I had a sudden sense of having missed something, perhaps my only chance to know the real Ben, the man the clown disguises from us all.

12 November 1974

Preparations for the Minister's visit started a week ago, when two circular flowerbeds in front of the Administration building, neglected for months, suddenly overflowed with bedding plants of an expensive and weatherproof kind. No one saw either the digging or the planting, which must have been carried out overnight.

Other unusual happenings include an attempt on the part of Locke to get the care staff to wear white coats, with separate small badges on them indicating name and status. Very few have accepted the white coats, and no one, so far as I know, has accepted a badge.

My newly transformed relationship with Lynn has made the Minister's timetable easy to find out. His tour is to start at 2:00 p.m. with the Administration block where he will be welcomed by Gomez, Paigle and Locke. Then he is to be shown two selected wards, Waverley and Midlothian, the latter chosen, I imagine because its once appalling lavatories are new and spotless following renovation.

The two wards will, at that hour, be totally empty of their residents all of whom will be still at school. This does not seem to have occurred to Locke, but will the Minister mind? A call to the therapy department will close the visit; Dr Fermatt will be offered tea there, and he is scheduled to leave us at 4:30.

A tense calm brooded over Sladebourne as I made my way this afternoon to therapy. In the car park for Admin sat a big, strange car: I had heard its driver earlier loudly fraternising with Aitkin, in the porter's room near my office. In therapy itself, frantic preparations went on for a luxurious afternoon tea.

Margaret, when I saw her, was preoccupied, but not by the catering. Only last week, she had succoured a wailing, heavily pregnant cat which duly gave birth in the storeroom, and was quickly moved, family and all, to the home of one of Margaret's friends. At 1:00 p.m., today another pregnant cat, also wailing, appeared in therapy.

Vicky shut this one up in the boiler room with a rag-lined box and a saucer of water. Audible cries, however, continued at intervals and took Margaret's mind off everything else. She confessed to me that she didn't know what to do about her lodger.

"I can hardly throw her out, poor thing, but the Minister? Do you think he'll be able to help notice?"

I tried to remember anything I'd read about Dr Fermatt. I was pretty sure there had never been anything about his attitude to cats, but it was hard to think he could ignore that noise. Tentatively, I suggested music to conceal it. "He may think you always have music here, after all, isn't it therapeutic?" Margaret went to borrow a tape and something to play it on.

Vicky conducted me to a small room, occasionally in use by visiting therapists, which adjoins the large central area where afternoon tea was laid. Empty-headed and dry-mouthed, I awaited the coming of the Man of Power. Presently, as his entourage approached the building, I could hear Gomez rather high voice addressing Dr Fermatt, who responded with a sort of growl.

Gomez was excusing himself, explaining that he had to go now; his patients awaited him at Riverdale, where he deputises for the paediatric registrar sometimes. Otherwise, Gomez said, he would have been eager to remain.

As it was, however, he would hand the Minister over to the wonderful Mrs Tobias. I heard Margaret's tactful response. I began to pray, silently and confusedly. Music began—could that possibly be: *In a Monastery Garden?* Yes, it could. Voices became louder. The door opened.

Dr Fermatt was not at all as big as he looked on TV, but he was of striking pneumatic plumpness almost (to be unkind) as if somebody had inflated him with an air pump. A mat of thin, sandy hair barely covered his large head, at the sides of which his ears looked surprisingly small.

The little grey eyes in his smooth pink face regarded me shrewdly as we were introduced, and he accepted a seat. I felt that he took in my pathetic glance toward the door as it softly closed behind Margaret.

"As you know, Minister," I began, "I'm the social worker here, the first one they've had. As change takes place, well, all the time really, there are always concerns one has—"

"I have been deeply impressed by the motivation of the staff here at, er, Sladebourne. They are all obviously devoted to the welfare of these unfortunate children, are they not?"

211

"In general, Minister, yes, but the fact is that none of them was trained in child care, and very few trained to nurse children. When they first came to work here, it was assumed that all the child patients were ineducable, and moreover, that none of them would live past puberty. Today, we know differently, that it's not sufficient to just give basic physical care and the odd cuddle! Local authorities are offering places in small group homes, where children can have something more like family life.

"Such homes have different standards to large institutions—and they are inspected to help staff keep these standards up. Sladebourne does not have such inspections. Here, for example, the children don't even have their own personal clothes or their own toothbrushes. The people caring for them are not, apparently, able to change the system—"

"Miss, Miss—"

"Delancy."

"Miss Delancy, I hear what you say, but all these are issues for management. Any complaints, any concerns of this sort, need to be dealt with by management on the spot. Not by me."

"Children's homes are inspected and reported on, Minister, according to the law. Why not inspect the long-stay hospitals, where children have to live for years?"

"The Hospital Advisory Committee visits, Miss Delancy, and I have seen their report. They did not mention any major problems here—"

"They don't look at children's needs, Minister when they come. They only look at Fire Precaution and the Accident Book and the condition of the buildings. And they give notice of when they're coming. They don't interview care staff or anything like that—"

Then the Minister told me that he appreciated my concern, he did really.

"But, if you should find the management doesn't listen to you, first of all, it is necessary to re-evaluate your own approach. After all, you share the same aims, the same common goal."

And I could not tell him outright, that this idea was at least questionable. Dr Fermatt, certain that he had said just the right thing, got up to go. The office chair creaked oddly as he took his considerable weight off it, and the plaintive incidental music outside changed to *In a Persian Market*. The Minister's large pale paw enveloped my limp hand as he took his farewell. Desperation made me reckless, to the last I pleaded.

"Dr Fermatt, I wish that things were as you say they appear to be. That the children always came first here—and everywhere—"

He did not seem to hear me. The door to the main room opened, Margaret reappeared with Victoria behind her. Dr Fermatt, just leaving the room, turned and faced me for an instant.

"Miss Delancy, you will never get anywhere in this life if you don't use the proper channels!"

And then he was gone. I slunk out through the back regions of the building, and as I passed near the door to the boiler room a wail from within suggested that Margaret's protégé was still suffering. As I left the brightly lit therapy building for the gloomy outer world, dank air caught me by the throat and what began as a slightly hysterical laugh ended in a coughing fit.

So much, I thought, for my efforts, not to speak of Ben's. He chose a most ineffective messenger, and if in future I remember these last weeks before Christmas, this is the happening that will always come most vividly to mind.

Returning to the flat on that evening, feeling as I did, I was so dejected and preoccupied that I forgot, until she rang the doorbell, that Nilla was coming over to help sort out our Christmas plans. Silently, I let her in. First of all, I told Nilla all about Dr Fermatt, and she said that I shouldn't keep feeling responsible for everything.

She said that Fermatt must have been human once, but it was obviously a long time ago because he was now no more than a political robot, spouting the most conservative party line for generations. I agreed with her at the time but afterwards did not feel so sure that she was right. I suppose that it's a characteristic of us *Chicken Lickens*, that we always feel that it is we ourselves who have pulled the sky down to fall on our own heads.

20 November 1974

Although, of course, neither of us has ever yet spent a Christmas at Sladebourne, Nilla and I find we share an idea of what this experience might be like. In a fairly tolerant, liberal, secularised society you don't *forbid* the externals of faith; no, no, but you seek to trivialise and diminish them. Since anything that is not tangible lacks value, whatever is considered to be transcendental must count for so little it can hardly even be rubbished.

So Christmas is: a time when the arrival of the Midwinter Solstice is celebrated with excess shopping, food and drink, and its importance is just that of any regular commercial opportunity in an industrial country. Nilla and I have both worked in institutions at Christmas. We know all about expense claims for buying decorations, and for extra hours worked putting them up.

We have seen from the corners of our eyes the stacked beer-crates and collected wine bottles in the kitchens, the last year's tatty streamers, the skinny synthetic tree with sweets cello taped to its balding branches and drift of ill-wrapped dummy parcels beneath it; the neighbourhood gift shop's contribution of unsaleable toys and board games with pieces missing.

"I don't know," said Nilla, "that I'd be willing to share my too-small wheelchair with an outsize fluffy pink dog smelling of synthetic carpet."

"Well," I said, "on Christmas morning something like him will be given to each child. As well as washing, toileting and dressing the children, the staff on duty will have to cook breakfast for them because catering staff here won't work on bank holidays. Distracted by their extra tasks, care staff will actually have less time than usual for the kids.

"They will be interrupted by Hanafin and Paigle, making a ceremonial visit to each ward; inspecting the dayrooms, where the children able to do so are already ripping up their gifts, to the sound of deafening rhythmic music—playing for the benefit of the younger staff. Then H. and P. will adjourn to the ward office, to be offered stale mince pies washed down with anything from ginger beer to Scotch. When all four houses have been visited, they'll go for much-needed proper drinks to Paigle's flat."

"Meanwhile," Nilla joined in, "some parents turn up, to collect their children for the day. They're sorry for those who won't even be visited, so they bring big tins of sweets which they distribute in handfuls to everyone. By the time reheated turkey, dried-up Brussels sprouts and pale grey mashed potato are put in front of the children, most refuse the meal. And the ones without the strength to do so are afterwards terribly sick."

Only Waverley will be different. And the workshop will be different, we can surely make it so. Donna is scheduled for Christmas duty; she is sympathetic to our aims. What are those? I suppose if you come down to it, to show at least one child that there are people who care about her enough to offer her something more than she has in the silver cage.

Behind all the tinsel and the shiny paper, the Crib, the little real Christmas Tree Nilla has bought and adorned, the cards from us and from Margaret and Vicky, the little presents we've got for Stella, behind them, something else of which they are the symbol.

And yes, we do feel guilty about going to trouble like this for only one child. There are upwards of ninety at Sladebourne, and here we are concentrating on one. Mostly in my flat, we've spent several evenings now talking about Stella and what we can do for her. Coming away from theory toward the practice is such a relief that in these sessions we've made all our practical plans, covered everything, I hope.

Armed with Tom Grace's permission, however grudging, I'll turn up first at the workshop on Christmas morning with Stella's presents and maybe something especially nice for her breakfast. Nilla will come later—say, about ten—and we'll take Stella out to the nearest church with a Crib, to see that. Nilla's able to offer me help now because things have changed for her.

She left the commune when she got the tutoring job and rented a flat in the same building where she tutors Stella. Liam joined her there recently. I don't know for certain how things are for them both, but they seem a lot happier. Liam's on call over the Christmas holiday, and he says he's certain to be called out. This is why Nilla feels able to help me with Stella.

After we've had a special lunch with Donna in the workshop, we'll all go to see Waverley—the decorations will be out-of-this-world—and Stella's never even been to Waverley before! Daroga's having a troupe of local carol singers there—that will be another good experience.

I did think of taking Stella to mass, but felt it might be pushing our luck—we can't tell yet how she will react to new situations and unfamiliar places. The rest of the day, we'll play games with Stella—I'm teaching her draughts and Donna's giving her a card game and teaching her to play it—now, that will be completely new for both of them!

2 December 1974

The Social Work Department party this year was the earliest and one of the biggest.

A late arrival, I negotiated with difficulty the crowd near the door. Encumbered as they were with plates, glasses and cigarettes, I went struggling through them with a chocolate roulade on a double-size plate held at eye level. The roulade, outsize and French, is one of the few cakes I can make that look edible. Single-mindedly I bore it along, aiming for the table at the far end of the room where we were supposed to leave our offerings so that they could be under the critical eye of Lillian.

That plate was very heavy, and I was trying to avoid distractions and elbows on the way. A hand suddenly hovered above the plate, a plump hand, which paused before it seized the slice adorned with most of the marzipan holly leaves.

"Hello, Minister," I said before I thought, "I didn't expect to see you here!"

Perhaps Fermatt looked embarrassed just because he hadn't recognised me beneath my cake. But greed is, after all, an unattractive vice. He spluttered a bit, trying to answer but not succeeding very well. I had mercy, smiled sweetly and passed on my way. Blessed minutes later, I was sitting between Joan and Celine, drinking white wine imperfectly chilled and catching up on hospital gossip. The sausage rolls melted in the mouth, the tobacco fug was warm and somehow, soothing, even for one who never smokes. I felt safe, anonymous, and relaxed.

"There's Lillian's new man," said Joan, "Mary, did you know she's got someone new?"

"You mean, that over there? But that's Dr Fermatt over there."

"So you know him, Mary? Then maybe you can tell us a few things about him. Like, if he's still married. And how they met. Yes, I know he came here on a state visit and not long ago either, but we never get to meet any politician like that. Only hospital administrators and maybe consultants get to speak to *them*. But how Lillian—"

"He did but see her passing by."

With this typical cryptic remark, Liam joined us. We looked at him with suspicion.

"Did you mean that?" came from Celine.

"Is it literally true?" Joan was already having trouble with long words.

"Of course, literally. No, I mean it. She just happened to drift into the Psychiatric Unit last month, while I was explaining to Fermatt the business I had there. Seems, he thought I was a patient. Lillian was able to explain to him both my true status and her own—and he was deeply impressed. I don't think he'd met any social workers before."

"I wish Lillian would explain my status to me," muttered Celine viciously, "sometimes I think she regards me as a dumb animal."

"Why?" began Joan, but left the question half-formed as Lillian, rosy and convivial in Kelly green, appeared among us and asked if we were all enjoying ourselves. We made incoherent noises; Lillian moved on, and shortly afterwards, we noticed, she left the party, to be followed in seconds by the Minister.

I was now beginning to feel uneasy. Lillian in spite of her joviality had made no eye contact with me and had ignored my nervous greeting. Moreover, I've discovered myself to be the only one in her flock not to receive an official Christmas card from her. These signs are not good. I must be in trouble.

When, a little later, I drove back to Sladebourne, replete with snack food and only a small bit tight, Steve emerged from the lodge to say the Cassatti's were waiting to see me. He'd shown them into my office, he said because, as he told them, he didn't know for how long I'd be held up at Riverdale. I looked at him narrowly and decided that he wasn't being sarcastic and really hadn't noticed the smell of drink from me yet.

But why were the Cassatti parents here? I knew that the boys were to leave Waverley tomorrow morning, travelling by special ambulance to their new residential home in Manchester. The relevant documents had all been sent off, including my social report, a copy of which had gone already to the parents. *Oh, God. That report. There must be something in it they don't like.* Approaching my office, I paused to offer a fragmentary prayer before opening the door.

"I'm sorry you've had to wait so long for me," I said with what I hoped was an unobtrusive belch, "I've been detained." (I was glad to note that Steve had had the sense to turn on the gas fire for them, and draw the curtains.)

Leo stood up and shook my hand, and began to make what sounded like a classic speech of farewell. (I was so surprised, that it hardly sank in.) They had already, it appeared, said goodbye to Sister Daroga, Dr Gomez, and the Waverley staff. All were wonderful, but they would be unable to forget me. The counselling sessions. The Parent's Association. The information-giving. They had been comforted, they said and given hope.

"You talked to me like a sister," murmured Fiorina, pressing into my hands a small, heavy parcel, "and *this* is to remind you of us." I made the usual polite protestations to which they refused to listen. They said they had come to see the boys before their journey, and then just to say thanks to the people who had helped them.

It's always like this, in this game. The people you are able to do least for, think the sun shines out of you, and the people you half-kill yourself for, never notice it enough even to resent it.

When they'd gone, I looked at my present. It was so beautifully wrapped, and in a paper resembling silk, that to open it seemed a destructive act, but I had to know what was inside. It was the bust of a Madonna and Child in some kind of whitish, silkish stone, maybe alabaster. Two faces, two heads, inclined lovingly towards each other, a glance holding a glance.

Had Fiorina known I'm a Catholic? How had she known? For I had told no one at my place of work that much about myself. Being Irish is often a giveaway, of course, but my accent has worn as thin as an old penny, and I could pass for anything and reflect anywhere.

Did it show in one of our counselling sessions, perhaps? They were the times when this pretty, sophisticated woman used me to ask—of something or someone, ultimately, I think, of God—what meaning could be made out of what had happened to Leo and herself.

The two of them were compelled to live double-sided lives, one side revolving around work and daily life in a wealthy, fashionable suburb; the other side, the concealed one, taken up with their two grievously disabled children.

Evidently, whatever I have said to Fiorina, it cannot have sounded as glib as I often feared. That is a relief but only the temporary relief of someone who, anticipating the 'drop' on a roller coaster, has unaccountably missed falling off this time but knows the 'drop' is coming back all the same. You may feel great on the upward path, but that's the time to prepare for the next descent.

Later in that afternoon, Margaret Tobias rang. She wanted to see me, and it sounded urgent. I thought of some new disaster of the Mark Shine kind—we are still halfway to negotiating an Accident Procedure for Sladebourne and there are many interim complications. But it was not quite like that. This time, the victim appeared to be me.

Margaret said she had accidentally met Lillian at Riverdale yesterday. Lillian took her aside and said to her, after much circumlocution, that she had heard disturbing reports about me. I was concerning myself with matters which were properly the job of Sladebourne management.

So concerned is Lillian, that she proposes to carry out an investigation. She will interview a number of people at Sladebourne, to find out from them if what she has heard is true. Then, she is going to speak to me about it.

I do not know what my expression was like while Margaret was telling me all this. I should have felt surprised, maybe shock, but my main sensation was anger. After asking Margaret a few questions, I found enough courage to ask her what she really thought about the whole business. Margaret paused before replying.

"I think Mrs Saye's is not a way I would choose to go about anything, but no doubt she has her own methods of acting—"

"That wasn't what I meant. I'm not bothered about her methods. I meant, about my interfering. Do I really do so much of it? Tell me, for I need to know."

"You cross boundaries. That's not really the same as interfering, is it? But some people might think it was. You do all kinds of things people never did here before. Anyone who works like that, can't avoid making some mistakes, even making some enemies, but they'll get things done. Well, things like children from Waverley going on to a day centre when they're too old for school.

"Matthew going to live somewhere nearer his family and a place that will suit him better—a whole lot better. Parents coming in so regularly—that never used to happen. But we've been all over this ground before, Mary, you are as you are, you speak as you think, and I agree with most of what you say and do. But now it seems as if Mrs Saye might need persuading of the advantages of your approach."

I thanked her, though it wasn't easy to do because I couldn't help feeling that her warning comes too late. Passing the car park on my way back to the office, I had a sudden wish to just get into my car and go home to think, to sort out my own mind before any necessity arose to do anything else whatever. But I knew I could not go home yet, for Stella was expecting me, and I could not disappoint her.

Each time now that I come to the workshop, I feel the smallness, ugliness and isolation of that place like a series of blows. More and more it seems a prison for one single prisoner, placed there without trial and impossible to free. A prisoner of ten years old! What will she be at twelve, at fifteen, if we can't help her? Tom is the official director of Stella's destiny, but I am losing faith in him. I don't believe he cares enough about what happens to Stella, and several recent incidents have led me to that unkind conclusion.

There was the time I asked him about the delay in allocating her a Hoxton social worker. He explained to me, in his tight, patient way, that there were 'many children even more needy' than Stella. They took priority over her. She is safe compared to them and must wait her turn.

She has waited three years already, as I reminded him. And he said that in my situation (he meant, I suppose, what he thinks of as my comfortable little existence) it's impossible for me to realise what life can be in that big, bad, busy world outside of Sladebourne. That real world, Tom knows, is full of danger.

When I counter that by saying there are even more urgent human needs than the very obvious ones, like safety—he doesn't like to hear that. More recently, when I've rung him about Christmas money for Stella, I referred back to the review and said I had put together my part of the report, but needed help from him regarding Louise's contribution, for which originally he took responsibility.

"I remember," I said at last, in what I hoped was a nonchalant, non-threatening way, "you spent some time with Louise beforehand teasing out her work with Stella, as I did with Donna. Neither of them had attended a review before. Now, I have Donna's report on file, but nothing to reflect what Louise has been doing. We know she's not literate, but we know you interviewed her and took notes. Can I ask you to send me something about Louise's work?"

"Why does it matter so much? Why don't you just go and ask Louise what she thinks, Mary, and put that down?"

"Because," I said slowly, "I also need to know what you think of Louise."

Silence. Then Tom replied with forced patience. When he does this, he sounds to me like the would-be-fair-minded colonial administrator reasoning with the uppity native clerk.

"Mary, I don't see why you are so worried about something of minor importance. Louise had little to add to what Donna said, so far as I can remember."

"That wasn't actually what I wanted to ask. I wondered if you knew more about, well, Louise as a person than I do—for instance, if there's anything you've noticed that you could share, that we both should know…. Stella's odd with her, so tense, so altogether different to what she's like with Donna. Or even, with me."

More silence. Then: "Louise brought some personal matters to me, which it would not be appropriate to disclose to you. Or to anyone else. I was in a position to ref—to advise her. Nothing to do with your client's review."

"I see. Sorry then to have bothered you about it, Tom."

So Louise discussed her personal problems with Tom, who has nothing to do with her really, rather than with me, right on her doorstep. Well, that is understandable, in a way. And Tom refers her on to someone else, someone from another agency, it sounds like. Now, he is annoyed with me because I'm probing him. Or is that the reason he does not want to let me know much about what he has done? Or can there be another reason?

Tom is a powerful man, on whom I rely for help with Stella. My one source of help, really. Then I thought: to hell with it. This isn't good enough. If there is anything, anything at all, that makes Louise unsuitable to be Stella's carer, I should not have to pick it out of Tom like a splinter. He's got a duty to let me know, Hanafin as well, and Paigle. Everyone.

Then I thought, maybe he has already done all this. Told them, I mean, not me. But no, he hasn't, for I've checked out with Lynn. Because I was expecting to receive a cheque from Hoxton towards Stella's Christmas present and feared that in the general pre-Christmas rush and confusion it would be re-routed to Locke or Paigle and never seen again, I asked Lynn to look out for any such communication.

Lynn said the cheque has come all right, from Hoxton's social services Finance Division, but nothing else has come from Hoxton. She sent Ray along to my office with the cheque straight away.

I feel the urge to phone Tom again, to show a bit of courage and challenge him properly, but whenever I try to do so recently his extension just rings unanswered.

11 December 1970

Just before the start of December, I bought Stella an Advent calendar. It wasn't one of the ones with a jolly Santa and the elves, but a pious one from Austria, with sparkly angels revolving around the roofs of a medieval town.

It was well-received, but like nearly everything else in life had unforeseen effects, for it had not occurred to me until I heard Stella refer to 'babies with wings' that the word 'angel' was not part of her vocabulary. I tried to explain angels to her, and soon was in the water so deep that I looked for help get out.

Stella, as should have been obvious to me very much earlier, does not know anything that is not Sladebourne. So she knows about rules and punishments, 'on duty' and 'off duty,' staff and patients, wards, medicines, treatments, injections. She does not know anything much about families, where food and clothes come from, or what worlds might lie outside of South London.

And even at the most sketchy level, she has been given no idea of any system of religious belief. In the seventies, it is part of our professional code of welfare ethics, all the more precious since relatively new, never to discuss religious beliefs with clients and more especially to avoid doing so with the young. Those of us who still hold to unfashionable concepts like a faith-based moral system must be careful to avoid influencing others, especially the disempowered, a vogue-word mainly applied to less educated people than oneself.

More so than any political theory, religion is seen as of its nature divisive, even destructive. Other people must be allowed to make up their own minds, free from influence by our rag-bag collections of beliefs and principles.

I wonder, and can't help it, what content there can be in the others' human minds already? And how, working directly with human need, you can honestly forbear *ever* mentioning why you are doing it, and how you think and feel about doing it?

If I'd asked this of Lillian, I can guess at her probable answer: In each society, there is a consensus morality that provides framework, or rather, foundation, for the road towards terrestrial bliss. I am sceptical about the nature of this road and its direction, seeing (as I do) plenty of potholes, boulders, and almost total absence of signage. But there are people for whom that identical way gives them a chance to skim, apparently happily, over life. They don't feel the unevenness, nor do they always want to know where they are going.

Such a way is not for Stella, to whom I find myself giving a crash course in St Luke's account of the first Christmas. First, she wants to know if it is true. Yes, I said, putting out of my mind the claims of revisionist historians. Then, she wants to know where all these people are now. I tell her that so far as I know, they are with God—in Heaven. And no, that is not a place to be found located anywhere on this earth.

"You mean, they're extra-terrestrial?" I agreed that Yes, in a sense, you could say that they were. (And how Nilla's improved Stella's language!) Starting to feel a bit desperate, I sent an SOS to Sister Bonaventure, one of the nuns who long ago had the task of educating me.

They've diversified from the academic schooling which was my lot, to the instruction of the children of the Republic's out-group of people who were once called Tinkers and are now known as Travellers. Bonaventure should be able to give me some new ideas on the instruction of an outcast little girl.

I am ashamed to write that I've concealed what I'm doing from Nilla. However, she's helped Stella's vocabulary, I don't feel it's tactful to distract her from Liam and expect her to go against her agnostic principles in order to advise me on methods of teaching religion. Nilla has enough going on at the moment.

Besides, I want to keep her sweet so that she will not be tempted to give up her part in the Christmas plans for Stella. So this evening, after what Margaret Tobias told me, I put all my feelings on hold and went to Stella in the workshop, with the expectation of being given a hard time there too.

And somehow, it wasn't like that at all. As I emerged from the cluster of low-roofed therapy buildings and looked over West, where my path lay, there was a great sky of pink and gold, and a gentle gust of air carrying the scents of wood-smoke and fresh-cut trees. A little holly bush I'd never noticed before, in a sheltered corner between the workshop and a part of Waverley, now bears improbable yellow berries! Against all reason, there's a feeling of joy and expectation.

It's Friday and also Stella's last day at tutorial class before the holidays. Stella met me at the workshop door, wearing a silvery tinsel wreath on her blonde head. I had a sudden vivid memory of myself at about the same age wearing a similar wreath because I was an angel in the school nativity play. Today's angel looked up into my face with an expression of concern and said to me: "Did you have a hard day?"

Taken aback, I answered her as I would an adult; thanking her and saying that the day had, on the whole, not been too bad.

"She did that to me too," said Donna laughing, "she's learning it at school. Politeness."

"Politeness," echoed Stella, turning the word over in her mouth as if tasting it and finding it strange. "I've been wrapping up presents," she said, "I had to do it at class instead of here because (she mouthed the words silently, rolling her eyes at Donna) one of them's for someone here."

I smiled what I hoped was a complicit smile. Then something occurred to me.

"I haven't seen Louise here for a long time. Is she all right?"

"Louise is gone away now," Stella said quickly, without looking at anyone.

"She's on annual leave," confirmed Donna.

"But you'll be here over Christmas, Donna, they won't put in anyone else? Who's going to be here on nights?"

"Michelle, it's her turn that week. From 7:00 in the morning, I'll be here, certain."

Now, Stella was at my elbow, holding out a plateful of shrunken, greyish objects.

"These are mince pies, Nilla and I made them. Would you like one?" She was being a polite, grown-up lady. I took one of the objects and put it in my mouth, where it tasted as it looked. The mincemeat filling was all right, but Nilla has no real interest in baking.

"Isn't it nice? I ate four of them, but I kept these for Donna and you."

"That was a good thought, but I couldn't manage another one just now. What's this? Not more goodies?"

"This is marzipan dates, we made them too. With our hands. We washed them first of course, and that brown bit, that's cocoa."

"Well, I'll have just one, thank you, to take away. Now, what would you like us to do?"

"You can read a book to me while I'm wrapping Nilla's present. But when the clock is—no, when the hour hands at the five—when it's 5 o'clock—there's a story on the Tele Nilla told me to be sure and watch."

Nothing is as easy as at first, it seems. Reading about the bloody history of the Holy Innocents introduced the topic of a future life. I don't know where I found the things I said, the answers I gave. I suppose they must have lain buried in me for years.

Something spoke all right, but not what I think of as my present self. How orthodox it was, I don't know, but Donna listened as well as the child, and that threw me somewhat. When we'd finished, it was after five and Stella had been actually concentrating, listening to somebody reading for a full thirty minutes! As long as that—I must tell Nilla.

Now, Scrooge loomed on the screen, with a Bob Cratchit who looked somewhat like a younger version of Locke. Stella pushed the big armchair (newly borrowed from Riverdale's geriatric unit), into a forward position before the set. Then she positioned a smaller armchair beside it, saying:

"This is for you, Donna. You're to sit here. The big chair is for me and Mary."

So, for the second time, Stella sits on my lap. She squirms and pulls my hair when Marley's Ghost appears and shakes his chains, but she really likes arms holding her, once she has arranged them to her satisfaction. And I'm unprepared for the rush of tenderness I feel, intensified by the discomfort of trying to hold someone of Stella's size as if they were a three-year-old.

When leaving, I explain to Stella that I will not be coming to see her again until Christmas Day. She follows me to the door to say goodbye. She hasn't done that before.

Tonight, I was out with Nilla and Liam and a few others until pretty late, and the local pub was absolutely crowded. If the combination of that with semi-darkness, heavy music, and a lot more than I drink normally was confusing, added to it came one of those sudden intrusions of silence which we used to call 'angels passing'. And during it, I distinctly heard, from the other side of the partition on my left, a voice so like Donna's that I jumped.

Was it her voice? It was so sad and almost tearful, that I could not be sure, and readily thought myself mistaken. I could not get at the words, which were responded to by a deeper, reassuring voice. A moment later, the angels had passed and the impression was gone, but I was now being fumbled discreetly by

Albery, the group menace. Dealing with his tender advances took some time and skill, while I did it, the incident of the voices dropped through a hole in my mind, and was temporarily lost.

When I came back into the flat the 'phone rang almost at once. Without fear, I went to answer it, knowing that Mr Lewis is still in hospital and won't be coming home for Christmas. So I spoke my name, and again, Oh God, there was that sickening pause before the caller hung up.

In the holly-wreathed mirror before me, my face looked bleached and strange. "Never mind," I said to the mirror. On the doormat near my feet lay a sheaf of envelopes and circulars, the day's Christmas post. When I'd hung up my inherited coat, I took the post into the sitting-room and started to open it, giving first preference to items with Irish stamps.

After a while, I noticed an envelope that was different—bigger and squarer than the others, addressed in a large flamboyant hand, and with a North London postmark that meant nothing to me. This is what the letter said:

Dear Mary,

Circumstances making it unlikely that I shall get a chance to speak to you, I have decided to combine Season's Greetings with an explanation and an apology. I owe you both.

My plan—for it was mine, not yours—to talk some sense of reality into our dear Minister about Sladebourne, was ill-judged from the first and now appears to have unfortunate consequences. Mrs Saye, who has been tracking me for some time, has finally caught up with me. With regard to the Minister's interview, about which she appears unusually well informed, she is seeking a scapegoat and has chosen you.

I have accepted full responsibility for whatever the Minister didn't like, but I shall not be around to do this for much longer. Forgive me for this. I won't be part of the scene at Sladebourne anymore, or for that matter at Riverdale either.

Why should I conceal it from you, whom I have learned to regard as a friend? I have cancer that no longer responds to treatment. Everybody is being very careful about what they say to me, but the fact is: my remaining time is measured in weeks rather than months.

I have always felt that your diffident exterior hides a warm and loving nature. May you live happily in the future, Mary, happy ever after, as the stories say.

What you are experiencing here and now is not going to be the whole of life. You will be able to look back on all of us with tenderness one day.

Farewell, dear Mary and a happy Christmas and New Year!

Ben Morgan.

PS. *I shall arrange for your book to return to you when I no longer need it.*

The postscript was set so low down on the page that I almost missed it. When I looked higher up, the address on the letterhead was that of a private clinic in North London. The sort of place where rich people go to die.

24 December 1974

This morning, Christmas Eve morning, was rainy, dark and cold. I overslept, got up late to the sound of radio news, and over breakfast read some of my posts, which included a packet from Mother Bonaventure. She sent me copies of two articles she thought might be useful, but her letter was what I really wanted. After the usual enquiries about health and well-being, she wrote:

I can't say, dear Mary, that I have had the precise experiences you describe with regard to poor little Stella. You may, with your professional experience, know some of the harm done to her as certain. I may, in the case of certain children here, suspect similar happenings in their lives, but without the ability to prove them or do anything openly about them.

Attempts at proof would indeed be difficult, given the age of the child and the tendency we all have to wish to play down and deny the darker side of human nature. The concept of Original Sin lacks entertainment value. Not everybody responds positively to challenge—people who don't may even see it as an insult or a threat—and this may go some way to explain the difficulties you have described with the different agencies involved. But how will knowing this help you to help Stella?

I would think rather that she needs to know more about the love of God for her, and that is something she can only learn about with the help of you and other people. This is where we all begin. We learn from parents who show love when they respond to our needs. At present, the situation seems to be that Petronilla and yourself are parenting Stella. Don't worry about not being good enough. No one is good enough on their own. When we realise that, we can ask God for help, and take each day as it comes....

I finished her letter, and sat thinking, trying to remember what Stella was like when I knew her first. She looked different, for sure, she did not look as though anyone cared about her. And she acted out like a much younger child, unable to express herself except by pushing and pulling, shouting and struggling, and running away.

Now, Stella is quieter and more thoughtful, but at such times appears almost depressed with as I suspect, the aggression she once directed at the rest of the world is now directed against herself. I do not think that this is for the best. In fact, I do not like to think of it at all.

Bonaventure wrote about Stella's need for reassurance, for the conviction that she is valuable and loveable. In some ways, the suggestion was, Stella needs the sort of attention you'd naturally give to a much younger child. Were we giving her that?

"Well, Nilla is maybe, but I don't think any of the rest of us here give enough," I said aloud, "Donna's kind, but not really committed to Stella in the long term—she has, she would say, her own life to lead. Louise has a lot to give; she's warm, empathetic, sensitive—but she too seems to be taken up at present with her own needs."

That leaves me. As far as I'm concerned, Stella has only the crumbs of my time, the leftovers from a demanding if the curiously satisfying job. *If I didn't work full-time? Or if I were a foster parent, for instance?* Nilla has tried this briefly—caring for the child of an African student couple who was her friends. She managed financially—though I've never asked her exactly how—and she did say she'd learnt a lot from the experience—but she showed no wish to repeat it.

Something has always made me reluctant to ask Nilla for more information. That's possible because of the impressive life experience she seems to have already. The eldest of five, with an absent father and a tubercular mother, her whole childhood seems to have been spent as a step-parent to her siblings. She came to England as an *au pair*, trained as a nursery nurse, then as a teacher.

She's taught in residential special schools. Her whole life is a good reference, a record of commitment to children. All that I can bring is motivation. All that I can say is: I want to do this. Now, according to Bonaventure, in some circumstances that is enough. But I am not sure yet what those circumstances are.

One thing I do know is that whatever my own future holds, Stella must not remain at Sladebourne. It is no place for her, and it never has been. With every tiny gain, she makes, she is moving away from the institution and into an unknown future. *I think as well, of what it would be like to be without her, to have no one to see off to 'school' in the mornings, or visit regularly in the evenings, no one to read to, play with, chatter to, listen to, take out, scold, cuddle sometimes, a nurse on my lap.*

And the space of time which I have had in which to learn to do all these things has been eleven short months!

Much later in the day, as I was wrapping up to go out to midnight mass, the phone rang again. I was sure it would be Nilla, but it couldn't have been, for by the time I answered, the caller had gone. After the mass, I went up to look at the Crib.

Someone with artistic pretensions has evidently taken it on; they have been unable to do much about the ugly plaster figures; but the background scenery, instead of consisting of the usual straw and conifer branches, is all in fabric— green roof and walls, dark blue sky with puckered gold foil stars, hanging high over a crumpled brown cloth floor edged (surely dangerously) with fairy lights.

The indispensable collecting box is for the Catholic Children's Society, and a picture on the box shows a little girl remarkably like Stella but smiling. It occurred to me then, with some pain, how seldom it is that Stella smiles. But I think that anyway Stella will smile to see this Crib and I'll take her there, maybe on Stephen's Day.

I missed out on dinner today but don't feel hungry. Just cold. What matters is, to get warm. Now, I've finished this, I'll go to bed.

25 December 1970

There was a forest of cloth. No sky, but the light coming from somewhere, light enough to see folds like soft felt, hanging every single way I turned. The fabric had little colour, but its weight oppressed, stifled me, holding my limbs so that I could hardly move them. I cried out, and the cry hurt my throat but made no sound.

I knew then that I was asleep and having a nightmare. I knew it, and for time, that was endless struggled to end the dream, tried to wake up, tried to breathe. My mouth, dry and useless, formed the words: *God Help, Help Me.* I saw the words glowing on the dull cloth-like smouldering traces. My limbs could not push away the dead weight of the cloth on them, and again I soundlessly wept: *Help Me, Help Me.*

And was suddenly awake, with my own tears warm on my face. Grey light showed beneath the window slats, my head was spinning, and somewhere there was a ringing sound. Shivering, I lifted the receiver, half-expecting the caller to hang up. Instead, I heard a familiar voice, speaking very quickly and with a kind of furtive excitement.

"Miss Delancy, is that Miss Delancy? He's here again. Sorry to call you so early, but he's here."

"Who is?" I said, "And who's this speaking?" But even as I spoke, I knew the answers to both questions.

"The bloke with the green MG, he is here again. Now, mind, no one told you, not anyone. You didn't know, you just come in by chance." And Steve hung up.

I still held the receiver, staring at it as if I'd never seen one before. That was certainly Steve, with his Dartford Loop twang, I'd know it anywhere. Why in hell was he pestering me, ringing me at Oh God before 7:00 on a Christmas morning? Then my mind took in the implications of what Steve had just said.

I fell out of bed and blundered around turning lights on, splashing my face, finding the clothes I'd thrown off the night before. Michelle, I thought. Michelle might be there still, and Donna will surely be there before I come. Maybe she's there now!

At the back door, I grabbed the old duffel coat and struggled into it before meeting the freezing outside world. Then I was out, breathing into the car lock, opening it, scraping the windscreen I hadn't bothered to cover last night. As I started, subdued sunlight showed me roads misty and empty, and all traffic lights seemed to be fixed at the green.

Green, green, my hope is green, my hope that winter spoiled, is seen... Sladebourne has no seasons of hope. And John Priestly, the man with the green car. What shall I do, whatever am I to say? But Donna will be there too, so what's to be afraid of?

My head was starting to ache, a familiar, one-sided ache, attended by nausea and a certain creeping chill. My left hand was slowly turning numb. Truly a migraine, but I could still see, and now I was nearly there.

The main gates were open, but there was no sign of life at the lodge when I passed it, jolting sickeningly over the ramps. Slow down. The drive, now. Like a small back road with no one anywhere. Not a stir. A village of the dead—or the sleeping—lay all around me.

Stella's asleep still. *Sweetly she sleeps, my Alice fair, her cheek to the pillow pressed, sweetly she sleeps, while her golden hair like sunlight streams over her breast.* Stop the car now. Leave it here, get out and walk. They shouldn't know you're coming. Don't let them hear you.

At the far side of the workshop, on a patch of cement about the size of a big tablecloth, stood the MG almost concealed, with only its antique bonnet trim showing a glint or two in the thin sunlight. There was no sound from the workshop, my view of which was confused by the migraine. My mind was not working, and I could not think what to do next. *Open my heart, open my lips.*

The idea came to me at once to approach, not the front door, but the window of Stella's bedroom at the back of the hut. Stella never draws her curtains, preferring to be woken by the daylight. So my intention was to waken her and get her to open the window, which was big enough for her to climb through. With this in mind, I stepped off the path.

There had been frost the shadowed grass felt crisp as I walked on it, my feet left dark tracks. Migraine distorts almost everything of the little you can see, and as I came nearer to the workshop, the whirlpool effect altered to a jagged lightning edge surrounding whatever was there to focus on. I got to the window, and I looked in.

The man on the bed saw me first and turned his face away. Stella cried, a cry of pain, and I think she saw me then. But before I could even move, a hand-pulled the curtain across the window, and I saw, on the third finger of that hand, Louise's tiger's eye-ring.

"Can't I get you anything?" asked the black woman whose gentle face bent solicitously above me. I could see properly again but still felt sick, cold, confused as well as empty. And my mouth was so dry...

"Please, could I have something to drink?"

"Sure. Your little girl's safe now—Sister's with her and the doctor's next door but he's on the phone. I'll bring you tea." The nurse went out again.

I couldn't ask about the police but wanted to know, for it must be the next thing I'd have to do, talk to them. Although some of my memory seemed to be missing, I knew I hadn't seen the cops yet. There were screams when I hit the window with the big stone I'd picked up. Then there was Daroga, and her son with his limousine, and I was sitting in the back of it with Stella in my arms wrapped in a blanket and struggling and sobbing.

She smelt of beer. I wasn't able to see her very well yet but I did hold her tight as tight and made my voice fierce as I told her she was safe now and nothing could hurt her. I said it over and over until her screaming stopped and then we were at Riverdale A. and E. with Stella holding on to me.

The on-call Casualty Officer, in slippers and with her chignon falling apart, persuaded Stella to let go of me and hold onto her instead. Blood came from somewhere and my right arm hurt. Then there was another blank. I couldn't work out what had gone on between *that* time, and *this* time when I was lying down flat on a slippery surface in a small room with no windows.

After the nurse went, I did try to sit up and then I saw the dressing on my right forearm. It hurt, but not much. Suddenly, there was a man in the room, a man who I seemed to have seen before. He stood at the door but moved very quickly to stop me from falling off the couch.

I thought even then, he's pretty strong because I'm not a lightweight, but he lifted me and put me in a chair with no trouble at all. He had brown eyes, not the Stoney but the warm kind, like Paul Gomez has.

"You," I started to say, "you must be the doctor—"

234

"I'm Frank Ledwidge and you're Mary Delancy. This looks to be your tea—couldn't they find you anything to eat?"

"I don't want it, only tea. You worked with Ben."

"Temporarily, yes," Frank explained that I'd fainted while he was examining Stella. When he saw my arm was bleeding, he stitched and dressed it, while I was still out cold.

"I can't remember any of that."

"And you're not anaemic, are you? All the red hair… and you're not pregnant either?"

I started to laugh, and then he added: "Just by the way—what were you doing with this?" and he was holding something up. "That's my coat," I said, "that grey duffel."

"No, it's not," said Frank Ledwidge—"it's mine!"

It can't be. But he says it is. He says he left it in the flat that I'm renting before he went to the States almost a year ago.

We talked quite a bit, and he told me Ben is dead. He died two days ago. Then we talked about Stella, they'd keep her in the Paediatric Unit for the present. Frank has spoken to someone about a Place of Safety order. He wanted to know about her family background, and I told him.

He will oppose her return to Sladebourne as she obviously isn't safe there. She must only be discharged to some form of local authority care. In the short term, he said, he wants to make certain she 'has not been infected with anything'. In answer to my questions, yes, he thought she had been sexually assaulted 'and possibly not for the first time.'

After the tea, I was feeling much better and was just saying so, when it suddenly got through to me, the reality did, about Stella and the whole horror of what had happened to her after we'd intended her to have her First Happy Christmas. My chest seemed suddenly to fill with one enormous, irrepressible sob. When I had to begin to let it go, I found myself holding on to Frank, and he was still drying up my tears when we heard Nilla and Liam outside looking for me.

I said a temporary goodbye to Stella (who refused to look at me at first,) and then the others took me back to their place. Nilla rang Sladebourne and spoke to Steve. According to him, it was Daroga who had called the police, and he thought they were still there, interviewing people. Attempts to contact Max Paigle were unsuccessful, but Liam was really great and got hold of Tom on the Out of Hours team, to let him know what was going on.

Over succeeding days, we all pieced out the course events had taken. They hung together in the peculiar way such chains of dreadful happenings do. You could say that Ben opened Pandora's box all right when he planned for me to meet Dr Fermatt, and that was the start, but there is much more.

On the day Lillian started investigating me, she first interviewed Mrs Bailey, who told her that I was an interfering bitch unable to forget my nursing past and like she thinks all nurses are, terribly bossy. Lillian next interviewed Locke, who said I wanted Sladebourne to close (true!), and Paigle, who said I had it in for him and was always upsetting his staff (not true!).

Unfortunately, Lillian also traded some information. She told Paigle and Locke that I told her I possessed evidence about serious misuse of facilities in Midlothian (the staff parties). The two evidently nailed Donna as the most likely informant, and late on the Sunday just before Christmas they fired her. They knew I would be on leave for the whole of Christmas week, and reckoned I wouldn't find out.

Donna was completely taken unawares. She truly had intended, as she told me, to leave Sladebourne shortly anyway, but not like this, without notice, references, or even a chance to say goodbye to Stella. No wonder she was upset when I heard her that night in the pub, telling her boyfriend about it. Donna, never the most organised of people, lost my phone number and on account of Mr Lewis and his phone calls, I'd anyway gone ex-directory six months ago.

Someone who had not lost my number was Steve. He says, that on several occasions recently he tried to call me with the information he felt I should have, only to be frustrated by the sudden appearance in the Lodge of one of the less sympathetic porters. Whenever that happened, Steve always hung up, fearing trouble for himself or his cousin, Ray.

Told by Michelle that Donna had been fired, Steve first intended to call me about it, but when he saw John Priestly's car coming in he only thought of the importance of telling me about that. When he knew I was on the way to Sladebourne, Steve did two other things, though. He called Daroga at her home, and he went and let the air out of the MGs tyres. Thanks to his actions, Priestly did not get very far before the police got him.

Having gotten rid of Donna, the conspirators (as I think of them), had to replace her at short notice. So Paigle (I'm sure it was he) rang Louise. All this, of course, became common knowledge later, so I reckon I can mention it now. Tom Grace, when he interviewed Louise before the review, sussed out that she was abusing drugs.

Not grass, which nearly everyone has tried at some time, but cocaine. Tom began his career working with people using hard drugs, so he knew the signs. But, apparently, he did not feel at liberty to tell me about Louise. I still feel angry about this.

I maintain he didn't have any right to keep silent, especially to a colleague. Yes, he had a right to be discreet and to refer Louise for whatever help she might accept, but no right to put a child at further risk of rape, and that's actually what he did.

Louise, well, she was at the point when she couldn't pay for her habit without selling herself. And, as it turned out, selling someone else too.

I'd like it to have been otherwise with her. I do not think that Louise set out to do any of this deliberately. She had begun to get help for herself, and, like Donna, she wanted to move on, away from Sladebourne altogether.

I'd like to think the changes taking place there played some part in that decision, as far as opening her mind to other possibilities went. But as long as Louise is an addict, she cannot put anyone or anything else before her short-term needs, and that, as I have realised, is what you certainly always have to do where children are part of the equation.

Louise knew John Priestly. They may have been lovers at one time—anyhow, she was aware of his obsession with little girls. Here we get to the heart of the matter: she did not see anything very wrong with it. All sex was good, that was an article of her faith.

Any kind of sex was good, whatever, whatever. It just couldn't be bad. I suspect experiences from her own childhood contributed to the grown-up Louise's life view, but to date, I don't know if that really was the case.

January to April 1975

Stella left Riverdale after a few days. Now, the full responsibility of Hoxton, she's placed out-of-borough with foster parents on the western fringes of London. As often as I can, I go to visit her.

Madge and Fred Lucas are large, even-tempered people, Madge somewhat larger. They like you to use their first names. Both have gentle, rather placid natures, and retain the attractive speech of their native Dorset, left without apparent regret many years ago. Fred works shifts at a local engineering set-up, Madge and he brought up four sons on his earnings plus overtime.

When their youngest joined his father at work the Lucases, inspired by the example of friends, applied to Hoxton to become foster parents. After several years during which their expertise increased, especially in regard to difficult teenage boys, Madge and Fred decided to try fostering a girl next.

Stella was a new experience for them, but one they wanted. At first, they had felt confident that they could help her, and the reports they gave Tom were encouraging. Stella adapted to what must have been a great change in her life with surprising ease. She was on her best behaviour.

Although the Lucases would have known all about the 'honeymoon period' and the 'try-outs' which inevitably succeed they were not, it seems, prepared for the ways in which the sexualised little girl confronted them. Her lingering caresses of Fred or indeed any visiting male; together with her penetrative kissing technique might be taken as demonstrating little more than a natural and unsatisfied craving for affection; her attempts to seduce their adolescent youngest son were not so easily dealt with or explained away.

The major threat to the placement came, though, from Stella's treatment of a pet. At first, seemingly entranced by Lulu, Marge's long-haired tortoiseshell cat, Stella became obsessed with hugging the creature so as to near-throttle her, then releasing her and professing to be unable to understand why the persecuted

238

animal fled at the sight of her. A day came, finally, when Marge discovered Stella trying to conduct a hanging in the garden, with Lulu as the trussed-up victim.

Tom knew the signs. He had realised that sooner than later, he would be getting a call from the Lucas's asking to meet with him ASAP. He did not tell me any of this, but I knew it because I was allowed to visit Stella regularly. Marge liked me. I think she enjoyed being able to unload her feelings to somebody outside the fostering system, and the fact was that Stella didn't yet have a social worker of her own. Everything was on a temporary basis.

When I asked Tom about Stella's possible future, he stalled. But then, he began to hint. There were, it appeared, units attached to psychiatric hospitals, where a disturbed child could be contained safely. Places where the opportunities to injure anyone including themselves were reduced.

Where they could be educated, if not very intensively because it was more important to iron out difficult behaviour first, was it not? Learning could not take place if a child was disturbed. I don't agree with this opinion but held my tongue. Casually, I asked Tom what happened when a child thus cared for was no longer a child, and became an adolescent? He said he didn't know—but there must be places for them—on adult wards, perhaps.

The thought caused me a pain that was almost physical as I thought of Stella's vulnerable face, her skinny body and bony limbs—causing me anxiety anyway—her hair, even, how long would it take for it to become neglected again—but more, more; her awaking interest in the world around her, in stories, in other people, in the future, in doubt and in belief. What would be left of her after years in a psychiatric unit, another institution?

But I did not say anything about that to Tom. I felt it would be useless. He was not going to fight for her in the way I would. I know that there are risks in taking on a damaged child on a long-term basis. But somebody has to try to do it.

With February in this New Year came a second winter. As I went inching my way through the slushy car park at Riverdale one morning, it became evident that no official space in it remained any longer for me. So I made for the alley which, as I recalled, on its way to the perimeter road passed a boiler house beside which, but only just, was room to park a small car.

Snow was beginning to fall again as I got out of the car; loose, feathery wet snow, penetrating the seams of my boots as I walked about looking for a shortcut, a likely way into the sprawling hospital complex. At last, there it was, the flappy plastic door leading to a corridor. Kitchens were near, and the gusts of steam fetid with overcooked cabbage met me passing internal wall louvres on my way toward Administration.

As I strode up an incline, a man pushing a trolley at speed from a side entrance and barely missing me with it swore, not at me I think, but at himself. When I looked at him, he turned his head away, but too late. It was angelic Ray, and he was moonlighting, a thing Sladebourne workers were never allowed to do.

Returning my greeting with a yell: 'Oh! Shit!' he crashed through another door, into a scullery where, to go by the noise, the trolley hit somebody who dropped whatever they were carrying. Poor Ray! He must have thought I would inform him to Locke. After all, that's my trade: I'm an informer.

Lillian's office was a long way from where I had parked. On the way there, I got lost for about a quarter of an hour, and I know that it was partly due to my state of mind, and not all because I had not come that way for weeks. And when I found her, Lillian did not promise any coffee and biscuits, or good cheer of any kind.

In the brief light of that winter day a display of greenish-white hellebores, witch's flowers, exhibited their premature perfection in containers along her window ledge. Their owner was today no smiling flower. So far as she could she suppressed her dimples and looked grim enough to be intimidating.

"I have sent for you, Mary," Lillian said, "to discuss the future. After the recent, regrettable series of incidents at Sladebourne House you, must have realised that it would clearly not be in your best interests to remain there." As she spoke, Lillian fiddled with a pencil, lowered blue eyes watching her own plump hand make holes in the blotter before her.

"I do not feel," she went on, "That children are exactly your line. Not what you're best at, let us say. The late Dr Morgan was complimentary about your work but perhaps over-generous, as were the younger people at Sladebourne, therapists and so on.

"They seem anxious to say, ah, only good things about your efforts. But where tact and sensitivity and, prudence, indeed, are called for, a certain lack is evident. Oh, not of goodwill, I am sure. But a certain lack, nonetheless."

That sense of panic which had threatened me a few minutes earlier had gone. I felt able to speak now but could wait a little longer before doing so. A single gold hair detached from Lillian's coiffure lay, lightly and conspicuously, on the dark sleeve of her blouse. Suddenly, it was all I could do to restrain myself from leaning forward across that desk, putting out my hand and picking that hair up….

Lillian went on talking. She had decided to suggest to me, she said, a New Direction. She had been offered a place for one student on a course for social workers who wanted an additional psychiatric qualification. This course was currently being set up at the Maudesley, and she felt convinced that I would be suitable for it.

And, by fortunate coincidence, that course was starting in one month's time, just giving space for me to finish off whatever few little things I had yet to do at Sladebourne, and take the rest of the annual leave owing to me. Afterwards, hinted Lillian, there might even be a job going at St Dismas, the local psychiatric hospital, where Dr Walter Woebegone—'you'll have heard of him, Mary'—and indeed I had!—despite holding out a long time against letting social workers into his territory, recently seemed more receptive to the idea of trying one.

"I'm sure he is," I said, "his secretary has given in her notice after seventeen years plus a knife attack from a patient which nearly finished her off, and he can't find anyone else to do her job. He thinks social workers will take dictation, type letters and answer the phone for him. He's rather like Dr Hanafin, in fact, except that Woebegone's older and more set in his ways."

Lillian reddened and looked nearer to anger than I have ever seen her. I interrupted her again; I couldn't help it now:

"Look, Lillian, we have to talk, and it may as well be now, today, about what's happening at Sladebourne. The present has to come before the future, and I think you need to know what's going on there at the present. I told you after New Year, all about Stella Wilson being placed with foster parents after the Place of Safety order ended.

"Well, two weeks ago I got a phone call from Hoxton's solicitors. They want to free Stella for adoption and for that they'll have to go to Court. They'll also have to involve me. They want an affidavit from me, as well as my presence in Court, in case anyone there wants to question me about the child and what happened to her at Sladebourne.

"As you know, I've no experience of court work and as I'm sure you can guess I've a lot of anxieties about the whole thing. I'll need a solicitor's help with the affidavit. And later on, there'll be no doubt a criminal prosecution as well, leading to a trial. I suppose I'll be subpoena'd to attend that, since after all,

I'm the main prosecution witness, for nobody can, apparently, accept Stella's testimony of itself.

"And over the last month, I've tried and tried to get you on the phone! I've left messages with your secretary—she says that you're very busy, and away a lot. Because there wasn't a response from you, I rang the Director, I felt I had to.

"That was last week. Mr Sawrey gave me an early appointment to see him, and when I came he asked me all about the case. He said that as my manager, you would accompany me to court, and arrange for me to have any help and legal advice I needed. He said, managers always do that. It's usual, it's part of their responsibility, he said."

Lillian had already tried to interrupt me several times—but I hadn't finished yet, and I wasn't going to let her stop me now.

"When Mr Sawrey finished explaining what I would be entitled to in the way of help, he asked me what I intend to do when Sladebourne closes. He said this is likely to happen earlier than we thought. 'Do you want to stay in the hospital system' was how he put it.

"He said there is a vacancy in the Fieldwork team in Longhurst. I told him I'd like to know more, and an appointment's been made for me to see the team leader next Monday. I appreciate your efforts to find a place for me, but it seems unlikely that they'll be necessary."

I stopped, not from lack of more to say, but because my mouth had gone dry as it does when I'm stressed. Lillian did not look me in the eye at first. When she did, her face seemed to have lost its usual high colour, and her eyes to have changed their normal radiant blue to a colder shade.

"You've already made up your mind, I see. You don't want to listen to me, Mary, and actually, it seems to me now that you never *have* listened. I am here to help you all—and my only intention has always been to help you. I cannot imagine, cannot really imagine, why—"

And so she went on, and on, while I sat stunned, gradually understanding that I had been given, in the last few seconds, the key to Lillian. She could not use her imagination, really could not, and that was all there was to it.

I said nothing. Lillian went on to seem bewildered as to why I had consulted Richard Sawrey. Didn't I know that it was unprofessional to do so? That all requests for transfer must come through her, as my line manager? Lillian did not mention my coming court experiences, which were building up such anxiety. I could feel that anxiety beginning to stir again. I knew it would impel me to speak, probably to say too much. And it did.

"Lillian, this has to do with a child's future, not just with mine. I have to give evidence. And all you're talking about is putting the lid on everything. If you look at what's happened, how it all happened, and why it happened as it did, that morning—things could have been even worse. And now when I need help—"

I stopped, appalled at the implication of what I had said, shocked at the sound of my own words which seemed no longer consciously mine, rather, coming from somewhere else. But Lillian did not seem to have taken in my accusation. She was still saying that she couldn't imagine, couldn't understand why I was saying all this to her.

Point by point she dealt with what I had said, in her own way, while I sat helplessly and still transfixed by her phrase, "I cannot imagine." It was a statement that she could never put herself in the place of any other person. She could not allow herself to guess how they might feel, fear, hope, act. Lillian is, then, without empathy; because you need the imagination to have any of that.

Some minutes later, on my way out through the lower regions of Riverdale, a woman greeted me as I passed her. It was Celine. We both stopped, then she looked at me intently, a habit she always had.

"Mary, are you all right? You look just as if something shattering has happened!"

Something had. For the first time, I was feeling sorry for Lillian as well as for myself.

I never saw Lillian again. All our further necessary negotiations were conducted through her secretary, for the rest of my time at Sladebourne, which has stretched from weeks to months because Gomez demanded a replacement for me, and insisted I stay until one was found.

I did, eventually, get to see the reference that Lillian sent to my new manager. It was a masterpiece of ambiguity, saying nothing good but implying everything bad as politely as possible.

And Dr Fermatt? His divorce is, I believe, going through quite smoothly. Celine and company are sure that Lillian will make him the most capable wife. For a time, anyway.

The Court hearing takes place next week. Thank God, I won't be accompanied by Lillian, but by my newly appointed fieldwork—team leader, Adrienne Shorter. We remembered each other—from the Deptford College lecture. Thinking of what could have happened if I hadn't managed to stand up to Lillian, I feel really grateful not to be facing the might of British Justice all alone.

Already I know from Ted Grace and the others in the fieldwork team what is likely to happen. Permission will be sought to seek long term foster parents for Stella, with a view to adoption. There are already several people interested in caring for her. Unknown to any of my new managers or colleagues, one of these people is myself. The fostering application form came yesterday, in the same post as my marriage annulment.

I've already told Nilla, and I'll have to tell more people. Frank first, he'll be so upset if I do not come straight out with the situation now. He's so bloody honest, is Frank. People like him are really vulnerable. Asking me on our second date if I liked children! But of course, the thing is, I believe his ex-didn't.

It is such a relief to be with someone like that, in spite of all the fears you have, and the knowledge that nobody is ever as uncomplicated as they seem at first. The thing is, I can't believe, somehow, that all we've all gone through is without purpose. And if there's a purpose. I am not absolutely sure yet how Frank will feel about taking on Stella as a long-term commitment—if we ever get the chance, that is. But that, of course, will all have to be another story.